CAVALCADE

CAVALCADE

BRUNO DE STABENRATH

Translated by Sonia Soto

LITTLE, BROWN

A *Little, Brown* Book

First published in Great Britain in 2004 by Little, Brown

First published in France 2001
by Editions Robert Laffont

A CIP catalogue record for this book
is available from the British Library.

ISBN 0 316 72770 9

Typeset by M Rules in Sabon
Printed and bound in Great Britain
by Clays Ltd, St Ives plc

Little, Brown
An imprint of
Time Warner Books UK
Brettenham House
Lancaster Place
London WC2E 7EN

www.TimeWarnerBooks.co.uk

to François Truffaut, Jean-René Huguenin,
Dennis and Carl Wilson

to the 'Stab' tribe

No one rises so high as he who knows not whither he is going.

Oliver Cromwell

1

Alizée

I can't stand. I can't sit. But I'm very good at lying down. I'm tetraplegic.

A year before I shattered the bones in my neck, when I didn't realise how lucky I was to be *homo erectus*, a young man walking on air, my legs went on strike. I don't know if it was an unconscious choice or a premonition, but I took to my bed for several weeks and refused to get up.

I weighed a ton. I'd been a zombie for months. Alizée was gone, Alizée didn't love me any more. Her departure had left destruction in its wake. Her absence filled my soul, my brain, my penis, my spine with lead; I was paralysed, but only temporarily because I was sure she'd return to set me free. At night she came and danced on our bedroom ceiling. With nights following mornings, my life was back to front. I pondered the matter deeply: how could I get her back?

I thought of something spectacular: a car accident. A pint of blood splattering the front of my torn dinner jacket, smashed fingers, a gashed brow and a broken leg. Three lines in a Biarritz newspaper.

*

Midnight in my convertible. I'm driving very fast along the Basque coast, leaving behind the lights of Saint-Jean-de-Luz. I never reach the Spanish border. I'm drunk, I've made big losses at the casino and having a hard-on is depressing me. Too bad for Michelle, the redhead who's caressing me. Even she can't distract me from the thought that, handsome, well-off fool that I am, my life is as flat as the dance floor at El Divino – the club where I picked her up – and as dull as the pathetic creatures twitching to the techno beat. Sad puppets! Who or what are they looking for? Nothing can replace lost love. Nothing can make up for Alizée's absence. Nothing and no one will ever give me as much pleasure as her hands, her mouth, or the way her naked body, entwined in a white sheet, shuddered when I surprised her in her sleep.

I accelerate, while Michelle uses the bends in the road to do an octopus impersonation, gluing herself to me. She slides her leg over mine. Another couple of minutes and she'll be climbing on top of me. I don't feel like slowing the car down or stopping by the side of the road. I'm in too much of a hurry, I've got an appointment with death.

Michelle turns up the volume on the radio to maximum and undoes her bra. I've often noticed how Mick Jagger's voice has a very bad effect on young women. Still, I could easily calm things down: I've got a copy of *Revolver* by the Beatles in my CD loader. A flick of the wrist and McCartney's hormone-suppressant voice would ooze from the metallic pores of my Sony hi-fi, dampening the girl's ardour. But I do nothing. The CD's been pre-set, I'm on autopilot, the car's on autopilot, and I glide along the cliff in the warm, light air.

Half-naked, Michelle flings her stilettos at a poor bloke passing on a moped as the Rolling Stones work themselves into a frenzy. I've had enough of these noisy, tiresome passengers. I'm lonely, I'm miserable, and I've got six hooligans in my convertible: five guys and a girl, Michelle, who's now licking my neck. She starts working at my ear with her tongue. She rips my shirt, scratches my chest and dives under the dashboard, giving me a great excuse for missing a bend in the road: *Ricaner sous les étoiles, quitter la route à poil . . . Michelle, ma belle . . . sont des maux qui vont très bien ensemble.*

Like a giant mattress, the sea cushions our fall. I am thrown out of the car and would have drowned, but for an insomniac fisherman.

At the hospital in Bayonne, Dr Langlois operates on an open fracture to my right femur. I've lost a lot of blood but it doesn't matter, given its alcohol level: it wouldn't have been much use, except perhaps for conserving prunes. Michelle's fine – just four stitches on her tongue, which make her slur her words. She sounds as if she has a mouth full of banana. I can't understand a thing she says . . . Oh, yes I can: she's furious, she's lost her engagement ring.

Alizée hears about the accident halfway between Saint-Martin and the Grenadines, and she turns her yacht around. Two night flights and a high-speed train journey later she's at my bedside, tanned and with espadrilles still full of sand. 'I will survive,' sings Gloria Gaynor on the rented TV, while I come back to life, snuggling between her breasts.

A month at a centre in Quiberon and I'm back on my feet again. Our love is now free of splints, drips and antibiotics. By the sea, Alizée, my wild pony, holds up her Indian dress and runs along the water's edge.

'Léo, I love you!' she yells, chasing a seagull.

I make a momentous decision: I'll make love to her less and talk to her more. I'll pay attention to her soul. She undoes her dress so she can wade into the sea. My bronzed blonde is as breathtaking as ever. I run, I limp, I feel horny. I'm in pain, but I'm cured.

'Alizée, I love you!'

We fall down on the sand.

I was purring in Alizée's arms when the night nurse shook me awake. 'Sir, calm down, it's just a dream! I'll turn the oxygen back on, you're having trouble breathing.'

I didn't care whether it was sea air or air from a machine filling the lungs of my shattered body, as long as I was left to my dreams. At that moment the only thing I wanted was a one-way trip.

Never wake a sleeping tetraplegic.

2

Happy birthday

The unscheduled flight in my car that annihilated my motor and sensory functions happened on Sunday 17 March 1996, three days after my thirty-fifth birthday, on the road to Melun. I've always hated Sundays, birthdays and B roads. And to think I crashed when I wasn't even drunk, driving too fast, or suicidal!

Who knows why a car comes off the road? Mine skidded, rolled, and fell down a ravine. Under the weight of the car, the convertible top was forced out of whack and I found myself trapped upside down. I appeared to be alive but I was unable to make the slightest movement. I couldn't even get a fag out of my crumpled jacket. 'Think positive,' I said to myself. 'This might be the ideal opportunity to give up smoking.'

I'd just have to wait patiently to be rescued. Anxiety gnawed at my insides. And anger. This accident wasn't scheduled in my Palm Pilot. A muddy taste of blood was burning my mouth and nasal passages, swallowing and spitting were a huge effort. My nose was poking into freshly cut grass and the gashed earth was getting soaked with my blood.

'Is this the end?' I wondered.

Bad joke. What about my destiny? What about all the years spent trying to become the Jacques Dutronc of the Rue du Bac? As Gainsbourg said, 'We'll only make it once our elders are gone.' But Jacques 'the opportunist' was still alive and I was about to croak.

It was so unfair. My band had just been signed up by Capitole, a record company that launched new talent. Goodbye gold disc . . . scratched disc, more like. The only mark I'd managed to make was in this fucking field beside a B road. What good were songs if they were never recorded, sold, played? If they just stayed compressed inside my skull, which was now squashed inside a big crushed box?

I waited. In a few seconds my life would flash before my eyes: François Truffaut's images recounting the tale of Léo, the wild child. Truanting from school; losing my virginity; learning to play the piano; going to New York for the first time; Alizée. Full stop.

Nothing happened, I could just hear silence and the approach of death. In a panic, my brain was channel-hopping furiously and throwing all its files into chaos, as my thoughts bombarded me mercilessly. Questions popped up one after another: should I cancel my dinner tomorrow night with Carla Bruni? Had I collected my shirts from the cleaners? What about my debts, my taxes, my overdue rent? My friends, my lovers, my hassles? Why did I take drugs and subscribe to *Karate Weekly*? Had I ever told my parents that I loved them? Who'd get my Beach Boy albums? Could I consider all the young women I'd enticed to my flat under the spurious excuse of a dinner party to be willing victims?

Why was I in so much pain?

Suddenly, I remembered there'd been someone else in

the car: Gwendoline had been sitting in the front with me. What had happened to her? I didn't want her beautiful corpse on my conscience, or my CV. I rewound to the minutes before the crash. I'd tried to kiss her, she'd turned her face away (I can't imagine why), I'd put my hand on her thigh . . . I'd let go of the wheel! The car had somersaulted and landed on its roof. The impact was pretty violent and I was now crushed beneath the weight of my own body, which was pressing down on my cervical vertebrae and gradually suffocating me. If Gwendo was half dead too, there wasn't much hope of either of us surviving on this little B road. My mother always said to me, 'Stay on the motorway!'

Right, maybe this was a good time to pray: 'Our Father who art in Heaven . . . I'm on my way! There'll probably be two of us. I wonder, oh sweet Lord, could I have the cell next to Betty Page's?' I got an immediate answer: 'You'll be here in ten minutes? Yes, I'll stay on the line!'

Gwendoline, my angel, you always do the opposite of what I expect. I'm dying, you're alive. I'm upside down, you're standing up. I'm suffocating, in pain and in distress, you're chatting to the Fire Brigade on your mobile. Luckily, you've never said you love me, or this really would be a joke.

'Léo? Don't worry, the ambulance is on its way!'

She managed to crawl inside the car and grab my hand, but she gave a start and let go of it quickly. That worried me: 'What's the matter now?'

'Hurry!' she told the person on the other end of the line.

Petrol was leaking from the car. My body wasn't responding and I was going to fry while Gwendoline looked on helplessly, providing live commentary of my cremation on her mobile.

For some reason the ambulance siren made me think of the last judgment, prison and O. J. Simpson's words in that court in Beverly Hills: 'All this, gentlemen, is the absolute truth! As for the rest . . . it must be an incomprehensible chain of fortuitous events with unfortunately dramatic consequences.'

But what was I being tried for?

What a mess! And the day had started so well.

3

Gwendoline

I'd been dragging Alizée around in my head for a year and I felt I'd only forget her if I fell in love again. The problem was, I fell in love every day, every hour, sometimes every second. I just had to sit outside the Café de Flore from the end of April, sipping a strawberry milkshake, and watch the latter-day Amazons walking down the Boulevard Saint-Germain. I always chose the end table on the corner of the Rue Saint-Benoît. The girls slowed down to cross the road. Some stopped at the newspaper kiosk, others dawdled outside La Hune bookshop or, better still, turned back for a drink at the Flore.

Gwendoline was chatting to some muscle-bound idiot on rollerblades when I first set eyes on her. She rested a pink lizardskin court shoe on a car bumper, hitched up her pleated tartan skirt and adjusted her flesh-coloured fishnet stockings. A Japanese guy took a photo of her and she slapped him so hard he went flying. A Greenpeace tin-rattler came between her and the Jap, who was doing karate chops by now. Quite a brouhaha. The police turned up and arrested the true culprit: an Argentinian refugee massacring Francis Cabrel songs on the guitar.

This little scene delighted me, so I invited the pin-up and the body builder over to my table. Gwendoline's companion was called Ralph. Tanned, he had a crew-cut, a long-sleeved t-shirt stretched tight over his pecs and abs, his backside squeezed into Quiksilver cycling shorts, and rollerblades grafted on the ends of his muscular, hairless legs. I couldn't believe that someone would go to so much trouble to look like a poof on wheels. The '80s penchant for encouraging doubts about one's sexual orientation was over. Nowadays, if a man put his hand on your arse it was to tell you to go and reshape your buttocks on the treadmill at the gym. It wasn't about sex any more but about bodies. Straight guys wanted to look like surfers and the problem was, girls loved it. Girls wanted to look like Pamela Anderson and the problem was, guys loved that.

Gwendoline was quite a beauty, and the spitting image of Anna Kournikova. Gwendo was from Toulouse, she was the daughter of a food manufacturer – *El Rey del Pollo Salsero* they called him, because the Cubans loved his chickens. She was doing a master's degree in History of Art at the Sorbonne and was a member of the women's swimming team.

I've always been crazy about sporty girls. Scantily-clad athletes at full tilt, tennis players, skaters twirling on the ice, floating words of caution on the rush of air in their wake: *ce jeu de dupes . . . voir sous les jupes . . . des filles . . .* More intelligent than me, richer, more beautiful and more selfish, Gwendoline could even beat me at the hundred-metre sprint. I didn't have a chance. But the second my eyes met hers, I knew she was the only woman on earth who could drive every last remnant of the searing memory of Alizée from my soul.

At that time – five months before my accident – I was going out with seven girls: Caroline, an actress in a sitcom;

Vanille, from Guadeloupe, a salesgirl at La Perla; Soraya, a part-Greek, part-Indian dress designer; Kaori, a Japanese girl studying French cuisine at the Ritz; Sibylle, a press attaché from MCM; Anne, from the Camargue, who showed her paintings in the Rue de Seine; and Dagmar, a part-time receptionist, who was bored. I really hadn't intended to build up such a collection but, for the first time in my life, I'd opted for honesty and was quite open with all these young ladies.

'Don't expect anything from me. My head's still full of my ex. If you like, you can sleep at my place and leave a few pairs of knickers and a toothbrush there. I'm weak, cowardly and unfaithful, but I've got smooth skin, I'm clean and healthy and I don't snore. OK?'

'Kiss me, you idiot!'

Girls of all colours passed through my bed: blondes, brunettes, redheads; white, black, yellow, red, green ones. They followed one another in quick succession under the duvet and I avoided calling them by their name in case I got it wrong: 'Are you coming, baby?'

'Why do you always call me baby?'

'Are you coming, my little slut?'

Sometimes I was even asleep before, during and after. 'I'm sorry, darling, but I completely forgot to fuck you last night!'

'Don't worry, baby, I've only just arrived!'

'Why do you always call me baby?'

Actually, I was bored of three-step sex: enter, move it about, ejaculate. I was more inspired by erotic situations – I never tired of watching the face of my partner in the throes of pleasure.

I was a devotee of the slimy little sheath. Most people's dicks shrivel on contact with the rubbery tube, clumsily unrolled – not mine! A girl who took the initiative really fired up my libido. As submissive and malleable as a prostitute, I let her handle my cock. I was a rubber-clad fornicator. Condoms are love-proof. They're like plastic raincoats: showers of love, fertile monsoons, simply slide off them.

By sheathing myself I stayed faithful to Alizée and her sacred pussy, and saved myself for Gwendoline's. Since our meeting at the Flore, the nature of our relationship had become clear: I was madly in love with her, she made sure we were never alone. That drip Ralph, the moronic boy-band wannabe, was never more than a turn of his rollers away and came with her to our every rendezvous. I myself brought along a different girlfriend every time, curious to see Gwendo's reaction. She never said a word to them. A woman who isn't jealous? There's no such person, apart from Madonna or Sister Emmanuelle. Or, maybe there is: Gwendo never turned a hair. I could have had a python, a bus or a Louis XV sideboard with me, it would have made no difference to her.

One thing, however, was encouraging: Ralph, the super-supplemented brontosaurus, was showing signs of weakening. Gwendo treated him like a lap-dog and, so far, that had been OK. But he lost his cool – flushing, going pale, stammering – when she had one of her laughing fits. Mostly Gwendoline was coldly condescending, but when she was euphoric she was completely out of control. She opened her mouth wide and let out a loud stream of 'Ha ha ha . . . hee hee hee . . . hee hee . . .' She writhed, lost her balance, fell to the ground hitching up her skirt, then, as if she were raping herself, flung off her jacket, tore the buttons off her blouse and ended up half naked. I'd never seen anything like this mix of madness, indecency and exultation. She was so wild during these fits that it was impossible not to picture her making love.

'Is she often like this?' I asked Ralph. In a sulk, he was making ever more minimalist turns on his rollerblades.

'No, never!' he bleated. 'She hates laughing. She can't stand TV comics or funny men in general.'

'Yeah, it's weird . . . maybe she's ill?'

'No, no. She must be making fun of you! She was never like this before she met you!'

'Of course, it's obvious, Gwendoline's taking the piss out of me. Thanks, Ralph. Hey, look out! You've just rolled in dogshit!'

At the beginning of March, she turned up alone at the bar of the Hotel Lutétia where we'd arranged to meet. I didn't ask any questions. After dinner we went back to my flat, but nothing happened because Caroline, after a hard day's work on her sitcom, was asleep in my bed. Again, Gwendoline didn't inquire. She just pulled back the sheet and uncovered my mistress's naked body.

'She's attractive. Nice bottom, nice hair. Her skin's soft.'

She sat down beside Caroline and stroked her leg. Caro, thinking it was me, snuggled up to her. Gwendo smiled.

'Does this turn you on?' she asked, twirling a strand of Caroline's hair.

'Maybe, if you made love to her and she didn't realise what was happening . . .'

'Shall I take my clothes off?'

'What for?'

Caro groaned, stretched and opened her eyes. 'Screw you, Léo! I have to be at the studio tomorrow. Get off with her somewhere else.'

The following week was a turning point. I was going to Switzerland to play some gigs, so I decided to break up with my seven girlfriends. Dagmar cried, Vanille couldn't finish her meal, Anne fell asleep, Soraya gave me a blow job, Kaori shredded my sheets, and Sibylle flung herself into the road. As for Caroline, she never found out.

I flew to Geneva on 12 March. On the 15th I left Montreux and returned to Paris. Gwendoline met me at the airport. She refused my offer to use a rubber and I made love to her for the first time.

That night, I made love for the last time.

4

Darius

Darius was there to meet Léo when he arrived by ambulance at the hospital in Garches, around 1 a.m. He made jokes to his unconscious brother. Graduates of the Ecole Polytechnique often use humour to comfort the seriously wounded: 'Playing at being a stuntman are we now, Léo?'

But no one was laughing, so Darius followed the stretcher in silence, taking in the scene – it's not every day you find yourself in Casualty in a big hospital in the middle of the night. The night staff barged through the double doors. They were heading for the 'rest and observation' ward. Darius stayed close to his brother. He searched his face, his body, his hands, for signs of blood or bruising, but he couldn't see any. The paramedics had cleaned up the superficial wounds in the ambulance.

'You look fine,' he whispered in his ear, thinking Léo would open his eyes, smile and get up.

They hadn't seen each other for three months. Darius didn't know that Léo had only just got back from Switzerland: music, skiing, sunbathing, clubbing. And anyway, Darius thought his brother was always on holiday.

A junior doctor came for the patient and told Darius to wait in the corridor. He'd been hanging around by the coffee machine for an hour when a nurse came up to him. 'Are you related to the patient?' She read the notes: 'Mr Léopold Champollon.'

'I'm his brother.'

'He's very badly injured. Please come with me, Dr Ezri would like to see you.'

She took Darius up to the first floor. Outside the operating theatre, a handsome young surgeon, his gown as white as his smile, said cheerfully: 'He'll pull through, he's tough!'

Then, taking Darius by the arm, he added more quietly: 'Is he in a band, by any chance?'

Taken aback, Darius nodded as the doctor slid a big lump of hash into his hand.

'This was in the pocket of his jeans. I haven't got his test results yet. Er . . . d'you know if he injects, or sniffs anything?'

Darius stared at him, frightened. The doctor didn't push it and gestured to the nurse. They had a lot of work to do on Léo's body: haircut, general anaesthetic, fusing of cervical vertebrae, tracheotomy. As the trolley disappeared into the operating theatre, Darius grabbed the nurse by the arm: 'What's the matter with him?'

'Please, you'll have to ask the surgeon.'

But the surgeon had disappeared behind thick glass doors. As they weren't answering his questions, Darius realised suddenly that Léo's life must be in danger.

Now he was alone, slumped in a plastic armchair. He took off his shoes and socks – he didn't know why – buried his face in his hands and started to cry, his head full of questions.

On the phone, the police had mentioned an accident.

Was it a suicide attempt, an overdose? Maybe even a settling of scores? Léo moved in the twilight world of showbiz. Darius looked on from a distance but suspected his brother kept bad company. He had once seen a photo of him in *Gala* having dinner with David Hallyday and two Russian models.

'I should have phoned him more often,' he thought guiltily, blowing his nose.

There were five brothers and two sisters in the Champollon family. Léo was the black sheep. He'd failed his baccalaureate three times, flunked his military service and never got married.

'One day he'll bring home a negress,' predicted Champollon senior, a former General. 'My boys are as strong and handsome as temple columns!' he'd say, but he'd always add, 'I've got four beautiful marble ones and one rotten timber, but luckily my house is solid – four are enough.'

Darius was a graduate of the Ecole Polytechnique; Charles was a monk; Antoine worked for Vandenberger Bank; and Louis was a doctor ranked captain in the medical corps of the 1st Foreign Cavalry Regiment. A few years earlier, when Louis had told his father he wanted to be a doctor, Mr Champollon objected: 'Doctor? That's not a career! Or do you mean an army doctor?'

Louis went to the Army Medical College in Lyons.

Léo, on the other hand, took a course in sex, drugs and rock 'n' roll. This was a surprising choice for a family that had served France since Louis XIV. He left home early on.

Darius felt guilty. Staring in despair at his bare feet against the lino of the hospital corridor, surrounded by the reek of disinfectant, he remembered their last family Christmas.

5

Brothers

Work was being done to the house in Poitiers where the Champollon family gathered for the holidays, so mother Champollon put the five boys in one room, in bunk beds. The arrangement made Léo smile. 'It's been ages, hasn't it, since all five of us shared a room?'

'The last time was the twelfth of June 1978, at Montmorillon, the day of Uncle Witold's funeral.' Darius's brain was infallible.

They'd emerged from the village church, ready to follow the coffin to the cemetery. The organ was playing J. S. Bach: 'Jesus shall remain my gladness'. The hearse was just about to set off when the fire brigade arrived. First, the truck with the big ladder, then the truck with the pump, then the truck with the water tank, then the truck with the hoses, then the first-aid Renault, the fire chief's GX, the jeep with the axes and saws, the ambulances, the gendarmes . . . It was never-ending, a thundering convoy of thirty vehicles drowning out Bach and the kids' yelling. The villagers watched anxiously, the priest crossed himself. Only the Champollon crew cheered: 'Fire, fire, house on fire!'

But once they saw the family mansion, they didn't feel like singing any more. The whole place had gone up in flames.

'That night we all slept together in the games room, at the cousins',' ended Darius.

After dinner that Christmas Eve, Léo sat at the piano with his folder of songs. It was a family tradition. His four brothers stood round as he handed them each a part: bass, mezzo, tenor and alto. Léo had nothing against Frère Jacques, Gregorian chants, or Basque choirs, he simply preferred a more Anglo-Saxon repertoire, rhythm 'n' blues, soul, gospel, rock: 'My Girl', 'My Sweet Lord', 'American Trilogy', 'Suspicious Minds', 'California Dreamin'', 'Proud Mary', 'Surfer Girl', 'Paperback Writer'. After all, the Bee Gees, the Beach Boys, the Osmonds, the Neville, Doobie and Everly Brothers all consisted of at least two or three brothers. There had to be room for the Champ' Brothers!

During rehearsals, Léo lost his temper, accusing his brothers of having as much rhythm as a sack of potatoes. They weren't going to sell millions of records sounding like that. The General suggested that the world tour be postponed to the following year and sent his little monkeys off to bed. But Darius hung around in the library and it was 1 a.m. by the time he got to bed. His brothers were already asleep, each in a different position, breathing quietly. Antoine, the banker – serious and neat in striped pyjamas – hugged his pillow: the miser's stash. When he counted sheep, he probably added up their value in francs and converted it into dollars. Louis, the doctor, still looked like a little boy. Charles, the mystic, lay with hands crossed over his rosary, ready for eternal rest. Léo sprawled across the bed stark naked, arse exposed like a baboon, hair tousled, muttering restlessly in his sleep. For some reason he'd left one sock on. Darius noticed the tattoo on his right shoulder: a dolphin leaping from the waves into the sun. Léo had always had dreams that were bigger than him.

Darius undressed quietly, still watching his brothers. Time passed so quickly. Yesterday, they had been running around in short trousers, today they were men. He felt stronger than usual. Was it because he was the one, as the house slept, to turn this page in the family history? Or because his parents were getting old and he knew that as the eldest, he would one day become head of the Champollon tribe? That night, Darius repeated a promise to himself, not because it ever occurred to him to neglect his family duties, but because some vows are always worth renewing: 'Nothing will ever drive us apart. I'll always stand by my family . . .'

6

C6–7

Léo came out of theatre at four in the morning, his head and neck held in a brace, his body under a white sheet, stitched and pierced with drips and catheters. Darius jumped to his feet.

'How is he?'

'He's going to Intensive Care,' the auxiliary answered, manoeuvring the trolley as easily as a shopping cart full of joints of meat. He headed for the lift and Darius followed. A voice called after him.

'Are you a relative?' asked the anaesthetist, throwing his mask in the bin. Darius said yes.

'I'm Dr Plisson. You have to sign a consent form and fill out an admission form as soon as the admin department opens. Then you'll need to talk to the surgeon.'

With that, he paused, leaned against the wall and searched his pockets. Darius offered him one of his cigarettes.

'Thanks,' said Plisson, again searching his pockets, this time for a lighter.

'No, thank you for taking care of my brother,' Darius said, holding out the flame of his Zippo. He waited politely while the doctor took two long drags and then asked, 'Should I wait for him to wake up, or come back in the morning?'

'He won't wake up.'

Darius gave a start. The doctor added quickly: 'No, I simply meant he won't wake up straight away. It was a major operation. One of his cervical vertebrae was dislocated and was pressing on the spinal cord. We're going to keep him in a kind of therapeutic coma for quite a few hours, so that he's not in pain. He'll be completely out of it.'

Darius crouched down and tried to get his breath back.

'He's presenting all the symptoms of tetraplegia at C6–7.'

'C what?'

'Cervical vertebrae six to seven. There are seven cervical vertebrae. The higher the injury, the worse it is.'

'You mean he's going to be paralysed? Is that it?'

Plisson threw away his cigarette and put a hand on Darius's shoulder.

'You must be exhausted. Get some rest and come back tomorrow.'

Darius stayed with Léo until morning. At first light, he went home for a shower and a coffee. In the kitchen he wrote a list: phone parents, family, friends, an uncle who was a surgeon.

Towards midday, for the first time ever, he went to his brother's flat in the Rue du Bac. It all looked very tidy. 'How can he afford a cleaner?' he thought.

He saw a large diary on the desk. He flipped through the address section and noticed a list of around fifty names on the last page: all girls! 'How on earth does he know so many women?' He wondered if he'd have to ring them all.

Suddenly, the sound of his brother's voice made him jump: it was the answerphone clicking into action.

'Hi, it's Champ! I'm not here, so leave a message! If it's about work, get in touch with Almira Solers at the ANPE. She might be able to find you a job!'

A girl left an irritable message: 'OK, Léo, it's Sylvia. We were supposed to have dinner together last night to celebrate your birthday, remember? I waited all evening for you to call. If you've decided to play dead, it would be nice to be warned.'

Darius recorded a new outgoing message, giving his mobile number and the address of the hospital. As he was leaving, the phone rang again. It was their brother Louis, the doctor. Conveniently, he was on a work placement in emergency medicine with the Paris fire brigade.

'Louis? I'll meet you in the Patel Wing, second floor, Intensive Care. I'm expecting Mum and Dad too.'

To his surprise, he drove back slowly through the streets of Paris. It was a beautiful day. On café terraces, girls in short skirts, lounging nonchalantly like lionesses, stretched out their bare legs in the sun.

'Léo'll pull through,' he muttered, lighting a fag, his first of the day.

7

Mickey

Mickey stood before Léo's body.

He'd jumped in the car as soon as he got Sylvia's call, even though it was late. Darius met him at the hospital and helped him put on a sterile gown. He entered the silent room. An oxygen machine was beeping at regular intervals. Léo's bed was bathed in the gentle glow of the emergency night-light. Something indefinable pinned Mickey to the spot. He couldn't take another step. His friend's face looked terrifying. Its flesh was swollen from the operation, his eyes rolled upwards showing only their whites, his neck was bent back; his teeth chattered in fits and starts, and the entire upper part of his body was vibrating from inside, expressing an intense, desperate struggle, as if he were trying to escape – a man buried alive.

Mickey moved closer and whispered to him that everything would be fine. He promised to come and visit him every day. Léo flinched; his face was a mask of despair and supplication. Two fat tears rolled down his cheeks. He'd recognised a friendly presence and was expecting something from it. But what? Mickey fidgeted helplessly. He stepped back and leaned on a chair, hoping for an answer. The instant he moved away, Léo's upper body shook in protest.

A nurse came in: it was time for him to leave.

'Can you help me?' he whispered to her. 'I think he's trying to tell me something.'

'He's agitated, but that's to be expected.'

She leaned over Léo's face and placed a hand on his forehead. His teeth were chattering, his mouth was working frantically.

'He's angry with you,' she said, still scanning his face.

Mickey asked why.

'Because you're going to leave,' said the nurse.

'So?'

'He wants you to help him to die.'

As she was leaving the room, she added: 'I'll put it in his notes.'

In the waiting room, Léo's mother was donning a sterile gown before going in to see her son. Mickey signalled to Darius that it would be better if she didn't, but it was too late.

Mickey took a long time to find his car in the hospital car park. He sat in it for over an hour, gripping the steering wheel, staring fixedly at the shadows through the windscreen.

He had glimpsed death.

8

Morphine

What was going on? I wasn't dead – you can't be dead if the pain's unbearable. And what a noise! People partying day and night. I'd been left in a corner and poured into a block of concrete. Even my head was trapped. My eyes, my ears were all that remained alive. Nobody to protect me. There were the nice people and there were the nasty people. When they pounced, there were at least four of them. They lifted me to change the sheets and then jumped on me, laughing.

The nights were terrifying. They came in pairs to tell me that I was going to die. The first time, they wheeled my bed into a freezing warehouse. The other beds were empty. There was a group of people waiting: they came and stood around me in a circle. They prayed, wept, pleaded and, one after another, slipped pieces of paper under my sheets. They were messages to their dead and I would be taking them with me. One old woman was staring hard at me.

'They say my son committed suicide. They're lying. You'll tell Daniel, won't you? His room is just as he left it.'

A weird old bloke of around sixty asked them all to

leave. He handed a two-hundred-franc note to the auxiliary standing by my bed. He took off his trousers, lay down beside me and masturbated. I screamed for help but nobody heard.

At dawn, a doctor came to see if I was dead. He sent all the people back into the shadows.

'Forgive them, they don't know what they're doing.'

He looked confident so I felt reassured. He added sadly: 'But you have to pay sooner or later. Everyone has to go through the check-out. Today it's your turn!'

'Please, let my family know!'

'Don't be silly.'

He touched my forehead. 'You've got a temperature. That's odd! I'll be right back . . .'

'No, don't go!'

I was lying naked on the cement floor of a garage, shivering. A brazier spat out red embers that burned my face and eyes and throat. Ninjas in black kimonos sprang from the ceiling, the floor, the windows. One of them took out a knife and held it to my throat. He cut the carotid artery and blood spurted everywhere. It formed a thick brown puddle on which I floated.

The leader shouted an order and the ninjas went crazy: they tore off my nails; they held pokers in the flames of the brazier and used them to burn my feet; a Sumotori hoisted up my body, which was hanging by the legs, chest and shoulders from butcher's hooks that distorted my flesh. The pain was unbearable, but I didn't want to lose face. 'Hey, it's not so bad . . .'

A gong sounded. Thick smoke filled the room and a big fan started up. A hatch opened in the ceiling and an avalanche of polystyrene granules filled my mouth and nostrils and lungs, suffocating me. One of the ninjas came over and cut my nose with his credit card, then turned to his leader: 'Sensei! The little white man . . . he's still breathing!'

'Never mind. We'll come back!'

A walkie-talkie crackled: 'Foxtrot, Charlie, Bravo! We're right above you! Ready for evacuation, repeat, ready for evacuation.'

'Sensei, the helicopter's here! Evacuate!'

Medical evacuation. The ninjas left and were replaced by two male nurses, sinister types with tattooed forearms and nicotine-stained fingers. They were obviously not interested in me. They put my body on a trolley and wheeled me down a cold dark corridor. They talked about drugs and sex. A woman came up behind me. I could see she was preparing a syringe.

'Don't forget to give me back the key to the pharmacy. And next time make me a copy, but be discreet about it.'

They shot up and then – sitting on the edge of my bed – they asked the girl if she'd brought the stuff. From a bag, she took dozens of little transparent plastic packets containing multicoloured pills.

'Of course I did. Here are your sweeties. But you've got to fuck me first!'

They lay down next to me. Their breath stank of alcohol. Their clammy hands moved over my body. The girl kept on moaning and pulling at my penis to make it grow: 'He can't get it up! Look at his cock, boys! It's tiny!'

Naked on my bed, the two junkies sniggered: 'Let's stick a needle into this piece of shit! Kill him! Hold his arm!'

The pain of the needle made me scream. I struggled.

'For fuck's sake, shut your mouth and keep still!'

The girl was furious. 'Get it up, you filthy little faggot! Make me come or I swear, I'll break your arse!'

'Go on, Madeleine, teach the little bastard a lesson!'

A group of people emerged from the lift at the end of the corridor and headed towards us. It was my family.

'Excuse me, we're looking for Léo's room.'

I caught a glimpse of my parents. The girl who'd been straddling me let go of my penis, put her blouse back on, slipped on her mules and took my father by the arm.

'I'm sorry, sir, we had to move your son to another ward. He had pleurisy. Come along with me, I'll take you to Reception, they'll tell you where to go.'

'Thank you, that's very kind of you, miss.'

And with that, my family turned and left, abandoning my poor tortured body.

'Dad! Daaaad!'

I was alone now. Day was dawning, but was that really light coming through the window? My body, free of its bindings, was floating up towards a square of sun, a luminous opening cut into the wall. I was warm, comfortable. Below, a group of high priests stood around a table watching my ascent and, one after another, raising their right arm. They were sentencing me unanimously to death!

Big old manuscripts lay before them containing the famous red list, written in blood, the list of my sins: deflowerings, sodomy, orgies, debauchery, cross-dressing, drug-taking, mind games, adultery. But mainly, too much time spent listening to the Beach Boys.

An old priest watched an hourglass, counting aloud: 'Ten, nine, eight, seven, six . . .'

'By zero, I'll be dead! Well, good! I've had enough of all your crap!'

'Hey, you up there! No swearing! You'll only make things worse for yourself!'

My lift stopped level with the window. Beyond it, I could see a golden prison awaiting me. I struck the plexiglass. It wouldn't open.

'Four, three, two, one, zero! Hosanna in the highest!'

The bearded old priests rejoiced at my entry into eternity. But the prison doors were about to shut and I was still outside! There was a commotion below, as my astro-body landed back on Earth. My limbs were tied down. A nurse came for me, pushing the old dodderers in purple cassocks out of the way. They complained, tearing at my hair and demanding a second lift-off. But it was too late. I was already outside, right in the middle of a funfair, my body in a bath of ice.

Why was I so cold?

9

Emergency council

Everyone arranged to meet at Léo's flat in the Rue du Bac. Darius's mobile had been ringing non-stop for three days. The news was getting around that Léo had had a serious car crash.

'Shit! You mean, he can't move anything? That's terrible!'

The men added: 'What was he driving? A Peugeot 604? How did he manage to overturn a 604? That's typical of your brother!'

And the girls asked: 'Was there anyone else in the car? Gwendoline? No, never heard of her. You know him, he had a different one every week.'

An emergency council was organised. There was plenty to do:

1. Liaise with the medical profession and monitor the development of Léo's condition and diagnosis (this was Louis' role).
2. Keep the family informed, answer letters and organise hospital visits (Camille, Léo's younger sister).

3. Go to the bank, ASSEDIC, Social Security, the insurance company, compile a file for the hospital and make sure that Léo's affairs were in order (Darius).
4. Bring together friends and family to form a support network (Mickey, Sylvia, Ambroisine, Patrice, Alix, Henri, Richard, Amélie, Ludovic and Eric).

Soon, Darius could count on a close circle of his brother's friends. Since Léo had been admitted to the Raymond-Poincaré Hospital, they'd phoned every day to offer help and there was nearly always a throng of them in the waiting room.

When Darius met them all for the first time at Léo's flat, he realised that his brother had real friends with real jobs – some were even married and had children. They weren't drug addicts or criminals; they wore normal clothes and paid their taxes.

Darius explained the situation: things were pretty bad. The doctors were pessimistic and they couldn't say how long Léo's stay in hospital would last, but it was likely to be lengthy and gruelling. He ended by saying that Mr and Mrs Champollon were obviously extremely distressed and needed to be comforted and reassured.

They waited for Louis to arrive. He knew one of the doctors at Garches and had spent the afternoon there. Darius handed round documents showing the costs so far: rescue from the car, ambulance transfer to hospital, surgery, twenty-four-hour intensive care, sterile room. They were all agreed – Léo's little flight off the road was proving expensive!

'Hey, he is covered, isn't he?'

'Yes,' said Darius waving a plastic card, 'he's registered with Social Security!'

This set everyone talking.

'You're sure it's not his travel card?'

'It hasn't expired?'

'Check it isn't mine.'

The relief of the gathering only confirmed Darius's opinion of his brother: what an unpredictable man!

They all thought that if Léo wasn't in bed with a girl, he was sitting at the piano, and that he only ever got up to play the guitar like Elvis, brush his teeth or answer the door to a chick who was there to get laid. None of which brought in any money. But now they had to acknowledge the truth: though only an occasional performer, Léo did actually work and earn a living.

Later, Darius realised that he'd seen only part of the puzzle that evening. Léo compartmentalised his life. At this first meeting, Darius had been dealing with the 'Friendship, Small Secrets, Films, Girlfriends, Acoustic Guitar, Holidays and Logfires' gang, which was in turn part of another, larger group, the 'Dinner in Town, Games of Castel, Cocktails, Private Viewings, Opera, Sunday Brunch and Weekends in Cabourg' set. In the world of pleasure, work was never mentioned. The following week, he met Laurent de Gasperis from the 'Rock 'n' Roll, Musos, Shades, Gigs, Backstage, SACEM, Canal + and Polygram' tribe, a whole other world which included most of Léo's employers and sidemen.

Like a doorman at a private club, Darius soon learnt to tell the difference between good mates (male and female), mistresses, colleagues, band members, traders, former mercenaries, inveterate party-goers, neighbours and Left-Bank intellectuals.

'How on earth does Léo know so many people? But above all, why do they all care so much about how he is?'

It was more than a puzzle to Darius, it was a human

mystery. True, Léo had never been shy; he was an opportunist, curious, insatiable: he wanted to see everything, drink everything, read everything, experience everything.

You might, over the course of your life, be able to list the names of five, ten, fifty people who are close to you, and state that you love and care about those women, those men. But can you be sure they feel the same about you? And what about those who love you but that you've left off the list because you don't love them and have never taken any notice of them? Or those who've never dared tell you they love you and whom you don't know exist? Or those who died without knowing you loved them?

One question persisted in Darius's highly organised brain: was it only when tragedy struck that you realised how much you loved someone?

10

A baby

Two male nurses came for me in the middle of the night and lay me face down on the operating table. One of them whacked me on the head with a baseball bat to knock me out, the other one tied me to the table.

'Sorry, mate – just doing our job!'

They left me alone in the gloomy operating theatre.

Gwendoline was with them. Why wasn't she horrified at the sight of my naked body lying on a metal plate, like a carcass that's just been chopped up? She stood at a distance, wearing a black suit. She was upset about what had happened to me but she couldn't deal with my suffering, she was too wrapped up in her own. All she could do was wring her mascara- and tear-stained handkerchief.

'I'm going to have a baby.'

This wasn't really the time or the place to break it to me.

'You know what this means, don't you, Léo?'

She pressed her hands against her flat stomach.

If this child was coming into the world, it was to take the place I was vacating. Its life or mine. So I was going to die. I'd never planned to leave behind an orphan, or a widow.

'It's the law of nature,' Gwendoline repeated. 'Some are born, others die.'

She added that she hadn't had her period since the night we slept together. I'd been about to pull out but she'd gripped my hips between her thighs. Instead of giving myself up to the pleasure, I fought to the end, surprised by her cannibalistic urge. Her body sucked mine in, her nails tore at my buttocks, her lips pressed against mine so that no breath could enter. She wanted everything – my sperm, my blood, my saliva, my sweat – so why not my life?

I'd gone from being a free man to being a prisoner, trapped by Gwendoline's sex, by the crushed metal of my car, by my own body, and now by these henchmen in white coats. Was she part of the plot?

Gwendoline lit a candle, placed it on the trolley and kissed me on the forehead. At the door, she turned and I made out the words 'I'm sorry' on her lips. I knew I'd never see her again.

Instead of giving in to despair, I made a quick mental calculation. Assuming she really was pregnant, it would be nine months before the baby saw the light of day, so that left me a little time to escape from my drug-induced haze. I had to find the tunnel exit before the foetus grew legs, but I had to hurry: the first one out got to live.

I prayed that Gwendoline's period would start as soon as possible, the blood flowing between her legs from her infertile belly. This child could not be born. It was a product of her imagination.

11

Rue du Bac

The girls were laying the table for supper. Darius was standing in front of the bookshelves, lost in thought. He felt almost as if he'd broken into the flat. Here he was, surrounded by Léo's motley collection of objects and musical instruments while back at the hospital, in a sterilised room, his brother was struggling with death. What would become of him? Would he end up as a vegetable in an electric wheelchair? Or living in a physical rehabilitation centre for the rest of his life? Or should he go back to live with their parents in Poitiers?

These thoughts contrasted with the things on the shelves: smiling pin-ups, miniature models of 60s cars – Chevrolet, Pink Cadillac, Ford Mustang – standing alongside old forty-fives by the Beach Boys, fake gold discs and models of cartoon characters – Tintin, Spiderman, the Silver Surfer, the Seven Dwarves, the Simpsons. Lots of photos of lots of smiling faces and scantily-clad women.

His brother wasn't the type to build up a pension fund, that was for sure. He'd chosen a Beach-Boy lifestyle: sex, salsa, skiing, surfing, windsurfing. And it turned out he'd been right to enjoy it while he could.

'What are you thinking about, sweetie?' Camille came and rested her head on Darius's shoulder.

'Nothing. I was just looking at his photos.'

'By the way, where the hell has Louis got to? It's ten o'clock.'

They stood in silence for several minutes, arm in arm in front of Léo's little museum of exotica. He was poking out his tongue at them from one of the photos. Darius and Camille had to accept the evidence: they didn't really know their brother.

The doorbell rang and Sylvia went to answer it. It was the pizza man. A young white Rasta with flowing dreadlocks, dressed in fluorescent red, followed the girls into the kitchen. They had to ask him to turn off his Walkman because he was talking so loudly.

'No point,' he yelled, 'it's broken. I pranged my moped on the Boulevard Raspail. But I'm fine. Shit, not a single bruise!'

'That's good,' said Camille loudly, 'but there's no need to shout, we can hear you!'

'Can't help it, I'm deaf. I used to be a DJ!'

Ambroisine saw him out.

'You drive carefully now and make sure you wear your helmet. And slow down when it rains! Promise?'

'D'you mind me asking,' said Mr Pizza, 'the guy who used to live here, has he moved out?'

'Did you know him?'

'Well, yeah, I delivered pizzas here loads of times. It's my area. One night I had some time so we talked. He even played me a couple of songs he'd just recorded.'

'He's had a car accident,' said Ambroisine quickly. 'It's pretty bad.'

The Rasta looked down and wiped his shoes on the mat.

'Don't know if you're into karma,' he said, looking her in the eyes now, 'but your mate, I know he'll make it. He's got a warm heart.'

He shook his bag. 'As warm as my pizzas!'

'Thanks . . .'

'When you see him, make sure you tell him – Zorro sends his regards.'

'Zorro?'

'Yeah, that's what he used to call me. "Out of the night comes the horseman known as Zorro." He always placed his orders last thing. Sometimes he only just made it.'

They were tucking into the Sicilian pizza with peppers and chorizo when Louis arrived.

'Well?' asked Darius.

Louis sighed.

'I'm sorry I'm so late, but I've got news.'

A shiver went through the group, as if somebody had found a way out, a cure for their collective pain. This was the first time they'd been to a dinner party at Léo's place and the silly fool wasn't even there!

Sylvia, Camille and Ambroisine made room for Louis on the sofa.

'He's at serious risk of developing pleurisy, he's got a staphylococcus infection in his lungs. They're putting in a drain tonight.'

'What does that mean?' asked Sylvia.

'They're stuffing him full of antibiotics to kill the infection. But he's very weak. We've just got to hope his body can take it.'

'And if not?'

'He'll die,' said Louis.

Around the coffee table, nobody spoke.

The prospect of Léo dying was like a slap in the face. He'd be wiped from the map, leaving them to get on without him. Life was taking an obscene turn, tossing them about like rags.

Darius paced up and down, shaking his head, turning things over obsessively in his mind. Some part of his brother was calling to him. He could sense that Léo was in danger but still alive. He tried to give some order to all the ideas swirling in his brain. He had an unshakeable conviction that he had to share with the others, because his brother's life depended on it.

'Listen, I'm absolutely convinced that if Léo survived the accident itself it's because he was meant to live. But we've got to help him! Louis, from now on, we're going to organise a non-stop shift system at his bedside. We've got to hold his hand, talk to him, transmit our energy, and our love. He really needs us now. Camille, get a tape recorder, we can tape some of his favourite music and each record a message.'

An invisible wave crossed the sleeping capital, passing through walls and across roads and gardens. A breath as light as a leaf tossed on the wind blew through the hospital and up the stairs of the Intensive Care unit until it reached a silent room. In the darkness, the body beneath the sheets shivered.

Message received.

12

Vibrations

Around me, white coats moved to and fro. I felt vibrations in the air, cool invisible currents indicating a presence at my bedside, by my face. But I couldn't feel anything at the periphery of my body. It was detached, disconnected from the rest of the world. I was just a head lying on a pillow, trapped in a brace, with a plastic tube stuck in my throat bringing the oxygen that I needed to breathe. A humidifier kept the open wound there moist.

The important stuff was going on internally, beneath the surface. The thousands of branching nerves, disturbed by the shock to my spinal cord and my enforced immobility, were functioning chaotically now – transmitting only negative messages. My skeleton, weighed down by the inert mass of muscles, was compressing my blood vessels and tissues, and bony deposits had formed in my joints. And then there were all the external intrusions: drains, drips, tubes, catheters, needles – penetrating orifices, tearing into my skin, biting into me cruelly.

I was living inside a phantom submarine that surfaced occasionally, summoned by pain, only to sink again, stunned by massive doses of tranquillisers and antibiotics. Nightmares, paranoid obsessions, sordid hallucinations swirled around my brain, signs of my desperate subconscious battle to survive. The insane struggle meant nothing to me because I was no longer at the controls. My brain was sailing on auto-pilot; if it faltered, it meant my conscious mind was back in charge – for a few minutes, at least. But these precious moments, when I opened my eyes and was back among the living, only frustrated me since I was condemned to silence – I could neither call for help, nor ask for something to drink or to relieve the pain. Lying down limited my field of vision, and all I could do was blink if, by chance, anyone came to check on me.

Suddenly, there would be noise – shouting, talking, movement, touching, treatment. Who could explain to me what was happening and how to interpret it? They shook me but I couldn't react; they asked questions but I couldn't answer. So they tried again, then they got angry, as if testing my endurance, my ability to bear the unbearable. Sometimes, when they were moving me as though I was an empty shell, I could tell that they were on edge, exasperated by these futile rituals, quarrelling for reasons I didn't understand. So I tried to be docile, it was best simply to play dead. I wasn't sure if I was imagining the verbal and physical violence, the sadism. It was terrifying.

Intensive Care units are occupied by patients in a critical condition, at the mercy of the slightest infection, or of mutant killer germs, like staphylococcus, that lurk in these antechambers of death. Patients are totally vulnerable, dependent on the staff who care for them and the security guards who keep watch. At night – the realm of the unhinged and illicit – some members of the medical staff, who'd worked for years in casualty or Intensive Care departments, went off the rails at the expense of us poor bastards stuck full of tubes, or of young women lying alone in sealed rooms.

I could tell the difference between the teams that took turns by my bedside. The 'compassionate' ones tried to establish contact, to soothe my shattered mind – they called me by my first name, applied cold water to my feverish forehead and parched lips, and were gentle when they moved my limbs. The worst ordeal was cleaning the tracheotomy in my throat: the open wound had to be suctioned because it got clogged with pus and saliva which blocked the flow of oxygen.

And then there were those you heard coming from a distance, when it wasn't too late, that is. They woke you with a savage yelling. These were the 'bogeymen', zombies from a twilight world: junkie auxiliaries, alcoholic ambulance drivers, junior doctors who'd hung up their white coats, manic-depressive night watchmen, nymphomaniac nurses, psychopathic porters, disillusioned medical students. They worked in gangs, taking sinister pleasure in terrorising the patients.

Sometimes an alarm blared, alerting staff that a respirator had broken down. They had to move fast – someone somewhere was suffocating. I could hear them charging down the corridor calling out names. Then, silence. No, someone was sniggering!

How did we get through those long nights full of pain and loneliness? By holding out. And, in the storeroom on the first floor, there was always the drugs cupboard, full of magic powders and happy pills.

Each to his own.

13

Cafeteria

Darius, Louis, Camille and Sylvia were in the hospital cafeteria at Garches, drinking Cokes and watching the occupants of the neighbouring tables, the poor buggers who'd been smashed up on the roads and scraped up off the tarmac. Most were under twenty and they went around in gangs, just as they had before. Only now, instead of motorbikes, they used wheelchairs daubed with fluorescent paint and covered in stickers.

As soon as the sun came out, the residents of Garches headed for the cafeteria in wheelchairs, on crutches and artificial limbs, or flat on their stomachs on trolleys because of pressure sores on their arses. The former bikers raided the magazine shelves for copies of *Motorbike Review* or *Turbo Magazine* and sat around discussing the performance of the 1300 Suzuki Interceptor or the tests of the Yamaha Vmax 1700. Darius had heard them recount their accidents in all their gory detail and then move straight on to talk of chrome fittings, rallying and motorbike or motocross trials. For them, nothing had changed.

At first, the sight of these youngsters had shocked and frightened Léo's friends. But gradually they'd got used to them, and pity had given way to admiration. These kids had pluck. As they watched them manoeuvre their new machines, weaving between tables, they all thought of Léo. Unless he made a miraculous recovery, in six months' time he'd be joining this tribe on wheels. And he'd be their first friend in a wheelchair.

The first time Loranska came to Garches, Sylvia arranged to meet her in the cafeteria. She arrived wearing a close-fitting zebra-print suit, black stockings with seams up the back, and stilettos. While Louis fetched her a chair, the bikers looked up from their favourite magazines and checked out the female who was setting their ghetto on fire: 36-23-35 on five feet ten of flesh, bone and muscle.

With an unconscious wiggle of the hips, Loranska thrilled her admirers, who were zapping between her arse and photos of the latest Kawasaki, their devotion to the biker cause suddenly seriously compromised. Shit! What had happened to the creed of these studded and zipped knights of the road: 'A motorbike for life, a woman for a night'?

Loranska, the unattainable goddess, was making them bite the dust all over again. Whether it was motorbike magazines or porn, they were still straddling a void.

14

Loranska

Loranska had very precise views about Léo's recovery: she was an enthusiastic proponent of electroshock therapy, having once tried it herself. She'd been in a coma after a drugs overdose and had even had an NDE – near death experience – white light and all. Just when the neurologist (who had a bad gambling habit) was suggesting they pull the plug, her husband had saved her life.

The day Loranska turned up on the second floor of Patel Wing there were about ten people waiting to see Léo: Mr and Mrs Champollon, Aunt Laurence, a starchy old maiden aunt, Ludovic, Marco, Louis, Ambroisine, Amélie, Patrice and Marina.

The introductions over, Loranska set out her theory: 'OK, it's simple, this is what I suggest: we pay for a girl – a real bomb, with all the gear. She comes to his room, she sucks him off, climbs on top of him. She gets his engine started again, that's the main thing! When I was in Intensive Care after my accident, Alexandre, my ex-husband, didn't ask for anyone's advice! He just took me like an animal. He really shook me up, and he saved my life! We've got to do the same with Léo. I'm right, aren't I?'

In the stuffy little waiting room, faces fell. Loranska had a big heart and her enthusiasm was infectious, but she'd soon change her mind when she saw the state Léo was in. He was so out of it that even if Cameron Diaz got on top of him he'd mistake her for a giant syringe.

Darius started talking loudly, trying to change the subject, but Aunt Laurence, both absent-minded and a little hard of hearing, hadn't caught all of Loranska's speech.

'What was that, young lady?' she asked. 'My name is Laurence Morley-Plissonière. I'm Léo's aunt,' she added, holding out her hand.

Darius said quickly: 'Yes, Aunt Laurence, Loranska had a serious, er . . . accident, a long time ago and, imagine, her husband saved her life by . . . administering shock therapy!'

'How wonderful,' said Aunt Lolo. 'He revived you?'

'No, no, he fucked me.'

'I'm sorry?'

Loranska's phone rang and she moved away to answer it. Ludovic couldn't take his eyes off her. Mr Champollon asked Darius if she was Léo's girlfriend. For the past few weeks he'd been trying to work out which of these numerous young ladies was his son's fiancée; he'd never got beyond the ancient ideal of monogamy.

'Well, Dad,' said Darius, 'I don't know much about her, only that she was married. And that she and Léo . . .'

'But your brother can't marry a divorcee!'

Darius explained that, since the 70s, men had been able to spend time with women without contemplating sexual relations, or even proposing marriage. Léo had a lot of women friends.

Furious, Loranska ended her call. She was still wearing her sunglasses. She now lit a cigarette. Mr Champollon stood up and went over to her. She was standing by the window sounding off to Ludovic.

'I mean, Pedro's a nice bloke but for the last two months, I hate to say it, his shit's been crap!' she fumed.

'Hello, Miss, I'm Léopold's father. How kind of you to come and visit him.'

'I adore your son. Let me give you a kiss.'

Loranska took off her sunglasses. She had blue eyes and a full mouth, made for kissing, speaking Italian and licking ice cream.

Father Champollon was under her spell. He hadn't felt this excited since the time he'd turned on the TV and seen Brigitte Bardot dancing the mambo on a table. He'd immediately switched it off and got a priest to come and exorcise it. At home in Poitiers, what with the monks of the Abbey of Ligugé and his bridge matches, he'd forgotten that a woman could make you lose your head and stammer with excitement. His upbringing forbade him from even considering there might be any other woman on earth except his wife. Loranska was as sexy as hell but he'd rather not allow himself to notice it. He'd been programmed to find women charming and delightful. Léo, who was a slave to his libido, couldn't think where his own sexual appetite came from. He wished his father had transmitted a little spiritual gravity or some metaphysical preoccupations along with his DNA, instead of leaving him to struggle with his stupid fantasies about dirty girls.

Loranska took Mr Champollon's arm.

'D'you mind if I ask you something?' she said.

'Please do, young lady.'

'What do the doctors say? Can he ejaculate?'

15

Awakening

How long had I been there: a week, a month, six months? All that time, wrapped in my burning shroud, I'd longed for a way out. Now, my mind was becoming more ordered. It was able to surface and reduce the persistent field of pain.

The first time I woke up I could see fluorescent light reflected in the stainless steel bed frame. A nurse opened the metal shutters and it disappeared. There, at last, was the sun and the blue sky.

'It's going to be a lovely day,' she said brightly.

At that moment, as I came back to life, those words meant as much to me as the most beautiful lines of Rimbaud. She could have said, 'It's cold today,' or 'It's cloudy this morning,' or maybe, 'You can see the mountains on the horizon,' or, 'There's mist over the fields.' I would still have begged, 'Please say that again, it's beautiful!'

Noticing the effect of her words, she came over to the bed. She made sure to pronounce every word clearly, as if she were speaking a new tetraplegic language: 'And-how-are-we-today-Mr-Champollon? We've-been-miles-away-haven't-we? We're-giving-you-a-room-mate, it'll-be-company-for-you! By-the-way-my-name-is-Marie-Thérèse!'

And she left. But I had two treasures: I was slightly alive, and I was contemplating a new morning.

The door opened and a figure approached.

'Hello, little brother, it's me!' Darius, waving his hand like a puppet.

From my vantage point lying flat on my back, he seemed immensely tall. I strained to keep him within sight. He sat on a chair and came down to my level. Smiling, he lay his hand on my forehead and whispered into my ear: 'Everything's alright, Léo. You've come through the worst. But it's not over yet. You've got to fight.'

Why was he whispering? Was there a spy behind the curtains, or some poor sod about to peg out under the bed? And who did I have to fight now?

'You've been here a month. You had a car crash . . .'

Yes, I knew it wasn't my tonsils.

'There's loads of people waiting to see you. Mum and Dad are here, and Louis. We've got things pretty well organised!'

I blinked my approval. I felt as if I were setting out on a new adventure. I should have died, but I'd been given a second chance. Everything seemed new: my brother, my family, my friends, my room, my life.

Darius suddenly looked round. A group of people – a consultant, two doctors, two junior doctors and two nurses – came in and stood around the bed. Darius winked at me.

'It's Tuesday so the boss is here. I'm off. See you later, little brother!'

The day was definitely off to a good start. But all the faces were grave, so I quickly put away my blissful smile. One of the doctors spoke. He sounded detached, monotonous; he could have been reading out the inventory at Drouot the auctioneers. I thought I ought to back up what he was saying so I wiggled my eyebrows: not only was he calling upon me as his witness but, more importantly, I was living proof of his talent and skill. Difficult to imagine things otherwise: 'Now, this patient came in on the seventeenth of March and, er . . . well, he died!'

There was a young junior doctor standing beside him, a brunette with green eyes. Her ample breasts bulged beneath her white coat, which was unbuttoned to reveal a generous amount of cleavage. I wouldn't have minded if my very own George Clooney had taken her from behind, coolly screwing her while continuing to read out his notes. I didn't have a TV and there wasn't much else to keep me entertained, apart from surviving.

The doctor went on with my case history.

'Mr Champollon was involved in a road traffic accident. He was at the wheel and wearing a seat belt. His alcohol level was nil. It took over an hour to free him from the vehicle. From the outset, the patient presented flaccid tetraplegia, with sensory function at T4 and motor function at C7. He had an anterior dislocation of the cervical vertebrae at C6–7. On the eighteenth of March, a fusion of the vertebrae with a fitting of a posterior plate was carried out. Post-operatively he contracted pleurisy, and a tracheotomy was performed on the nineteenth of March.

'Initial neurological assessment revealed total paralysis of both upper and lower limbs, with no change so far. As for the condition of the skin, there is a slight reddened area on the coccyx, but no pressure sores. There is, however, evidence of a positive Babinski response on both right and left sides.'

The doctor paused and stared at me, perplexed, as if worried I might question his diagnosis. What was he afraid of? That I might get up without a word, stark naked under my hospital nightie, stand behind Vulvina, lift up her white coat, tear off her panties, grab her buttocks and take her, right there against the cupboard, humming, 'Let's talk about sex, baby, let's talk about you and me.'

I did nothing of the sort, of course, I agreed with every word, except for the bit about Babinski – I'd had no response from him, positive or otherwise. George Clooney cleared his throat and went on: 'He's being kept under observation for the time being. We're going to start weaning him off the respirator this evening.'

They stood round the bed whispering and giving me friendly looks, all except for Vulvina who was pissed off with me for being so stand-offish. Dr Clooney winked at me, walked over to the respirator, which was beeping plaintively, and pressed the OFF button. I felt my throat contract and I opened my mouth like a dead fish, trying to take in air. Nothing. It was a huge shock; the machine had been breathing for me for the last thirty days and nights.

Seconds passed. Everyone was wondering what George would decide to do. He had his back turned to me and was watching the flow gauges and dials whose needles were now pointing to red. It was a recent model, the Automatic Air Turbo Survivor 3000 TDI. I could hear him lecturing me: 'You've got to start breathing on your own. You're perfectly capable of doing so, aren't you? He is, isn't he?' he asked doubtfully.

The nurse made a face. I was going blue.

‘He’s still very weak, Doctor.’ She leapt in and switched the machine back on.

I was saved. But I’d have to stay on my guard. I hadn’t emerged from oblivion to be murdered by my doctor.

16

Mr Buzuf

My first night as a free man was a challenge. I was still on tranquillisers, but I'd crossed the boundary between coma and consciousness. I had remote control over the movement of the nurses and auxiliaries and I now knew who I was dealing with, having put a name and face to the voices that had hypnotised, terrified, reassured me. There were three teams, each working an eight-hour shift. I devised a personal alarm system to attract attention whenever anyone walked past my open door: I clicked my tongue, making a sound like a cricket.

When one of them came in to the room, I initiated the second phase of communication, using the language of the mute and armless with great facial mobility. I conveyed everything by my expression and by vigorous movements of the eyebrows: hot, cold, thirsty, in pain, more or less oxygen, switch light on or off, open or close shutters, sleep. The person present tried to confirm my meaning by reading my lips. I was still, however, subjected to errors of interpretation and jokes intended to take the drama out of my situation.

'Hello there, what do you need? Another blanket? A drink? A taxi? An overdose?'

I had no idea if they were pleased that I was getting better, or whether the extra work bothered them, but I knew that they weren't indifferent to my agitation. Perhaps, down the corridor, someone had even put a note next to my room number on the board: 'The little guy's alive!'

Like a Resistance fighter who meets his torturers years later, but says nothing because he's still afraid, I knew that while I remained in Intensive Care I'd be docility itself, especially at night. I greeted each member of staff as eagerly and delightedly as an old Labrador welcoming home its master.

'This one's sweet,' said a plump nurse to another as they gave me a bed bath.

'Not like the other one,' replied the second nurse, her look turning murderous.

The other one: I'd been lumbered with a room-mate. He was inoffensive at first, and seemed in an even worse state than me. On one hand, I was in no danger of him trying to grab me by the throat; on the other, he was lucky that I couldn't move because I would have happily smothered him with my pillow. Bloody Mr Buzuf. He was always moaning, calling for help and demanding an injection. He stopped me sleeping and bothered the night staff, even when they were on their breaks.

'Can somebody help meeeeeeee . . . help meeeeeeee? Why is there nobody heeeeere?'

Repeated over and over, his wailing had the effect of brainwashing me. And my brain being in a pretty fragile state, I started to believe his mad, paranoid obsessions. What was he on about? OK, he wanted a shot of morphine but why was he demanding REAL doctors, REAL nurses, and why did he want to be moved to a REAL hospital? (What if he was right?) The fact was, he was REALLY getting on everybody's nerves.

His serial pain-in-the-arse attitude had the advantage of making him the focus for all the bad moods on our floor. One auxiliary after another tried to get him to shut up, but they soon lost patience. I could hear their attempts at persuasion escalate. It was like the good old days of the Cold War and the KGB.

Intimidation: 'Shut your mouth, or else . . .'

Beatings and violence: 'Here, take that in your ugly mug. I warned you!'

Guilt trip: 'This is not good, you're not letting your room-mate sleep. He's in pain too, you know.'

Blackmail: 'We won't let you have any visitors. Your wife won't come to see you any more.'

Hints of a Siberian concentration camp: 'Stop it, or we'll put you in the cold store!'

Nothing deterred him, he went on mewling. Eventually, at her wits' end, the head nurse would stick a great big needle in his arse. The poor guy put up a struggle, waving his arms and yelling that they were trying to kill him, that the syringe was a fake, that the nurse was working for Mossad, that a real doctor must come and put things right. Gradually, though he was still complaining, his voice would become quieter, his breathing laboured, his speech slow, then suddenly, nothing. Silence.

Mr Buzuf had regained his artificial paradise. Sister Morphine calmed him down for as long as the shot lasted. There was three hours' respite before he woke up and started all over again.

Hell is other people.

17

Bob

I still needed the respirator but, as the consultant announced – and Louis confirmed to me the following day – I would only get better if I was willing to make my lungs work using my diaphragm.

Step one: breathing for myself. This meant suturing the tracheotomy. Step two: speaking. I'd regain the use of my vocal chords. Step three: eating. I'd get rid of the feeding tube inserted in my nose and be able to take in solids again, at last. Then, once I was strong enough, they'd get me out of bed, weigh me, and sit me in a special wheelchair. Meanwhile, the plastics people would fit me with a custom-moulded corset that extended from my chin to my lower abdomen, which I'd have to wear until my cervical vertebrae were realigned. And that would be the end of Intensive Care. I'd be moved to a transit room on another floor where my progress would be monitored. The healing of a damaged spinal cord, the regrowth of nerves, are unpredictable things, but signs of recovery can take from one to six months to manifest themselves. After that time, welcome to the world of tetraplegia!

After the intermediate post-Intensive-Care stage, my new body and I would be transferred to Dr Desmouches' physical rehabilitation department. I'd start on an arduous programme of physiotherapy, occupational therapy, hydrotherapy, ball games, Russian roulette and wheelchair racing. For the first time in my life, my diary would be booked up six months in advance!

Once the night nurse had cleaned my tracheotomy and replaced the dressing, she switched off the respirator. She stayed just long enough to check my reaction.

'It's always difficult for the first few hours, but you'll get used to it. Keep breathing gently, I'll be back in an hour.'

An hour? But I'd be dead in an hour. Panic-stricken, I clicked my tongue but the nurse turned and left the room. I was still clicking furiously when a hairy personage with a furtive manner came and stood at the foot of the bed.

'Hi there, kiddo, doing some scuba diving?'

I'd seen his hideous face before. He had black hair that stood on end, a thin body and powerful, gnarled forearms, and his aftershave made me want to throw up. Its sickly combination of pine and lavender reawakened my sense of smell, which had been out of action for the past month. He took a turn around my domain, kicking my room-mate's bed to see if he was asleep. Then, smiling strangely, he stuck a plastic tube connected to a container of water into my mouth.

'You were thirsty, weren't you?'

I drank compliantly while he watched the flow of water. As I was gagging slightly he smiled encouragingly and said, 'Hi! My name's Robert, but you can call me Bob.' He added quickly, 'Well, you can call me Bob when you can speak again.'

I was going to thank him for his thoughtfulness when a voice made him look round.

'Pleeease, Bob, give me an injection, pleeeease . . .'
Damn! Buzuf was awake again.
Bob's face darkened.

18

Musicians

At the entrance to the Intensive Care unit, there was a sign that read: 'Danger. Please switch off all mobile phones.' A mobile ringing unexpectedly could interfere with the electromagnetic codes of most of the machines keeping patients alive in Intensive Care.

Jeanne, a young nurse who worked the morning shift – seven till three – woke me gently by laying her hand on my forehead. Grinning delightedly, she waved Mister X's latest CD under my nose. Mister X, was a pop idol, a man with platinum discs, who was a hit on the radio, on TV, in concert, throughout France and the entire French-speaking world. Jeanne was terribly excited.

'I know it's not visiting time,' she said, pointing at her watch. 'It's only eleven, but your friends really want to see you, and it'll do you good! They say they've just got back from touring Canada with Mister X. I love his stuff!' She waved the CD again and looked into my eyes. 'Do they really play gigs with him?' I blinked. 'Wow . . . OK, I'll go and get them. Don't go away!'

Don't go away. Not much risk of that. And anyway it

would be great to see my musician friends, Laurent and Pierre Jean.

I caught sight of them in the doorway. They hesitated for a moment, during which their smiling faces froze in horror. I realised that they'd been prepared for anything, except this. They'd just dropped by between flights, and it was outside visiting hours so my brothers hadn't had a chance to forewarn them. Those first moments were devastating. Laurent came over to hug me, clasping a present, unable to say a word. How could fate be such a bitch, turning a life upside down like this, destroying hopes and dreams overnight? Only a month ago, we had all been together – on the ski slopes by day, playing gigs by night. We'd gone down a storm in Switzerland. People had come to our dressing room afterwards to congratulate us. It was supposed to be the start of great things.

I could see from Laurent's stricken face what a difficult situation I was putting him in. 'Can I do anything for you?' he asked, and stroked my forehead, his hand trembling. That same hand never hesitated on the neck of a guitar, making the strings sing. I'd never seen him so fragile.

Pierre Jean reacted differently. While white people weep for their dead, black people sing and praise theirs. I was alive, if a little burnt round the edges. What was happening to me was like a parody of a Blues song, a Cotton song, the lament of a slave in the old South. Tomorrow I'd be free, liberated. I just had to get through this difficult time.

After hugging me, he toured my little kingdom, examining all the machines with an expert eye. He was a real tech freak. Since the advent in the early 80s of MIDI – Musical Instrument Digital Interface – and home studios, which had revolutionised music production, he'd followed every stage in the development of computerised music: analogue and digital synthesizers, rhythm boxes, sequencers, samplers, music software, individual CD recorders, web music.

'Laurent, take a look at this!' he whispered. 'There's some KazWax stuff!'

This Japanese manufacturer of digital pianos also made medical equipment! Jeanne came in to change my drip and Pierre Jean started asking her about all the machines – their reliability, their working life. He pointed out that one of the control dials was off while the other one, on the right, was on. She explained that this was quite normal: the left one only came on if there was a problem. Every circuit had a back-up in case of a breakdown or power cut.

Laurent unwrapped his present, a small FM radio in the shape of a Harley Davidson. Pierre Jean got down on all fours to find a socket, providing a running commentary as he followed the connection cables: 'There's a big red thing . . . don't know what it is. Ah, here we are . . . No, the socket's full. This is the thing for the humidifier, and this is . . . What's this?'

I was terrified he might unplug the oxygen. The motorbike headlamp lit up as the radio came on, playing some pure hard rap – a somewhat brutal reintroduction to music. Laurent tried to find something a little more gentle. Watching to see how I reacted, he adjusted the volume and fiddled around on the FM frequency to find the perfect sound: a beautiful vibrato and a few notes recorded somewhere between California, Abbey Road, Memphis, Tennessee, New York and Havana. I ground my teeth as soon as a French song came on; a strange and unexpected revulsion. I found the words, even the most anodyne, painful to listen to. '*Si maman, si . . . maman, si tu voyais ma vie . . . Belleville ou Nashville? Où sont mes racines?*

Je ne t'aime plus mon amour, je ne t'aime plus tous les jours.'

I wanted the music to take me far away. Laurent landed on a beach in Rio where Antonio Carlos Jobim's girl was wiggling her hips to the sound of the bossa nova. We all winced: the bloody song had been played in lifts, airports, piano bars and three-star restaurants ad nauseam! To make me laugh, Pierre Jean danced a few steps of the samba around my bed, shaking his behind. He took his mobile phone from his pocket, grabbed a thermometer from my bedside table and shook them in time like maracas: 'Tall and tanned, and young and lovely, the girl from Ipanema goes walking . . .' He knew all the words by heart. And he was almost as good as Stan Getz on the sax.

It was painful to laugh. Tensing my throat squashed the tracheotomy incision. I could either suffer agonies or try not to listen. Laurent could either knock Pierre Jean on the head, or quickly find the perfect FM frequency.

Pierre Jean's mobile started ringing, setting off a deafening alarm in the room. Laurent meanwhile had found a gem on OuiFM: 'It's Oh So Quiet' by Björk. Jeanne and a doctor rushed in to find them sitting by my bed with their hands over their ears.

'WHAT'S GOING ON?' Jeanne yelled, hurrying over to my bed to make sure I was still alive.

Dr Rollin turned off the alarm.

'It's OK, it's just the back-up circuit for the oxygen recycler. Everything's fine. Jeanne, you can go back to Room 11.'

Rollin noticed the music on the radio and came over to the bed.

'I like the music. Makes a nice change for you from the usual racket in here. How are you sleeping at night? Not too well? It'll get better eventually.' To my friends he said,

'Are you the guys who play with Mister X? I've got all his albums! Tell me, er . . .' He took each of them by the arm: 'Is it true his wife's shagging the Minister of Culture? Or is that a load of crap?'

19

ICU

Everyone was told: Raymond-Poincaré Hospital, 92 Garches, Patel Wing, Intensive Care unit, second floor, Room 12.

They waited their turn. Sylvia acted as hostess. If she wasn't around, Camille or Ambroisine took her place. Alix and Amélie came in every day, so there were always at least three girls in the waiting room, in addition to Léo's women friends and exes and his girlfriends Dagmar, Vanille, Anne, Soraya, Kaori, Sibylle and Caroline.

As for Gwendoline, she'd fled to New York. She avoided being decapitated in the accident by a hair's breadth. All the other girls had turned up, to Darius's astonishment. He couldn't tell who was actually going out with his brother because they all acted like 'Miss Tetra 96', the cripple's official fiancée.

Doctors came by every single day to talk to the family and keep them up to date on the patient's progress. What Darius didn't know was that the second floor of the Patel Wing had been renamed the 'Chick Reserve' by their envious colleagues in the Vidal Wing. The medical staff got all hot and bothered at the sight of these emotional young women walking down the corridors in mini-skirts and stilettos. Some girls took several days to get to know their way around the maze of buildings, if they weren't first kidnapped by some lecherous doctor.

The daily parade of silk stockings and high heels brought joy and colour to the silent corridors of Intensive Care. The patients weren't the only ones who were sick: these female presences gave a much-needed boost to the carers' morale too.

One day, when Dr Rollin came to check Léo's blood pressure, he witnessed Loranska's show. Not in the least put out by the doctor's presence, she donned a red PVC catsuit and matching thigh boots, and started swaying her hips to a jungle bass and drums beat and clambering like Catwoman on to anything that would support her weight – stool, bed, table, washbasin, radiator – so that Léo, between naps, should miss none of the show. She uncovered his stomach and brushed against him, still in time to the music, licking his navel. Loranska's tongue, like a little pink serpent, moved lower. For the first time in his life, Rollin was momentarily sorry he wasn't a tetraplegic too.

The tale of Room 12 spread round the hospital. The second floor buzzed with excitement. If only Léo could spend a whole year in Intensive Care, maybe that would fix their love lives!

In the midst of all the flurry, Darius handed cigarettes to the more nervous visitors and, when there were fewer people around, went over his brother's papers. Louis explained to newcomers the rules of Intensive Care, and what they should and shouldn't do at Léo's bedside.

After putting on a sterile gown, once through the double doors, they should head straight for Room 12. The temptation to stop and gawp at some zombie in his terminal phase sometimes proved too strong, but this wasn't an episode of *ER*. Certain personality types were mesmerised by all the technology used in ICUs – Intensive Care units. Fascinated by the study of obsessive deviancy and pathological neurosis, Louis had once read in a survey of US hospitals in the *New Yorker* that people sometimes pretended to be members of a support group or charity, or clowns for sick children, or volunteer readers, in order to get into ICUs. They all had the following things in common: 1. They hadn't had any toys as children. 2. They'd been locked in cupboards or bathrooms by abusive parents. 3. They watched *Star Trek*.

These loonies – mostly men – found it exciting to hide in dark, sterile rooms stuffed full of computers, control screens, cardiac monitors with analogue print-outs, and high-precision apparatus monitored by miniature cameras, infrared sensors and automatic alarm systems. The journalist called his article 'The Challenger Syndrome'. When questioned by the FBI, these ICU 'junkies' all claimed that they thought they were inside a space ship, virtual passengers in a life-size video game.

Louis took notes, observing the behaviour of visitors, and found confirmation of something he already suspected: when faced with the suffering of others, women were less nervous, less afraid than men. Perhaps because they gave life? Having said that, not one of Léo's friends copped out; they all wanted to see him, hug him, touch him, bring him presents. When someone entered the room and whispered kind words in his ear, he opened his eyes, smiled for a few seconds and immediately fell asleep again, knocked out by the huge effort he'd just made.

Darius, Louis, Camille, Marco and the others watched as the daily pilgrims to Room 12 tiptoed out, faces ecstatic from their experience.

'I spoke to him. He moved his head a bit and smiled. It was wonderful, I think he recognised me.'

It was time to exchange all the drips, drains, intravenous injections and tranquillisers for love. A lot of love!

20

Taxes

At the tax office in the Rue de Grenelle, Darius was shown in to see Miss Victoire Lemercier. Forty-ish, with dyed red hair and a generous figure in a bright pink suit, she looked more like a 50s starlet than a tax department employee. In fact, she had a collection of framed postcard-sized posters for old films by Hitchcock, Lubitsch, Kazan, Truffaut, King Vidor, Minnelli, etc. on the wall behind her. Always keen to give his grey matter a workout, Darius memorised them all while she checked her files.

'How long has your brother been living in the area?' asked the Stranger on a Train.

'Almost a year.'

'OK, that makes it easier. I'll even be able to give you a copy of his council-tax statement. Does he have a television?'

'Er . . .' murmured Darius nervously. He knew that only two Frenchmen in three paid for a TV licence.

'Let's see what the computer comes up with,' said the Blue Angel. 'Let's find out if he's paid his parking tickets.'

Darius needed his brother's last tax statement for the

insurance company, but he hadn't been able to find it, despite searching all his drawers. Léo had moved three times that year: after leaving the flat he shared with Alizée on the Boulevard Saint-German, he'd stayed at his friend Marin's for three months, before finally moving into the Rue du Bac. During his wanderings he'd scattered his things all over the place. Léo's bohemian disorganisation was making things very difficult for Darius, who was tidiness personified.

'What was the name again?' asked the Lady of the Camellias, moving her mouse over a mat printed with a pattern of dead leaves.

'Léopold Étienne Marie Roger Champollon, born in Pau on 14 March 1963.'

The Pirate's Fiancée tapped away at the computer, taking care not to break any of her bright red nails. Darius watched her discreetly. On the wall Marilyn Monroe smiled down at them.

'I see you like films,' he said and read out, inspired: '*Some Like It Hot*.'

Angélique Marquise des Anges stopped typing and looked at Darius with surprise.

'I beg your pardon?'

'I was referring to the Billy Wilder film. You've got the poster behind you.'

The Mermaid of the Mississippi turned round.

'I'm sorry, they've been up there so long I don't notice them any more.'

'Happens to me all the time . . .' said Darius, nodding understandingly.

Cleopatra ignored this and began to rearrange her hairdo. Darius waited the length of a film trailer.

'I'm sorry to bother you with this, but my brother can't deal with his affairs himself, so I'm taking charge of them.'

'Yes, you mentioned it on the phone. He's had an accident.'

'A month ago.'

The She-Cat on a Hot Tin Roof shook her head to ward off bad luck.

'Oh, I know what these insurance companies are like. Always ready to take your money, but when you get into trouble – forget it!'

The computer grumbled away while Miss Lemercier typed.

'Ah, here we are! Your brother's file is coming up on screen.'

'Great,' said Darius enthusiastically.

'Hmm, you know what?' asked Babette Goes to War. 'My colleague the tax inspector is going to be pleased to hear from him.'

'Are they acquainted?'

'Not at all. I think your brother's forgotten to pay his taxes.'

'Really?'

The Last of the Mohicans sat back, looking sorry.

'Your brother didn't pay any tax in 1996.' She peered at the screen and added, 'Or in 1995 . . . or 1994!'

Poor Darius. She'd taken the wind right out of his sails.

'How long has he been in hospital?'

Darius wished he could say three years, but instead he had to plead mitigating circumstances on behalf of his brother: Léo was an artiste; a fragile, absent-minded, temperamental being, at the mercy of the caprices of a cruel business. Miss Lemercier knew how extravagant showbiz people could be! They lived from day to day and, if they had the prospect of a contract, they went out to celebrate instead of stocking up the freezer and paying off their tab at the butcher. Ah, if only she could have heard Léo's songs – they were so beautiful, so tender, so melancholy! His lyrics were so profound. And to think, he couldn't even raise his hands to a keyboard now! That might seem unimportant to her, but to him it was a tragedy. He was born to sit at a Steinway, and now he was as helpless as a plate of jelly and as silent as a tortoise. Music had been his whole life and now he couldn't even play a tin whistle! It was a horrifying blow. If he had money worries on top of everything else, he'd surely lose the will to live!

Pretty Woman, who never missed a charity concert on TV, said reassuringly, 'I'm sure things'll work out . . .'

Was she referring to Léo's recovery or to his estrangement from the tax authorities? Darius decided to make one last desperate bid to save his brother. 'Look what I received today,' he said.

He held out the hospital bill: 385,000 francs for thirty days in Intensive Care.

'My goodness,' whispered Mary Poppins, 'it doesn't come cheap, does it?'

Poor Darius. The day was costing him a fortune!

21

Yin and Yang

One morning, the ENT doctor came to suture Léo's tracheotomy. A nurse held up a pocket mirror and he peered at the cut at the base of his neck. He'd had his throat slit, but he really hadn't come off too badly. In a second, he'd be able to speak, to communicate at last. He tried to thank the doctor, but instead Bugs Bunny spoke out.

'What's that horrible sound?'

'It's quite normal, you haven't used your voice for a month. If need be we'll get the speech therapist to see you.'

Every time Léo said hello to a member of staff it felt as if his vocal cords were out of whack – his voice sounded all high-pitched. He made the nurses laugh, at least, and, since it wasn't his voice, he came out with all sorts of rubbish to amuse the young student nurses (he called them 'the novices').

'Hey, what's the difference between a noodle and a tetraplegic?' he asked one of them.

The girl shook her head.

'The noodle moves when you suck it!'

A nurse had to spoon-feed him, but he found it impossible to swallow lying down and he choked on his food.

He wasn't hungry anyway. The food stank, his mouth stank, his whole body stank. He just wanted to sleep. But his nursemaids were persistent; by 8 a.m., they were already trying to stuff him.

'You've got to make an effort, or the doctor won't be happy. You're much too thin!'

But Léo refused to eat. Two big strong auxiliaries brought a weighing machine to his room. They got him out of bed using a hoist and laid him on the metal platform. On contact with the icy surface his flaccid body went into spasm. This was the first time that he was conscious of being off his air mattress. So now, there he was, as naked as a skinned rabbit on a butcher's block, as skeletal as a prisoner in a concentration camp. He hated his physical deterioration. In the olden days, he'd have been left by the roadside. He never dreamt he might become a burden to society, to his family and friends, but that's all he was: a burden.

'Fifty-six kilos,' announced the auxiliary.

'That's no good at all,' said Dr Rollin. 'You must eat, or we'll have to put in a feeding tube.'

Léo had lost twelve kilos in thirty-three days.

'Shall we put the carcass back in bed?' asked the auxiliary, winking at Léo.

He now inhabited a different body, spoke a different language. Before his accident, he'd had flu occasionally and a couple of bad bouts of the clap, but apart from that he'd never been ill in his life. And he'd always kept well away from hospitals. In the old days he could run for a taxi, climb stairs, carry a suitcase, hold a woman in his arms and suck her tongue without getting in the least bit tired. It was in his nature not to waste energy on everyday things, but to throw himself body and soul into the frivolous stuff. It was a question of philosophy. Yin and yang.

He'd always looked much younger than his age. He was a kind of vampire: the older he got, the younger his girlfriends got. They had fresh blood, high spirits, the stamina of thoroughbreds and boundless imagination. Léo desired all the women in the world. He owed them so much. Even for what was happening to him today.

On the day of his accident, fate had stopped the clock – an old-fashioned grandfather clock with roman numerals, two hands marking the hour, and a big motionless pendulum.

Who would get it going again?

22

Don't I know it, Charles!

It would take another week before I was well enough to leave Intensive Care. I felt like sleeping less, which was a good sign. I had a nap after lunch and then waited impatiently for my visitors. I could see that the doctors and nurses were relieved I was out of danger, and I also noticed a change in my nearest and dearest. We'd moved to phase two. Now that I could speak again – my voice had completely recovered – I could express my feelings and wishes. The first of these was to ask for Charles, my brother the monk. I wasn't sure why. I'd been into the shadows, I'd seen death, and I wanted an explanation. I felt, however, very far removed from mystical or spiritual matters. I hadn't been to church in a long time and, when I thought of Charles, it was always as my brother, not as a priest. He could have been a car salesman, removal man or history teacher, it would have made no difference whatsoever to our relationship. We lived on different planets but we were very fond of each other. Indeed, inveterate hedonist that I was, I thought him brave to embrace a life of contemplation and seclusion in a cold, damp Cistercian abbey on the edge of the Jura. I couldn't imagine living without cable

TV, Caribbean beaches or Cuban salsa; without the delightful company of women or the latest Armani suit; without reading *Gala* or being invited to the Surrealist Ball at the Hotel Lambert.

While I was delirious, Darius, at my bedside, heard me call for Charles several times. He mentioned it to Louis, 'D'you think it's his brother he wants, or a priest?'

He concluded that I must be afraid of dying. Charles arrived, in a grey habit in the midst of all the girls in mini-skirts, with a shaven head, sandals with no socks and a rosary hanging from his belt. The first thing I saw was the top of his head.

It was late. The nurses had turned out the lights, leaving only the night light above the door. Drowsily, eyes half-closed, I noticed a round whitish shape with the pallor of raw pastry on the bedcover just beyond the edge of the sheet and my extended arm. I was still on barbiturates so I wasn't surprised by this weird apparition: an upside-down pizza whispering from Paul's epistle to the Corinthians: 'When that which is perfect is come, then that which is in part shall be done away. When I was a child, I spake as a child, I understood as a child, I thought as a child; but when I became a man, I put away childish things. For now we see through a glass, darkly; but then face to face: now I know in part; but then I shall know even as also I am known. And now abideth faith, hope, charity, these three; but the greatest of these is charity.'

The pizza looked up. Charles knelt and prayed by my bed. He took my hand and pressed it to his forehead. A smile lit up his face, so I knew we weren't alone: he'd brought along his old friend, the invisible prophet, the two-thousand-year-old bearded holy man. They must be pretty close, because he'd entrusted me to the care of his mother Mary, the little Jewess from Nazareth. While I was asleep, Charles had hung a luminous figure of the Virgin on the monkey pole above my bed, where it swung in the darkness. I was faced for the first time with our respective isolation, he in his cell, me trapped in a bed. I was about to say something but he stopped me. He was right, we didn't need words. What could I tell him that he didn't already know? It was the longest silent conversation we'd ever had. He stayed until the night shift arrived, around 1 a.m. I was interested to see their reaction, but nobody seemed bothered. My brother put an envelope into my hand, hugged me and left.

After seeing to my needs for the night, one of the auxiliaries, a huge West Indian called Barnabé, sat on the bed and, without my asking, opened the letter. Without straining his voice, which was a deep bass, he tried to make sure that every word stood out clearly as he read, as if afraid I might miss one.

Léo,
The entire community has been praying for you since your accident. Yesterday evening, I held a mass for you and we sang with all our hearts. I felt your presence very strongly. I reproached myself that it should have taken a tragedy to make me think of my loved ones and you in particular. Not that my prayers haven't been with you all since I've been far from you, quite the contrary. But I always picture you so healthy and full of energy that it's been hard to come to terms all of a sudden with just how fragile our existence really is. I can find no words, for the moment, to convince you that what has happened to you is a terrible test and that you must not lose heart. I grieve with you over the tragedy that has struck you. All I can do to comfort

you is to offer you all my love as your brother. I know that your heart is uneasy, but I want you to know that you mustn't be afraid of the light that your suffering has lit within you.
Charles

Hands trembling, Barnabé folded the letter and placed it on the bedside table. His eyes were so full of sadness that I wondered if reading the letter hadn't reawakened painful memories of his own. He wiped away a tear, said good night and walked heavily to the door. I'd never seen someone so big look so vulnerable, so wounded. Maybe he too was afraid of the night? Maybe he even wanted to change places with me? Charles's letter troubled me less than the auxiliary's obvious emotion. I hadn't realised until then just how desperate my situation was. The letter had caught me unawares. I'd been so afraid of death. Now that I was back among the living, and in pretty pleasant circumstances – surrounded with visitors, love, presents, women, flowers – I thought things would surely sort themselves out. I'd soon get my legs back.

Yet I couldn't see anything clearly. I was searching for a way out, a future, but for the time being all I could move was my head, which wouldn't get me very far. Charles's fervour had struck home. His letter had evoked the insane ordeal to come as accurately as any doctor's diagnosis. By taking my hand and accompanying me amongst the wounded and afflicted, Charles had only succeeded in fuelling my dismay. He had propelled me into a world that was bottomless, endless, because you could always find someone at a lower ebb, unhappier, more unfortunate than yourself. As I'd just seen with Barnabé.

The nameless chaos of the planet was no longer confined to the evening news on TV. No, it was here, right in front of me, on my plate. And I had to finish it all up, like when I was a kid. 'You can't leave the table until you've emptied your plate!'

Don't I know it, Charles.

23

Sylvia

I looked a real sight when they moved me to my new room on the first floor. Sylvia was already there, putting away in the cupboard the things I'd need for my stay: toilet bag, CDs, and that was it. In fact, I'd never been so much in need of . . . nothing. Apart from a razor and toothbrush, which someone else handled for me, I was bare of belongings, or almost.

The hospital provided me with a special cotton gown that buttoned down the back and could be slipped over my neck brace. Underneath I had to wear a corset; flesh-coloured, padded and oversewn, it stretched from groin to chest and laced up at the front – very Jean-Paul Gaultier. I also wore white support stockings that came to mid-thigh and regulated my circulation, especially when I was placed in a half-sitting position. I'd spent the last six weeks flat on my back twenty-four hours a day. As soon as my upper body was raised, the blood, accustomed to flowing horizontally, abruptly left my brain and I fainted. The white stockings (why white?) helped to maintain the blood pressure in the upper half of my body.

When Sylvia saw me in my hospital drag-queen get-up,

she burst out laughing. 'Serves you right, my love! We're getting our own back at last. Now you've got to put up with all the things you've inflicted on us for years! All you need is a pair of high heels and you'd look perfect, my little bitch!'

She was right. I was always getting my girlfriends to dress up as femmes fatales, always urging them to undress a little bit more: 'Unbutton your blouse!' 'Wear stilettos!' 'Shorter skirts, with higher slits!' 'Get rid of that bra!' 'Don't cut your hair!' 'More lipstick!' 'Forget tights, wear stockings!' 'Paint your nails!' 'Don't even think about knickers under your jeans, just a G-string!' 'Put on PVC thigh boots!' 'Keep quiet when I'm looking you over!'

Some got annoyed, others loved it and went along with it. 'Playful, aren't you?' said Sharon la Bianca, an American beauty queen on a trip to Paris. We'd just ransacked a leather, PVC and lingerie boutique in Pigalle. Miss Texas was into spanking and accessories.

Nature had spoiled Sylvia: she was dynamite, a real Latin bombshell. A sexy brunette with Argentinian blood, she attracted both men and women, which didn't bother her a bit. 'I'd rather do it with a beautiful girl than an ugly man!' she'd say.

We both had complicated love lives, full of ups and downs. We told each other everything, we were allies, complementary, hand in glove. I was much too fickle for her even to contemplate sharing my bed, and we were too close for me to try anything that might test her 'sex-control'. She'd be off like a shot. I found it more interesting to make her laugh, to make her feel happy and safe. She needed a big brother, hers had died ten years earlier in a car accident. Whatever happened, we planned to end our days together.

'See, Léo,' she said in hospital, 'I'm getting in training.

It's a bit sooner than expected, but you're my grumpy old man in a wheelchair!'

At least now she didn't have to worry: I could no longer jump her, or corner her in the changing rooms of Bon Marché. The ball was in her court from now on, and if I ever changed my mind and declared my passion, I was under no illusions: Sylvia would burst my bubble.

24

Physiotherapist

I had left Intensive Care but kept the newborn-baby lifestyle. It wasn't unpleasant. I lay in bed the whole time and, like the first months of my life, I was surrounded by women. I had one nurse to deal with my personal care, another to feed me, and I was assigned a young physiotherapist, Françoise.

She arrived on my second day, equipped with a little hammer. She tapped knees, elbows, fingers, checking my reactions and neatly entering the results, graded from one to five, in her notebook. She was pretty disappointed with my scores: legs = 0; arms = 0; hands = 0. I stuck out my tongue, but she said that didn't count. The doctors got mad when they saw my marks. I was bloody lazy. 'You're not going to move up into the next class if you keep this up!'

I was setting out on a career as a dunce all over again. The past always catches up with you. Only my mother remained encouraging: 'Don't worry, darling. Rome wasn't built in a day.'

No, but I'd destroyed myself in a couple of seconds!

On the third day, Françoise arrived with a box of

ergonomic tools. I was very excited. My young physio had a distant manner, an even voice, hair pulled back into a neat bun, and a close-fitting, perfectly pressed sky blue tunic with matching trousers. I'd given up on my old fantasy of a nurse wearing nothing under her uniform long ago. We weren't there to have fun. Françoise kept strictly to medical questions: 'What about here? What can you feel when I do this?'

I thought about it. I knew that she'd jabbed me somewhere, at the end of myself. Armed with a mini-icepick, my mini-serial physio was pricking a small area of my skin. But where? My left foot? My knee? I had no idea. I felt like saying, 'You could be pinching the end of my toe, I don't give a shit! Suck my cock instead and I'll tell you what's really going on!'

'Well?' asked Françoise.

'Er . . . I think there's something happening . . .'

'Which leg? Left or right?'

'No, down the corridor. Can't you hear it? Someone's shouting "Fire!" Let's get out of here!'

'Please try to concentrate, Mr Champollion, or we'll never get anywhere. Well?'

I adored her Marseille accent, and the way she smelled of soap; a good clean smell. She had white teeth, olive skin, and she didn't smoke. Since my internment, my sense of smell had become as accurate as radar, intercepting anything that came within range of my nostrils. The smells wafting from my meal trays made me want to throw up, but I sniffed the scent of women with delight: they reawakened pleasant memories. How old could my Mediterranean lovely be? Twenty-five? Twenty-eight? I asked her, but she soon put me in my place: 'That isn't relevant to our work here.'

Her job was to give me a sensory examination – in

other words to test the reactions of all the 'lifeless' parts of my body, awarding them a+ or a–. There are two levels of sensory awareness: full and partial. Full sensation is what most mortals – the able-bodied, the normal, the healthy – enjoy. Partial sensation, resulting from trauma to the spinal cord or brain, alters one's sense of touch and feeling.

The surface of the body has millions of highly complex sensors. Every shift, every movement, every touch, every temperature sensation is fed into our central computer, analysed and instantly retrieved, for example:

- cautiously dipping your toe into a swimming pool to check the temperature;
- burning your fingers getting a dish out of the oven;
- feeling your shirt soaked with cold sweat after a big shock;
- getting goose bumps when out walking in a cold, damp wind;
- feeling the gentle caress of a hand or a foot brushing yours under the table;
- putting on a pair of jeans;
- getting punched in the face;
- drying yourself after a bath;
- being kissed;
- getting a hard-on;
- coming.

The spinal cord, which looks like a long, fibrous, translucent noodle, runs down the centre of the spinal column, starting at the base of the brain and ending in a tail just above the coccyx. The spine is divided into three sections:

- The cervical vertebrae. There are seven of them, from the base of the skull down to between the shoulders, and they support the head. The neck is the most fragile, most vulnerable part of the human body. It's the fetish zone of the serial killer, the commando, the hanged man, the karate expert, the sado-masochist into slow strangulation, the polo-neck sweater and the tetraplegic. Strangulation, whiplash, and you've had it. The higher the injury, the worse off you are. Christopher Reeve, alias Superman, who broke his top vertebrae, can't breathe unaided – he's on a ventilator twenty-four hours a day. He's totally paralysed, even his head has to be supported. He has some movement of his chin with which, by means of a joystick, he guides his electric wheelchair. He can drink, chew and swallow, but he couldn't spit out an olive stone at you – you need your diaphragm, abdominal muscles and a strong push of air from your lungs to do that. And if ever an olive went down the wrong way, he'd die.
- The thoracic vertebrae. There are twelve of them, from the base of the neck to mid-back (at belly button level). This is the level at which bikers are most often injured. In a fall or a skid, it's your thoracic vertebrae that cop it.
- The lumbar vertebrae. There are five of them, from the small of the back to the coccyx. A fracture of the lumbar vertebrae can lead to paraplegia, or paralysis of the lower limbs.

Cervical, thoracic, lumbar. Specific motor functions and areas of sensation correspond to each of these levels. An injury at T1, the top thoracic vertebra, for instance, affects the use of your hands.

There are lots of paraplegic bikers, lots of paraplegic and tetraplegic car-crash victims, and in general, way too many dead on the roads. The All Saints' Day and August holiday weekends break all records for the number of mangled bodies in helicopters, ambulances, morgues and casualty departments. During peak periods, hospitals like the Raymond-Poincaré in Garches always leave a quota of rooms free for the 'fresh catch'. It can happen to anyone. If you're very badly injured, you're better off being taken to a major centre in Montpellier, Lyon, Marseille, Bordeaux or Paris than to some crappy little local clinic. Or, better still, just waiting patiently for an ambulance or a good Samaritan who's got a bit of sense.

Sometimes, the rescue helicopter crashes with a pilot (let's call him Jack), a doctor (say, Dr Mabuse), and a paraplegic (let's call him Phil), injured in a car accident, on board. After the crash, the information recorded on the CASCEV (Civil Defence and Sanitary Evacuation Air Control) tape has altered radically. Jack, the formerly able-bodied pilot, is now paraplegic; Mabuse, the flying doctor, has become tetraplegic; and Phil, the paraplegic patient, has 'become' dead. An unlucky passer-by, who became badly burned, then dead, is found under the wreckage. As he was HIV positive, the police think it may have been suicide.

It can happen to anyone.

Françoise decoded my medical notes for me: I was a C6 incomplete, therefore everything below the injury (from thoracic 1 to lumbar 5) was, for the time being, or 'forever', on hold. She could busy herself moving around my bed, playing with my body, tickling me and ignoring my questions, it didn't make much difference to me.

But there was one thing that she hadn't checked or assessed: my libido. It was still working. For the time being, my penis seemed very far away. Too far – a poor little shrivelled palm tree, alone on an island in a sea of ice, in need of a wave, an expert hand, a beautiful castaway to bring it back to life in this unfinished Eden.

But it wouldn't be Françoise.

25

Corkscrew

This morning they brought me a TV. I must be the only person in the world who has a human remote control: my room-mate, Maurice, fifty years old, divorced, no kids. He changes channels for me.

'Maurice, the remote control! Change channel!'

'Hang on a minute, son, I can't find it.'

Maurice has been in and out of hospital for years. He wears dark glasses. He's blind and has only one leg. When he was thirty he was working as a baker and he used to set off for work on his moped at the crack of dawn. 'I lived in a tiny village called Saint-Martin-sur-Hinx in the Landes, ten kilometres from Hossegor. I got up at five every morning to go and bake my bread. One Sunday I was on my moped, waiting at the stop sign at the crossroads with the A road from Bordeaux to Bayonne. It's always a busy spot, but there's a bit less traffic at weekends, particularly when it's still dark. In the distance, I could see a lorry coming pretty fast from the right. I decided to wait and let it pass. Just as it was about to go by, I felt a big jolt from behind and I was thrown into the middle of the road, right in front of the lorry. Its driver didn't have time to brake, he had to swerve to avoid me. He still ripped half my leg off and I hit the tarmac head first. They told me later it was youngsters coming back from a nightclub. They were hammered, they didn't see me.'

Maurice was in hospital for a week this time. He was having problems with his false leg, which was irritating his stump and causing sores and skin infections. He also had unbearable phantom pain. The lower leg and foot, left by the side of that road twenty years ago, still caused him pain. His blindness came later, probably because of the blow to his head and the ensuing coma. And his divorce. So now he was in for a general check-up, having his drugs reviewed, his liver, joints and blood tested, his skin checked (he'd had grafts), and trying out a new carbon alloy and Pyrex leg, followed by compulsory walking practice with a Zimmer frame.

Maurice had smuggled in food, rations from his native south-west, which made a nice change from supper at 6 p.m. as the nurses would insist on. After that we had the end of visiting hours, the news at eight, the film on cable and the final care routine at midnight, so that gave us six hours to digest our meal before going to sleep. My appetite was pretty poor anyway, what with having to lie flat on my back; the neck brace which chafed my chin when I opened my mouth; the drugs (Lioresal, Dantrium, Ditropan, Valium, Rivotril, Orelox, Xantrax, Smirnoff . . .); the padded vest, the stockings, and the lack of my ex, Alizée, who still hadn't shown up.

Maurice undertook to re-educate my palate. He waved foie gras, pâté, duck *confit* and red wine under my nose. He kept them stashed in his cupboard and I was his lookout, warning him if I heard a nurse coming. I had to give him directions so that he didn't crash into anything. Balancing on one leg, and hopping, blindly of course, with a bottle of Bordeaux in one hand and a jar of 'bon canard landais d'Esperolle' in the other should be a paralympic event.

'Two hops to the right, Maurice. Stop. Two hops to the left. Stop. Now, two hops towards me. Stop!'

He sat on my bed and set out his goodies on the trolley, feeling for the tin- and bottle-opener.

'Hand one inch to your right, Maurice. Stop!' He smiled at the ceiling and opened a tin at random.

'Here, take a whiff of that, son. What do you think?' It stank. Big mistake: it was a tin of sardines from Saint-Jean-de-Luz.

'Marvellous, Maurice, wonderful . . .'

'Smells good, doesn't it, son? I'll make you a sandwich.'

Maurice called me 'son' because of my voice. That was something, at least, to set against my galloping senility, my thirty-six years. I hadn't told him I was a tenor. I could sing really high. Nor did I mention my piano, or my guitars, or playing live on stage, or rock 'n' roll, or 'Surfer Girl' by the Beach Boys. It was still too early on in my illness to contemplate that it might all be over. I was still full of hope. It was only two months since the accident. 'Up to six, eight months,' the doctors had said, 'anything's possible.'

I was confident. And yet . . . Seeing Maurice, it was difficult not to jump forward fifteen years and picture my life as a Severely Disabled Person. Would I still be paralysed, an occasional inmate of rehab centres and hospitals? Would I be alone, somewhere out in the country, finishing off an old jar of duck *confit* and a bottle of plonk? No, that would never happen: I couldn't move my hands. You need quite a bit of strength to use a corkscrew.

You need strength . . .

26

Criminal business

Darius was in the office of Simone Lefranjus at Crédit Lyonnais, trying to sort out his brother's finances. He'd brought Léo's last few bank statements. The situation was calamitous. Not only was Léo overdrawn but, even with the fees he was owed, he couldn't afford to buy himself a wheelchair. Darius had made some enquiries: Social Security would contribute up to 3500 francs, but the average cost of a manual wheelchair (not even an electric one, they cost more like 55,000) was about 16,000 francs.

Luckily, Léo's friends mobilised themselves and clubbed together. So now there was a new problem: what to do with all the cheques coming in. Darius was being cautious: in addition to his disastrous discovery at the tax office, he'd found that Léo owed three months' rent and hadn't paid the hundreds of parking tickets lurking in the bottom of the wardrobe under a pile of multicoloured panties. Even if he paid all the cheques into Léo's account, there wouldn't be a single centime left over for his war chest. Léo didn't have a portfolio of stocks and shares, or a home-savings plan – only a babe-catching plan. He had lots of credit in that area, plenty of liquidity, particularly in the pelvic region.

And it got worse. As Darius went through the statements from September to March, he noticed a standing order for 185 francs that went out on the tenth of every month. Beside the debit column, it said: 'Criminal Business'. 'Damn! Another problem!'

This was the reason for his visit to Madame Lefranjus. She requested information about the payment from the main branch, but it would take six weeks to get an answer.

'Can the law seize an account?' asked Darius.

'Yes, we've got an official letter making that clear. In which case, there's nothing you can do. Couldn't you ask your brother about it?'

'Well, it's not really a good time. He's got enough to deal with at the moment.'

'I understand. By the way . . .'

'Yes?'

'Do you know if he's got a police record?'

Darius asked Sylvia, Alix, Marco, Ambroisine, Amaury, Guillaume, Pierre-Jean, Laurent, Charlotte, 'Tito' the tramp in the Rue du Bac, and at least fifty others who were close to his brother. Nobody knew of a crime Léo might have committed. There was one way of finding out, but Darius, who was neither a pushover nor a kamikaze, had no intention of throwing himself into the lion's jaws again.

The police station for the VIIth arrondissement at 122 Rue de Grenelle was midway between the offices of the Treasury and the Rue du Bac where Léo lived. Darius walked back and forth in front of the entrance several times. The policeman on duty kept a close eye on him. Darius wondered if he'd spotted his similarity with the photofit picture issued by the Department of the Interior of the serial lover of Bon Marché, a pervert who watched young women in the changing rooms of the lingerie department and strangled them with a Chantal Thomass silk stocking. Léo, who else?

Darius was very worried: what mess had his brother got himself into this time? Did this criminal business have anything to do with his accident? He remembered something, a possible clue: the garage mechanic had stated that in twenty years in the business he'd never heard of a Peugeot 604 doing 80 kph on a straight road, with a sober and seat-belted driver, overturning all on its own. It couldn't happen. Unless there was some external factor or deliberate interference. Or the driver was completely inept. Darius decided to consult an expert in the morning.

27

Video cassettes

A few days later they were all at the flat in the Rue du Bac, packing up Léo's stuff. He didn't know it yet, but he wouldn't be going back there.

Eric had brought champagne. He filled glasses, while Ambroisine played some songs Léo had recorded on the stereo just before his accident. '*Feux de bengale*', 'Sexy Girl', 'Saint-Germain Boulevard', '*Boum sur le corail*', 'Arizona'. Looking like a group of washerwomen, Sylvia, Camille, Alix, Virginie, Barbara and Garance folded shirts, underpants, trousers, jackets, singing along with their favourite crooner. The doorbell rang. Ludovic motioned to keep it down – it was nearly midnight.

'Pizza!' yelled Mickey hopefully. He hadn't had time for supper.

Louis opened the door expecting a complaining neighbour, but instead he found a beautiful blonde with legs that went on forever. She held out her hand to Louis, who wished suddenly that he were a chest specialist, then she adjusted her décolleté.

'Hi, is Léo here? I'm his neighbour, Marie Aymée. I'm

off to New York tomorrow. I promised to bring these videos back months ago,' she said.

Darius showed her in – Louis was rooted to the spot. Marie Aymée greeted everyone, perfectly at ease. When she leant over you could see that she wasn't wearing anything under her dressing gown. The two brothers offered her a seat and poured her a glass of champagne.

Poor Marie Aymée! She'd simply dropped by to return some videos and now she was weeping on the sofa between two Champollon brothers who were as upset as she was. This set off Alix, Camille and Sylvia, which put the men in an awkward position because all the handkerchiefs and boxes of tissues had already been packed away – there was only toilet paper left.

Marie Aymée told them how she'd met Léo. She'd got home one night after a wedding and found him asleep on the stairs. He'd lost his keys and was waiting for morning to call a locksmith. She offered to lend him money for a hotel room but he refused – it was already 5 a.m. and, besides, he had quite enough debts, he didn't want to take money from a stranger. Marie Aymée had been dancing all night, so she took off her shoes. Léo said he was just back from Thailand and offered to massage her feet. She thought that was a bit weird, but he wouldn't stop talking so eventually she sat on the stairs with him. Two hours later, they were still there, setting the world to rights. She invited him in and offered him the sofa.

Ludovic exchanged glances with Sylvia, who exchanged glances with Ambroisine, who exchanged glances with Eric: Léo had never set foot in Thailand! Another of his ploys to get laid! As he and Louis were seeing Marie Aymée out, Darius asked her what she did for a living. She said she worked for a mail-order video club. Their list of titles included a large selection of documentaries, news reports, magazines and investigative reporting: *The World of Hunting*, *Treasures of Egypt*, *Great Historical Mysteries*, *American Cinema*, *Flemish Painters*, *Wonders of the Indian Ocean*, *War Planes*, *French Gardens* . . .

'In fact,' Marie Aymée told Darius, 'your brother took out a subscription with us.'

'Do you know what for?'

'I can't remember . . . Our list is huge.'

'It wasn't *How to Hit on your Neighbour in Ten Easy Lessons* by any chance?' asked Ludovic, wondering if bloody Léo had managed to get his paws on her.

They were just about to kiss her goodbye at the door, when she snapped her fingers.

'I've got it! It was something horrible about serial killers, there were at least thirty videos in the collection. It was . . .'

'*CRIMINAL BUSINESS*,' yelled Darius.

The whole building heard him.

28

Ramona

Maurice had gone home so I had a new room-mate, Ricardo Martinez, a construction worker. He spoke three languages at once: Portuguese, French and 'Ayyy'.

'Ayyy! *Madre de Dios*! Ayyy, it hurts! I've been broken into a thousand pieces. Ayyy! A thousand pieces!'

Dr Azam had found a way to cheer him up. 'Now, now, Mr Martinez, that's not true! Not a thousand pieces, only eleven: one wrist, one collarbone, five ribs, one femur, one tibia and two ankles! The toes don't count!'

'Ayyy! Doctor, it hurts. I've been broken into . . . how many did you say?'

'Eleven pieces. You are allowed to say that, and "ayyy" too.'

Ricardo had fallen off scaffolding. Bandages, plaster casts, splints, traction weights – he was a living mummy. On the plus side, he hadn't damaged his spine and, though he was in a lot of pain, the doctors guaranteed that in three months he'd make a full recovery. On the minus side, he'd fallen on top of his boss Mr Gangotena's Renault Safrane. Mr Gangotena came to see him every other day, at around 8 p.m.

'Look, Ricardo, it's not about the car, it was only the bodywork, but still, it's no way to behave.'

'But boss, I didn't do it on purpose, I slipped. Ayyy, it hurts!'

'You weren't secured, Ricardo. If you'd been wearing your harness . . .'

'But boss, I lent it to Maurizio. Ayyy, it hurts!'

'Why did you lend it to Maurizio?'

'I can't remember now, boss. Ayyy . . . it hurts.'

'Ricardo! Answer Mr Gangotena!'

The worst was when Ricardo's wife got involved. Ramona Martinez always arrived five minutes after Mr Gangotena. Coiffed, made up, wearing sexy short skirts and stilettos, she looked like a streetwalker. At first I found it touching that she did herself up for her husband, but she was so horrible to him that I began to wonder what she was getting out of the visits other than satisfying an innate vindictiveness. Sitting at his bedside, wearing perfume that would wake all the living dead in Intensive Care, Ramona nodded in approval at every one of Mr Gangotena's unpleasant remarks, and then added her piece, arms raised to heaven, '"It hurts, it hurts!" What kind of an answer is that, Ricardo?'

She always brought him a little bag of cakes, which she put away in his cupboard. Then she went to the bathroom to redo her make-up. Meanwhile, Mr Gangotena would bring out a set of photos and hold them under Ricardo's nose.

'Look, Ricardo, this is the car before the accident. And now, look, you see the damage? Why did you do this to me, eh?'

At the end of his tether, poor Ricardo gave up and retreated into silence, interspersed with quiet 'ayyys'. He turned up the volume of the TV with his good hand, looking like a sulky child who'd just been told off. Mrs Martinez could be heard in the bathroom, announcing that she was leaving. I knew her lines by heart.

'Ricardo? Because of you, I'm going to have to run for the last train . . .'

She'd come back out, a snotty pout on her face, then suddenly she'd be all smiles. 'Mr Gangotena, would you mind doing me a favour and dropping me off at the Porte de Saint-Cloud?'

'I'd be delighted to, Mrs Martinez.'

I bet he would. It was the third time that week that he'd done her a favour.

29

Soap

On my last weekend before moving to the physical rehabilitation department in the Vidal Wing Dr Desmouches, accompanied by two junior doctors, came to introduce himself. He made me laugh.

'How's our rebel then? We're really going to whip you into shape, soldier, or it'll be the firing squad for you! Isn't that right, sir?'

He looked at my brother Louis who was in his navy blue off-duty uniform. Vanille, Marie and Garance, in skirts and trainers, were sitting on my bed reading *Gala*, *Voici* and *Jeune et Jolie* to me. They read out my horoscope. This was a promising time for us Pisces born in March. I just had to steer clear of draughts, beef and parking tickets. As for romance, it was as clear as day: someone was madly in love with me. Who was she? I'd find out soon . . . in next week's horoscope.

Saturday afternoon was quieter. Now that I was so much better, I could watch TV for fifteen hours at a stretch without getting tired. I'd discovered a brilliant soap, *The Fires of Passion*. At first I thought it was a documentary on the hairstyles of adulterous couples in Santa Barbara.

But no, the series and the actors were real, except for their hair – these people had indestructible hairdos! They looked like they had Yorkshire terriers sitting on their heads. They had rows, kissed, had sex under the sheets, rushed across the living room shrieking . . . and not a hair moved! I renamed the series *Tetraplegic Hairdos*. I tried to convert my parents, brothers, girlfriends, doctors and physio to the cause, but without success. They glanced absent-mindedly at the screen, but the images exerted no power over their imaginations and they got bored.

'Darling, we've come to see you, not to watch television.'

'Who's that big tart talking out of the side of her mouth?'

'You don't know where the remote is, do you?'

Louis was the only one who got to the end of an entire twenty-six-minute episode of *The Fires of Passion*. Just before it started, I summarised the story so far: Jennifer loved Kevin, who was cheating on Joan, who loved Derek, who was cheating on Priscilla, who loved Mike, who was cheating on Bruce, who loved Sharon, who was cheating on Brian with Jennifer, who ended up getting depressed and losing her self-confidence. Hence her affair with the handsome Carl.

At the end of the episode a nurse came to take a blood sample and Louis asked her if I was still on Valium.

30

Moving day

I moved out this morning.

Not back to the Rue du Bac. Darius has already told me that my stuff is in storage for an indeterminate amount of time. Anyway, I couldn't care less about my clothes, my furniture, my photos, my collection of cowboy boots and Hawaiian shirts. Apart from my guitar, my piano and the complete works of the Beach Boys, everything could go – they were just things. *Li fet met*, as it says in the Koran: time past is time dead.

This life in limbo doesn't frighten me. It's like a long journey, an exile. You leave everything behind on the quayside, keeping only the essentials. And anyway, how much do you really need? A healthy body, legs that can run for a train or climb the steps to a plane to escape to the ends of the earth, to start over. That's all.

I don't need to start from scratch, I just have to be patient and accept what my body lets me do. That's my journey. And the adventure starts today because I'm being transferred, after thirteen weeks in hospital, four of them in a drugged haze. Vidal Wing here I come! General mobilisation for Léo the immobile! Me and my army of frills, lace and mascara will be taking up new positions. Goal 1. Regain the use of my hands, shoulders, back, chest and abdomen. Goal 2. Regain the use of my penis, pelvis, hips, legs and feet, stand up again, run, and hold a woman in my arms. All in logical and neurological order: first the higher level (T1), then the lower (L5).

At night I dream that a cellular tremor reawakens my numb spinal cord, repairing atrophied networks and burnt-out neural circuits. And, as its healing molecules permeate the translucent cord, the nerve fibres for my sensory and motor functions light up level by level, like the windows of a skyscraper at nightfall. A little magical lift moves down the vertical bony structure of my spine, from my neck to my coccyx, reviving my inert body. My feet once again touch the ground, the churned-up sand of the Basque coast and the brightly lit dancefloors of Havana.

Monday morning is action stations! A nurse comes to wake me at 8 a.m. My things fit into a single sports bag. Two auxiliaries slide me from the bed on to a trolley. They cover me with a sheet, and then we're off down the maze of corridors. I say goodbye and thank you to familiar faces – doctors, junior doctors, nurses. They all wish me luck. At the lift we come across another trolley with a body asleep under the covers.

'Where's this one going?' a big black man asks the nurse at the desk.

'Room 12.'

That's my room, or rather, it was. Who cares? On we go.

In the lift, I'm filled with impatience. Outside *il fait beau, il fait chaud, la vie coule comme une chanson . . . aussitôt qu'une fille . . .* I'll feel the sun on my skin. Fresh air will rush up my nostrils. I'll see the tops of trees, maybe even some birds. En route, I'll encounter civilians, men and women who are neither visitors, patients, nor hospital staff.

The cramped lift with its graffitied walls make me think of a prison, of all forms of incarceration: lunatic asylum, monk's cell, high-security prison, plane/train/car crash, torture chamber, concentration camp; as a hostage; lost at sea, or up a mountain, or in the jungle . . . labyrinth of passion . . . bondage . . .

The lift doors open. My two pilots wheel me towards the exit. I pass curious, fearful, unfriendly faces. I suddenly feel that I'm a nuisance. I've swapped the quiet cocoon of Intensive Care for the unknown. Also, I'm virtually naked under the sheet. I'm worried a gust of air will lift it, exposing me to stares. I've become modest. The time when Léo showed his arse to anyone is long gone.

'Excuse us, please! Coming through! Thank you!' my two auxiliaries call out politely. Their speed is impressive. I must be number three or four on their list of transfers. Every year, they must have to move thousands of bodies. As we stop in front of the glass doors, my heart is pounding. In a few seconds' time, I'll be out in full sun.

But they steer the trolley into another lift and one of the auxiliaries presses the button for –1. This is pitiful, we're leaving Patel Wing by an underground route. A long corridor – dark, damp, cold, foul-smelling, dirty, noisy. Staff push carts of meal trays, rushing to the different departments. They pass one another, yelling, avoiding collisions by a hair's breadth. We wheel past transparent door flaps at the entrances to kitchens. Two thousand meals served every day. There's a great clattering of dishes, of glasses in racks. Faded coloured arrows on the sweating walls point the way to the Vidal Wing. Another lift, this time going up to level 1.

When we emerge, a change of décor. It's no longer the

static, sterile, peaceful environment of the Patel Wing, here things are really moving! The air is filled with voices shouting orders. Down the corridor I glimpse my first wheelchairs. Youngsters of fourteen, fifteen, eighteen, overtaking, crashing, racing, swearing.

Before abandoning me at the admissions desk, the auxiliaries place my bag on my legs. I'm left there for quite a while. How I wish one of my loved ones were with me, talking to me, comforting me. 'In your dreams, Léo. It's Monday morning. Your friends are at work, your parents aren't coming till tomorrow, and your women are taking a break.' I try to reassure myself – to check my impatience, my despondency – but it's no good. I'm in the middle of a world on the move and I have to take my place in it.

My rehabilitation has just begun.

31

Basque

Florence was getting ready in front of the big wardrobe mirror. She'd just got back from the hairdresser, having stopped off on the way at Sabia Rosa, a boutique that sold fine lingerie. She adjusted her basque before slipping into her sheath dress, taking care not to ladder her new tights. Her husband, Arno, arriving home from work earlier than expected, almost passed out when he saw her.

'Why is Florence, at six fifteen in the evening, getting dressed up like a call girl? Is she having an affair?'

He closed the bedroom door again. The children were playing with the babysitter in the next room. Arno checked to see if anyone was hiding under the bed, behind the curtains or in the wardrobe.

'What are you looking for, darling?' asked Florence, putting on a patent leather shoe with a five-inch heel.

'Er, nothing. But . . . er . . . what the hell are you doing in that get-up? Aren't we having supper here tonight?'

Florence turned round. She was a good head taller than him. 'Wow!' thought Arno. 'She looks much too sexy. Something's up.' She'd made up her eyes with eyeliner and mascara and her mouth looked like a big moist strawberry.

'Baby, I'm going to Garches, to see Léo. Don't you remember?'

Arno clicked. Of course! They'd talked about it last night.

'Ah, that's all right then, if it's for Léo!'

Florence peered at herself closely in the mirror. She had to get the finishing touches right – matching gloves, handbag, earrings.

'How do I look?'

Arno almost choked, and scratched his balls. 'Lucky bastard! If all it takes to get women to dress up like tarts and bring you chocolates is to overturn your car, throw me the keys now.'

He pressed up against Florence as she swayed on her high heels. In the bathroom, she leant over the basin. Arno eyed her cleavage in the mirror. He thought of Betty Page, the bumper of a 50s Cadillac, and a pearl necklace. The lace neckline of the basque barely hid the pink areolas of her overflowing breasts. 'You can see her nipples,' whispered Arno to himself, a finger in his mouth.

'Did you remember that it's our fifth wedding anniversary?' asked Flo, spraying scent on her cleavage and wrists.

'Yes . . . that's just it, I was hoping . . .'

'Too late, I've already got plans.'

Glumly, lustfully, Arno followed his wife to the lift. He said he could go with her, after all Léo was his friend too. And wasn't it a bit risky, her wandering around dressed like that? What would the neighbours think, and the concierge, Bernardo Riberoles, a real sex maniac? And what about the car park – the timer switch for the lights was on the blink down there . . .

Flo said Fabienne was waiting downstairs in her Mini

Cooper. She kissed him and disappeared into the lift, shouting, 'See you later, my love!' Arno stood open-mouthed for a few seconds. Back inside the flat he did a few dance steps on the carpet, put 'Sexual Healing' to play on the hi-fi, kicked his daughter's teddy bear out of the way and leapt on to the sofa, yelling, 'My wife's really sexy! My wife's really sexy!'

Without knowing it, Léo was bringing couples together.

32

Love

My room faces the door and has three beds, two of them unoccupied for the time being. When the door's open, I can see down the corridor, which is useful for when I get visitors. The good thing about my women friends is that I can identify them both by sight and by sound. The rhythm and pace of their heels clicking on the lino vary according to who it is. The ones who've been before (Sylvia, Camille, Ambroisine, Vanille) head straight for my room and make it in about forty-five seconds. Girls visiting for the first time take longer, depending on the height of their heels, the length of their legs, and their emotional state.

They're already nervous as they come through the hospital entrance for the first time. 'What state will he be in? Will he recognise us? Damn, I've smudged my eyeliner!' They do themselves up for these visits. The more absent-minded ones have to ask for directions a dozen times en route so it takes them about half an hour to get to the Vidal Wing. The department is a shock to them. They have to find Léo's section, putting up, while they do so, with the stares of sickly, shattered, aggressive or lifeless figures. By the time they get to the notorious room at the end of the corridor, their legs are shaking and their steps falter. They hurry past open doors, scared they'll be drawn in by faces desperate for any passing signs of life.

'Hey, girls! I'm over here!'

They catch sight of Léo; he's thinner, his head is trapped in a neck brace, but he's still smiling. On the wall facing the bed, friends have pinned photos, postcards, poems. He's even got a telephone, with a special control mechanism so he can answer without lifting the receiver. The girls have brought presents: books, wine, CDs, a shirt, sushi, cakes and, most importantly, kisses. The back of the bed has been raised. Let the party commence.

'What d'you think?' asks Caroline, twirling her skirt so that Léo can admire her lace garter.

'You're late,' answers the patient, glancing at the clock.

'But it was worth the wait, wasn't it? The bloke at the entrance sent me to the wrong department. Useless . . .'

'Yes, and it's good to see you, my dear.'

Léo is discovering the amazing power of female love, which is reaching its full expression at his bedside. The girls kiss him, touch him, hold him in their arms. They have no ulterior motives, they were simply afraid of losing him. You shouldn't wait until people die to tell them you love them. Léo represents the baby, child, son, brother, lover, husband, father or grandfather some have almost or already lost. In the past, he would have got the wrong idea about such expressions of affection and tenderness. How wrong he'd been all these years confining women to the role of mistress. They radiated love in a way he could never have imagined.

The accident is his chance to gain new insights in the field of love. Now that he is stranded, deprived of his physical assets, only huge emotional sensitivity will make up for his body's impairment. His days as the smooth-talker, nonchalant playboy, the piano-playing lover, are over. The sacrifice of his hands, his voice, his legs is an unquantifiable loss – a slow, searing, obscenely cruel execution. Beyond the unimaginable, this desert he has to drag himself across, there has to be a way out, perhaps a healing of the soul. Otherwise, what's the point?

Léo gives himself up to these affectionate women, these smiling angels, lavishing attention on him, savouring every minute in their company. But there's something he can't understand. What has he been doing all these years? Who has he loved, if not his own image reflected in the eyes of a female he was lusting after, idealising? Often, after an orgasm, he already wanted to move on to something new and, above all, to sleep alone.

Now, this tragedy is pushing his resistance to suffering to the limit, to the point of nausea, but it's also giving him a capacity for love whose existence he has never suspected. Perhaps because he's always seen love as a currency, never as a gift.

These women are teaching him a huge lesson, a lesson that you never forget once it touches your soul.

33

War

The department was very well organised. In addition to some thirty state-registered physiotherapists, treating both children and adults in a space that comprised a heated swimming pool and a physio area with exercise machines, there were occupational therapists, a social worker, a psychologist, a dietician, a pressure-sore adviser and a person in charge of the stock of wheelchairs, who loaned a super-machine on wheels to each new arrival for the duration of their stay.

A junior doctor in glasses, Harold Munch, came to examine Léo and to assess his motor and sensory functions. Apart from his hair, which had grown, there was no change; the unanimous verdict was 'condition stable'. Léo noticed lots of zeros lining up in the columns of Munch the pen-pusher's table.

'So, what's new, Doctor?'

'Would you like to see the psychologist?'

'Is she hot?'

'She can help you . . .'

'Really? Could she find me a hairdresser?'

Munch smiled sympathetically and, in the box marked

'summary' at the bottom of the page, wrote, 'Subject disturbed. See treatment.'

Mr Roger, the plastics man, made Léo a new, lighter, more comfortable neck brace, but he still had to wear the damned vest and ridiculous white stockings. Then came the turn of Dr Desmouches. He was a thoroughly good bloke, not yet fifty, unaffected, straightforward and warm, with a great sense of humour; he referred to his patients as his 'little blue rabbits'. He examined Léo's legs, chest, arms, hands and fingers at length. He knew all the secrets of the nerve paths and networks of the body. By feeling such and such a muscle, or such and such a nerve, he knew how, where, and why the course had run dry. He always answered your questions, without being flippant or making obscure analogies. He was asked every day, 'Doctor, will I ever walk again?'

Since the First World War and the Vietnam War, medicine has made huge advances in the development of drugs, treatment, equipment and psychological support for paralysed patients. Faced with patients and their questions, doctors divide them into three groups: those who want to know; those who absolutely don't want to know; and those who manage on their own. It's not easy telling a twenty-one-year-old that he'll have to push himself around in a chair for the rest of his life. Rebellion, anger, retreat into silence, depression, suicidal feelings, or fighting spirit – you get the whole range, the full palette of human pathos.

The attitude of the medical profession towards patients and their families can be brutal. This is the 'cold shower' approach. Some doctors give no hope from the outset. A period of despair and of mourning the body inevitably follows, before the desire for a social, professional and love life reasserts itself.

Léo didn't ask Dr Desmouches any questions, he just requested that the department recruit only blonde Scandinavian student physios in white PVC blouses, with panties and buns optional.

'Are you a patient man?' Desmouches asked, tapping Léo's left wrist.

'Well, I've postponed all my appointments to the next millennium.'

'Don't worry, from tomorrow we'll be keeping you very busy.'

'Great.'

Desmouches nodded to Marie-Jeanne. It was lunchtime. In the old days at that hour Léo was only just getting out of bed and starting his day. Now, a nurse came to tie his bib and feed him.

'We're going to sit you in your wheelchair tomorrow. You'll be having Micheline as your physio.'

'Is she good?'

'Very. She's been working here for twenty-five years!'

What a let-down! Léo had been hoping for Eva Herzigova; instead he was getting an old dinosaur.

The next day, at 8.17 a.m. on the dot, a woman of around fifty in a white uniform, with short, grey hair and forearms worthy of a wrestler, interrupted Léo, who was having his coffee watching the TV shopping channel: a sporty young woman in a thong bikini was lying on a massage table having her backside pummelled by two vibrating massage devices. Her buttocks, shaken by a fleshly earthquake, opened and closed, as if in a muscular act of coitus. The brunette, with her swimmer's physique, was being fucked by the invisible man.

The scene was a puzzling one. Firstly, she wasn't alone: some idiot was providing commentary and feverishly adjusting the power settings; secondly, she was pretending to read a magazine; thirdly, her arse was perfect already – tanned, rounded, without a trace of cellulite. What did it all mean? Was there a subliminal message here? Léo was pondering the matter deeply when a sudden wave of bitterness ruined his good mood.

This toned, brazen young woman reminded him of Gwendoline. The last woman of his life. He missed her. It sickened him not to be able to touch her skin, nuzzle her warm stomach, run his tongue over the bitter folds of her sex. He'd desired her so much.

And Alizée? Absence was cruel.

'Mr Champollon?' said Micheline firmly. 'You must be ready by nine thirty! Right, I'll see you in a little while.'

In a little while? But Léo wanted to die in a little while. It was 8.34 and his war had just begun. He'd been too young for the war in Indochina, too old for Central Africa. But for Garches . . . he wouldn't get out of this one.

34

On the table

I had passed out, fainted. When Jean-Luc and Gaston sat me in a wheelchair (with a headrest) and wheeled me around the maze of corridors reeking of disinfectant that was my new domain, I felt the winds of freedom on my face for the first time. But in front of the security guard desk things went pear-shaped. A black veil descended before my eyes and a rush of nausea burned my throat. Someone screamed and I fell unconscious. I came to a few seconds later with a slight headache. Gaston was tilting back the wheelchair and blood was flowing back to my brain.

'This is normal. Your body's got to get used to sitting up. If you don't feel well we can take you back to your room,' said Marie-Jeanne, tapping my cheeks.

'Ne . . . gative. They're . . . expecting me . . . downstairs . . . for . . .' I couldn't finish the sentence.

'Gaston, set the chair upright again, gently.'

'What's your name?' asked Jean-Luc, trying to get me to pull myself together.

'Champ . . . Champ . . .'

'Champion? Champagne?'

'Léopold Champollon,' said Marie-Jeanne, one hand on my forehead, taking my pulse with the other.

The wheelchair was upright again. I was feeling better. The telephone at the nurses' desk started ringing: it was Micheline, my physio, wondering where I'd got to. I was four minutes thirty-seven seconds late.

'He'll be right down. He just had a dizzy spell,' Marie-Jeanne told her. 'OK, boys, take him away, slowly now.'

The wheels rolled across the lino towards the main lift. In the corridor there was all the bustle of a day out at the zoo. Two species lived here side by side: walking creatures and smashed-up creatures. I stared at my new friends, inhabitants of the wonderful land of 'Catastrophik Park': Paraplegix, Mongolitus, Tetraplexus, Amputax, Myopathus, Hemiplegix, Traumatolox . . . Some of them were hanging out in their rooms, TVs blaring, while cleaning ladies mopped the floors. Gaston slowed down by the occupational therapy room. Inside, therapists busied themselves with a group of young people and adults, wheelchairs parked around a large table.

In the basement, as you emerged into the physiotherapy department, the overall impression was more cheerful. Everything was new, apart from the damaged patients and a few old physios. There were two big rooms separated by a rectangular patio – like a large winter garden – with a huge glass roof over the swimming pool. Fake plants climbed up to the glass ceiling. A pleasant space, it made you feel like having a swim, or drowning yourself.

'The water's heated to 29°C,' Gaston told me. 'And it's really clean! Better than at Aquaboulevard.'

I hummed: '*J'ai touché le fond de la piscine dans ton pull marine . . .*' They took me to Room 2. Empty wheelchairs were parked everywhere awaiting their owners, who were lying on big blue foam mats having their limbs mobilised for forty-five minutes. Others were standing, their bodies trapped in the metal claws of a verticaliser. Gaston explained that once my condition had stabilised (I didn't ask what that meant), I'd spend sixty minutes a day in the 'machine that holds a man upright'. The verticaliser does you a lot of good: it straightens and stretches out the skeleton, facilitates the circulation and blood pressure in the vertical, helps digestion, eases the joints, and relieves the pressure on the buttocks and lower back caused by constant sitting.

A few lucky ones were pedalling on exercise bikes or wandering about using walking frames, taking it easy. They looked like film extras compared to most of Dr Desmouches's critically injured 'little blue rabbits'. The worse the injury, the more intense the effort. In the case of a physio+head trauma case, the physio had to expend huge amounts of energy trying to get her vegetable of a patient going. By contrast, in your physio+paraplegic duo, it was the poor sod in the wheelchair who sweated blood on the tatami while the physio looked on like a trainer. In the case of a patient with only a slight injury, shuffling along between parallel bars, one witnessed the comical spectacle of the tortoise drawn on by the nonchalant physio: 'Come on, Mrs Benardeau, just a little bit further . . . That's good.'

Micheline was waiting for me on the battlefield, the square blue mat where, in a few minutes' time, the devastating consequences of tetraplegia would become clear.

'Take off his brace, please, Gaston. Now, hold him under the arms.'

She held my legs and counted to three. They lifted me and lay me on my back, my body as soft and flaccid as an octopus.

'Mr Champollon, we're going to lie you on your tummy and you've got to try to roll over.'

I was now face down, dribbling like a baby on to the plastic mat. My head felt as heavy as a cannon ball and my chin and nose were getting squashed. I tried to move my shoulders, raise my head, wake up my arms, but the messages didn't get through. I was literally crushed by the weight of my own body. A solid block that hadn't moved for fifty-five days. I was suffocating, struggling for breath. What an indignity! I never could have imagined that I'd end up so helpless, boneless, torn to pieces. I wasn't cut out to be an object of pity. I was, however, capable of compassion for my fellow men; I knew that a wretched life could precipitate the weak, the unlucky and the downtrodden into decline and collapse. There was only man to kill man . . . and to save him, perhaps. Me, I'd killed myself or rather, I'd failed. Until now, I'd suffered only from romantic troubles or thwarted ambitions, but there'd always been another woman, another project to make me bounce back. Life was beautiful and I had plenty of time.

I tried to hold back the tears as I lay there, like a gunman shot down by a sniper, face in the dirt. Micheline said nothing. The seconds seemed interminably long. At last, she slid her hands under my neck and chest and turned me over. She wiped my mouth with a tissue and, as the song goes, 'tidied my hair, out of habit'. I looked away, trying to focus on something to distract myself. I didn't want her to witness my grief.

There was a young woman strapped to a tilt board, her head bent at an awkward angle, eyes half-closed, mouth hanging open.

'What happened to her?'

Micheline sighed. 'She's been with us for three months. A car accident in Africa. Head injury. She's got two children. Her husband comes to visit her every day.'

'Any hope that she'll . . .'

The physio shook her head. 'I've been working here for years. I've seen too many cases like hers. We look after them and then their families take them home or put them in centres.'

'What's her name?'

'Jade.'

Jade, little Jade . . . what a strange name! Why not Ladybird or Butterfly?

'She worked in films. She was a wardrobe mistress.'

I noticed her use of the past tense. Micheline was rather terse and I was having trouble getting used to it. She had something of the old school about her. If it was her I had to confide my feelings to, we were off to a bad start. But things were looking up: I'd spotted a really hot little blonde physio across the room. When Gaston came to fetch me, I asked him to wheel me over to the brain-injured woman. She was moaning gently.

'Jade? Hello, my name's Léo. I hope you're not doing anything Saturday night. I've got two free tickets for a gig at the Barrio Latino. Jade?'

'There's no point in talking to her,' said Micheline. 'She can't hear you.'

How do you know, you old cow? I had a feeling Micheline wasn't going to last long.

Don't worry, my little Jade, we'll be alright, I promise.

35

Pascal

My new room-mate, Pascal – twenty-four, paraplegic – has terrible nightmares. At night he screams and wakes me up but during the day, because of my constant visitors, it's me who disturbs him. One evening he told me his story.

'I'd finished my shift at a motorway café near Paris. It was around midnight. I got on my motorbike, a 125, and headed home to Fontainebleau on the motorway. The road was empty. I was keeping to my lane when a car rammed me from behind. I was thrown on to the hard shoulder, but I was still conscious. My bike was caught under the bumper of the car – I could see the sparks as it drove away. It had to stop after two hundred yards. There were two of them in the car. They got out and managed to disengage the bike. I couldn't move but there was an emergency phone a couple of yards away so I thought I was saved. Then they saw me and headed in my direction. The two blokes grabbed me by my shoulders and legs and threw me over the guardrail into a ditch about thirty feet deep. I rolled down the slope and my head hit something hard. I lost consciousness. A fireman rescued me the following morning. A driver had seen the bike and called the police. It took them three hours to find me.'

Pascal's parents had reacted badly. They couldn't bear it that their son was an invalid, unemployed, depressed. My girls were nice to him and we shared all the goodies they brought. One evening shortly before he left, as he was transferring from wheelchair to bed, he asked: 'How d'you get all these girls? Did you use an agency or something?'

I explained that I'd lived in Paris for twenty years so I knew a lot of people. He nodded and said nothing for quite a while. The next day and every day after that, as soon as one of my girls came through the door, he handed her his card. 'I'm going home next week. Come and see me. We could go to the cinema and then you could have dinner at my place. Léo is OK with it, aren't you, my friend?'

My relationship with Micheline had become a cold war. I let her manoeuvre my corpse while she monologued; stopped to answer the phone; asked her colleague Muriel what days off she was having, what time *Questions for a Champion* was on; and was Mrs Pinaire's orthopaedic corset still hurting under the arms; and had Mr Lacote's Quickie TR300 wheelchair been found, she'd parked it in the corridor and it had disappeared; and Mr Floirat's crutches had been adjusted wrong, and her sister-in-law might have breast cancer. I didn't have time for all this crap.

The following Tuesday, Desmouches came round with his staff. Micheline was there too. He got straight to the point.

'Well, now, Mr Champollon, do you still want to change physios?'

'More than ever, doctor.'

'All right then, Hélène will come to see you after lunch.'

'You haven't got a picture of her, have you?'

Micheline raised her eyes to heaven: who did the little creep think he was?

That afternoon, my blonde appeared at last. Hélène was smiling. She had a nice little body. She was twenty-eight, a single mother with two children, and she'd once been in the French junior skiing team. She examined me carefully, occasionally brushing against my face. I let her scent wash over me – lavender. I watched her curvy figure and agile hands as she checked my muscle mass and joint mobility.

'What do you do for a living?' she asked.

'I play the piano, I write songs, I sing, I pester physios. What about you?'

'I look after tetras and, when they're back on their feet, I strangle them.'

'That's fine, I'm not in a hurry. When do we start?'

'Tomorrow.'

'Why not right now? I've got fuck all to do until supper.'

'Hey, I can see you could be a pain in the arse.'

'Fabienne, please!'

'Hélène.'

'I'll call you what I like!'

And she left me there, full of impatience. Joel, the occupational therapist, knocked at the door.

'You're late, Champollon. Come on, we've got work to do. Marie-Jeanne's going to help me get you into your chair.'

Occupational therapy was developed in the United States. It's an important part of a patient's rehabilitation. Both useful and entertaining, it's aimed at people whose movement has been affected by a brain injury or a virus – head trauma cases, hemiplegics, sufferers of Parkinson's – or at patients with limited movement in their upper limbs, or none at all, such as people with tetraplegia and muscular dystrophy. All sorts of games – puzzles, balls, cubes, Lego, darts, drawing, Meccano – are used in order to recover manual dexterity, as well as assistive devices made of wood, plastic or leather – transfer boards, fork and toothbrush cuffs, Velcro straps, joysticks – to make day-to-day living easier.

I watched my fellow tetras and noticed how much they used their mouths – to bite, catch, grip, move things, get undressed, blow. The jaw served as a hand, the teeth as fingers.

Very soon I learnt to do the same. I wondered how long it would be before I could unfasten a skirt, pull down a zip, tear off tights, rip off panties and undo a bra using only my teeth.

Stéphanie became the ideal accomplice. I hadn't known her very well before, but since my accident she'd become very keen on me. I wasn't sure why. When I was running around on two legs she'd told me where to get off, but now that I was only a quarter of half of a tenth of a shadow of my former self, she wanted me to screw her!

She always came to see me in the evening, around ten, wearing a short skirt under her silk mac, and making sure to close the door behind her. She climbed on to the bed and kneeled over me, holding on to the monkey pole. After massaging my tummy and chest, she positioned herself, thighs spread, about ten inches above my face, and slowly lowered herself. She kept her skirt on, so I disappeared beneath a pleated, perfumed curtain. In the darkness, I could feel her cotton panties rubbing against my nose. I nibbled her sex, which was wet under the fabric, and slipped my tongue under the elastic. Stéphanie prolonged the pleasure by offering me her belly, then her breasts. There too I had to struggle with the underwiring and lace of her bra – it was exhausting. Then, when she made up her mind, we returned to paradise and I tore her panties to shreds.

I was sure Pascal, my depressed room-mate, watched while we were engaging in cunnilingus. I hoped he enjoyed the show, and that it made him forget his fears and fall into a deep, healing sleep. But not everyone was an exhibitionist like Stéphanie, or a voyeur like me. I assumed that Pascal was, but if not I didn't want to upset him. I'd already shredded four pairs of Stéphanie's knickers before I said: 'Hey, Pascal, tell me if it bothers you when that girl comes round in the evening.'

He said nothing for quite a while. 'Did you get a big sum in compensation for your accident?' he asked at last, staring at the ceiling.

I couldn't see what that had to do with sex. 'Er . . . No, why?'

'She must cost you a fortune.'

36

Outing

Louis was having coffee with Darius and Sylvia in the cafeteria. The news was good. Léo was getting stronger. He still couldn't move his legs or hands, but he'd got back some movement in his shoulders and upper arms by building up his triceps and biceps. He no longer had to wear the neck brace and he could sit in his wheelchair without passing out. More and more friends were getting together to help him. Ludovic, Mickey, Ambroisine, Camille and Henri had a list of a hundred people who'd immediately agreed to contribute financially. Darius had done the sums: how on earth was Léo going to pay for food, accommodation, a personal carer, rehab equipment, telephone bills and transport when he didn't have a penny in savings and would be getting only 5000 francs a month in welfare benefits?

'By the way,' said Louis, 'I spoke to the consultant. They're going to start weaning him off tranquillisers. Emotionally he seems fine, but the good mood's artificial as long as he's still on Valium and all the other happy pills. It'll be hard for the first few weeks, but we'll be there to support him.'

'It's a stage they all have to go through, isn't it?' asked Sylvia.

'Yes. And they have to rely on their own natural defences. But Léo is tough. He'll get through it.'

'Has he mentioned the centre in Britanny to you?'

Léo wanted to see the sea. Kerpape, near Lorient, was an experimental rehab centre, open all year round. They had a place for him in August.

Darius tackled the next item on the agenda.

'Alizée called. She's in Paris and she wants to see him. What do we do?'

'Surely it's up to him to decide?'

'Should she come before or after he's off tranquillisers?'

'He's still in love with her, isn't he?'

'He's spoken to me about her,' said Sylvia. 'He has to know how things stand. I mean, it's his life.'

In the end, everyone agreed with Louis and Sylvia. Alizée was part of Léo's life and plans, even if they were pipe dreams. It was up to him to decide, and if their meeting ended in failure, at least he'd know for sure. There was so much in his life that he had to rebuild.

'By the way,' laughed Louis, 'have you heard the latest? We almost lost him again! Poor Darius, he did really well . . .'

Darius had come to have lunch with Léo earlier that week. He found him sitting in front of the open window, staring at the sky, following the course of the clouds. In the distance, he could just see the tops of the trees in the park of Saint-Cloud. The sun shone on the tiled floor and a warm breeze blew through Léo's hair. He was lost in thought, lulled by 'God Only Knows' from *Pet Sounds* by Brian Wilson and the Beach Boys. *Pet Sounds* was more than a subtle sequence of songs and instrumentals, arranged by a songwriter of genius on the edge of madness. Leo felt a metaphysical connection with it. 'I haven't yet found the woman of my dreams,' he often said, 'but I've found the music of my dreams.'

It had been with him since the age of twelve and had never let him down, and this was from someone fickle who was always falling for new musical trends. They'd grown up together and despite all the rock operas, the punk, disco, funk, ska, folk, blues, soul, reggae, salsa latina, hip-hop, rap, jungle, techno; despite being seduced time and time again by the glitter and videos of showbiz sirens, he always returned to his first love, to the vinyl album that a Californian surfer's girlfriend had given him in the summer of 1973. *Pet Sounds*. It was his personal anthem, his bible, his profession of faith as a musician. In the words of Serge Gainsbourg, '*Ce qui est gravé est grave.*' That which is recorded is serious.

Music was made up of notes, black and white ones, but above all it was stained red, from all the blood and tears. Darius knew that Léo used to spend hours at the keyboard, practising complicated melodies over and over.

'Eaten yet, maestro?' asked Darius waving a tray of sushi under Léo's nose.

'Not hungry.'

'OK, what do you think this is? Cow piss?' he said, taking a bottle of ice-cold Asahi beer from a plastic bag.

'Not thirsty.'

Darius stared at his brother a moment. Léo was still transfixed by the clouds. He seemed to be in a kind of trance.

'What's up, Léo?'

Léo turned to look at him. His eyes were glazed, his complexion pasty and the words came slowly: 'The student . . . Dada . . . nurse . . . got it wrong . . . whole pill . . . Valium . . . 5 mg . . . stoned . . . sleep now . . .'

'Wait here, I'll be right back'

'Damn!' thought Darius. 'Not a good start to getting him off tranquillisers.' In the corridor he had a word with Harold, a junior doctor, who confirmed that there had been a slip-up. He suggested Darius take his brother outside. It was sunny and warm; it would give him a change of scene, and a change of record!

'It's weird, since I've been here, your brother's listened to the same thing, all day long. Has he always been like this?'

'A musician, yes – a tetraplegic, no!'

Darius took ages to convince Léo to leave his room. He agreed to be wheeled down the corridor; at a pinch, he was willing to go as far as the next section, but that was it. Yes, OK, he'd happily pay Hélène a visit. She was on duty at the pool today; she looked delightful in her red swimsuit with her little whistle, which she didn't really need because the pool was barely the size of half a tennis court.

Poor Léo – he hadn't been outside for three months. Darius realised that he was scared. Scared of people staring, scared of the summer that was just beginning, scared of passing girls in summer dresses, scared of seeing the life that had gone on without him all these weeks, that had crossed him off the map of the walking. He was thin, sunken-eyed from all the pain, and his dull hair stuck out untidily from his head. He used to take such care of his appearance. If he could see himself in that yellow and orange tracksuit and those big swollen Nikes. In the end, it was Marie-Jeanne, with all her feminine tact, who persuaded the two brothers to get out of there.

'Come on, shoo, outside. Léo, you're getting on my nerves! Come back when you've sobered up. I'm fed up with you hanging around in your room.'

Darius tipped the wheelchair on to its back wheels and

set off at full speed making revving noises. After the first five minutes, Léo began to relax and enjoy the rays of sun warming his skin. His brother gave him the grand tour. 'This is the emergency entrance, where they brought you on the first night. That's the Patel Wing – you know, Intensive Care – over there. And that's the car park at the end, where I leave my car. The cafeteria's just next door. By the way, now that I think of it, I've got to go to the Admissions Office to get a hospital certificate for Social Security.'

Darius looked for somewhere to park his brother.

'Where shall I leave you?'

'Over there, on that bit of tarmac, facing the sun. I'll get a tan. Come on, give me a push, big brother!'

The red brick hospital building was topped by a clock tower. In front of it, a big lawn about the size of a football pitch welcomed visitors and emergency vehicles. Darius pushed the chair across the grass and parked Léo on the tarmac, well away from any driveways.

'Wait here. I'll be back in five minutes,' he said, applying the brakes.

Léo dozed. The effects of the benzodiazepine were gradually wearing off and what felt like a soft breeze, cool and gentle, made him open his eyes and look up. A giant, droning hornet was approaching, wings against the sun. Léo blinked, dazzled, wondering how he could drive away the horrible insect that was wrecking his fragile serenity.

'Everything's fine. The bastard'll fly away.' He tried to get rid of it by blowing at it. But instead of buzzing off the winged brute seemed intent on tormenting the unfortunate wretch in the wheelchair. It hovered above him, making a dreadful racket. Léo, who was no fool – even when under the influence of a soft drug – stared at it in alarm.

'Shit, it's *Apocalypse Now*!'

He'd been parked on the hospital helipad. The pilot was circling above him, getting more and more anxious. Léo wondered if perhaps he still hadn't woken from his nightmare. He'd survived a car crash and now a chopper was about to land on his head!

'Sir! Please move your wheelchair! You're not allowed to park here!'

'Can't. You'll have to help me.'

A man in white leapt out of the ambulance. Léo was removed and the helicopter was able to land at last. Two paramedics carried out a stretcher.

'Hey, we're full . . . no room,' Léo grumbled.

Darius was back. He thanked the ambulance man and then went to rescue his brother, who had now definitely snapped out of his drugged haze. Just outside the Vidal Wing, Darius suddenly started laughing uncontrollably. Léo joined in. It was the first time they'd laughed together since the accident.

'I was right. It really wasn't a good idea for me to leave my room.'

'What are you complaining about? You've had your baptism of air!'

Shaking with laughter, or shaking with terror – Léo was still alive!

37

Erection

Some coincidences are troubling. On the same day, ten minutes apart, Léo received the two phone calls he had given up expecting, from Gwendoline and Alizée. Two meetings were arranged. Léo was in heaven; what with his girlfriends, his exes, his new girlfriends, his sisters, his physio and his nurses, he hadn't felt so indebted towards womankind since the day he'd left the womb. They were giving him life a second time round.

Just before hanging up, Gwendoline said: 'I thought I was pregnant by you at one point. Just after your accident my period was late. I couldn't sleep. I was convinced that if the baby lived, you'd die. It was weird.'

She paused before going in the same tone: 'By the way, can you still get a hard-on?'

There had been new developments in that area. One evening, just after the nurse had been round, Léo had felt an itch that he couldn't pinpoint. He called Evelyne, the night-duty nurse. She pulled back the sheet, expecting to find a fork or something stuck under him.

'Well now,' she said, staring at his crotch, 'Junior's waking up.'

She raised the head of the bed and sat him up. Léo's penis was standing up between his thighs, swelling and lengthening. It was like a miracle! Léo remembered the first months of puberty, when he'd fallen madly in love with his dick. It was an almost autonomous part of him, a rather comical barometer of his well-being. This had less to do with his education than with the personal hygiene his mother had taught him: when he was very small, she had encouraged him to wash it thoroughly. One day, in the bathroom with his four brothers, he waved his prick around and pissed on them, declaring: 'He's called Alexander the Great and he's going to conquer the world!'

Alexander led Léo by the nose many a time – normally Léo couldn't see beyond the end of his cock. He jerked off every time he took a shower. And he showered three times a day: in the morning when he got up; at lunchtime after the gym; and in the evening before going out. His penis was clean, vital, powerful, natural; and it never broke down. The only times Alexander sulked in his cage were when Léo was ill, depressed or had the clap. As soon as Léo felt better again, Alexander was back in action.

In time, Léo learnt how to control him better, though Alexander often still surprised him by his independence. But Léo got along well with his schizophrenic body. And the women who shared his life helped to make Alexander blossom. They kept a tight leash on him, talked to him at night, woke him up in the morning and took him in their mouths when Léo was sitting idly in the car waiting at traffic lights.

Mickey was there the evening of Alexander's rebirth.

Mickey visited Léo every day. There was nothing particularly virtuous about this: he was single and he lived opposite the hospital. And it worked out pretty well for him – he met girls at Léo's bedside and took them home with him. He never turned up empty-handed. His mother cooked things for his friend, who was growing increasingly desperate with the hospital food. Mickey brought Léo some *poulet Basquaise* and he, in return, offered Mickey a nice plump goose on a plate. Léo sometimes felt jealous, but he'd promised himself that no girl would ever jeopardise what he held most dear: lifelong friendships. In their twenties, Mickey and Léo had rows, fights over women, of course, but, good God, there were enough women in the world for them not to be so stupid as to choose and quarrel over the same one.

So Mickey was the first to spread the news: Léo could get a hard-on! In two days it was all over Paris and it brought a new crop of visitors, the ones that had, until then, pictured poor Léo lying on his bed of pain, moribund and suicidal.

As soon as the male contingent knew that he was no longer lazing about under the covers and that his dick was performing like it had in the good old days, they showed up at the hospital and celebrated the event by cracking open champagne. But their enthusiasm was not without self-interest. 'If Léo can get an erection, the girls will soon hear about it and head straight there to check it out. There'll soon be a bevy by his bedside! Mustn't waste any time, summer's almost here . . .'

Léo's room became a dating agency where the wolves got out their personal organisers and took down the numbers of the innocent does at his bedside.

38

Alizée, mon amour

When Alizée turned up, after more than a year away, Léo asked Louis, who was on his day off, to stand guard at the door to his room. He didn't want to be disturbed.

She had changed. Léo was haunted by her memory. On contact with her skin, her lips, that scent which scrambled all his senses, he'd dreamt she'd erase all his suffering with a kiss. As if nothing had happened. He hoped she'd be the one to witness his recovery; they'd set off for the sea and she'd help him take his first steps.

'You're as beautiful as ever,' said Léo as Alizée sat on the bed and rested her head on his shoulder. She was wearing a short, sky-blue linen skirt and a white blouse that showed off her tan and perfect breasts.

'See, sweetie, I wanted to give you a treat.'

'I've always loved your style,' said Léo quickly, trying to stem the urge to cry.

She spent the afternoon in his arms, kissing him, stroking his hands and chest. She was relieved to see that he was well, but he was sad and anxious to see that she was so well. She was there, devoted and affectionate, but he realised that he played no part in her future. Tomorrow, Alizée would head off back to her islands, to some ship's captain, to her swimsuit design studio, against the dazzling backdrop of Saint Lucia. They were worlds apart. Before, he would simply have crossed that ocean, had the desire to win her back been strong enough, but now?

Alizée radiated sun, golden beaches, love under the stars and sex when you felt like it. And he bet she'd had her fill. Life by the sea had toned her body, turned her hair gold, left four little pale triangles on the flesh of her breasts and buttocks.

She went to light a cigarette by the window, resting her elbows on the sill. Léo stared at her profile against the light, the curve of her back. She leant out, standing on tiptoe, and her skirt rode up at the back. She looked up at the sky. 'You've got a wonderful view, sweetie. Next time, I'll take you to the park of Saint-Cloud.'

'I've got a wonderful view from here, too,' thought Léo, overcome with jealousy as he watched his beach babe's arse. He was dreading her leaving. The hands on the clock moved forward inexorably. He knew that when she closed the door behind her, she'd be closing it on everything – his hopes, his dreams, the will to get better. Until today, she'd been his main reason for doing so.

'I've got to go,' said Alizée, buttoning her blouse.

He felt he'd be hearing those words for the rest of his life, like the parody of a sentimental song: '*J'ai pensé qu'il valait mieux nous quitter sans un adieu . . . car je sens bien qu'au fond . . . tout est fini . . .*' I thought it'd be better to leave without saying goodbye . . . Deep down, I know it's all over.

He held her tight, then let her go.

Alone in his room again, his grief seemed like a big pile of dirty laundry that he wanted to throw out. In matters of love, he'd never had to beg.

But who'd want him, who'd love him now?

39

Freddy Cut-Cut

With Gwendoline, things were simpler: she sent a postcard cancelling their meeting. Every time Léo phoned her, he got her answerphone. He'd leave a message and, invariably, a week later, a card would arrive.

Dear Léo,

It was so lovely to hear from you! I'll come and see you as soon as I'm back in Paris.

Love you, sweetheart,

Gwendo

After the tenth 'Love you', he realised she'd never come. That crappy word, love, that he'd used so many times in his life and in his songs, now tasted like ashes. Things looked very black.

Still, when he talked to his fellow patients – some no more than fourteen – he realised how lucky he was to have his family and friends. In the evening outside the Vidal Wing the youngsters gathered for a powwow, smoking joints, trying to forget their amputated youth. They all dreaded the day when they'd be thrown off the reservation. It was a haven. During the week, they had special classes to keep up with their schoolwork, and at weekends some of them waited for parents who never turned up. But they bore no grudge for this neglect, this premature separation; if their accident wasn't down to bad luck, it must be their fault. They'd tried to be clever and lost. They alone were to blame. The authority of their teachers was a painful reminder of injuries that they managed to accept when they were amongst themselves, united as a group.

Léo could hear them yelling like Red Indians at night as they bombed along the hospital corridors in their fluorescent wheelchairs, pursued by overworked nurses. As the echoes of their wild cries faded in the maze of dark corridors, Léo thought of his own adolescence, which had been happy and beautiful. And he prayed to God and all his angels to protect these swaggering kids, orphans who had nothing but a life of struggle ahead of them.

Freddy Cut-Cut was their leader; barely eighteen and already a survivor. He'd had about twenty operations. An incomplete tetraplegic, he guided his electric wheelchair with his left hand; the other hand was dead. He'd had his right leg amputated above the knee. He had pressure sores on his backside so he got around lying on his front on a trolley that his mates piloted at full speed, passing him from one to the other like a rugby ball strapped to a skateboard. Freddy's tale was edifying, a horror story that made you writhe with laughter because you had to be a lucky bastard to dice with death not once, not twice, but three times – and still come out alive.

'Come on, Freddy, tell us your story!'

'I was staying with my father in New Caledonia. One night we had a party at a mate's house up in the hills. At four in the morning we decided to go for a drive. We were completely slaughtered. There were three of us in the front and this guy Michael was driving. We were so pissed that after a few miles we missed a bend and the car fell down a ravine. By chance, two big palm trees stopped us halfway down. They saved our lives. We were all fine, not a scratch, nothing!

'We climbed up the slope and got back to the party on foot. We celebrated our lucky escape, and a few pints of booze later we decided to go off in the gardener's van. I let my two mates sit in the front and I fell asleep in the back with all the bloke's stuff: pruning shears, lawnmower, billhook, electric saw, machete, toolbox. The two idiots in the front drove for a few miles and then, bingo, after a bridge they missed another bend and the car fell twenty yards and landed in a stream. I don't know how many times it turned over but I was trapped in the back so all the tools landed on me! I got stabbed, chopped up into little pieces! Blades, nails, the mower . . . I was a real mess! I was pissing blood, and my neck was snapped in two. And my mate Tonio was dead. But I only found that out afterwards.

'I woke up two days later in hospital. They waited two weeks before arranging to fly me back to France in a special plane. When the ambulance came to pick me up the driver was in a hurry – the flight had been brought forward because of the weather. He was driving too fast and when he tried to overtake a lorry, he slammed into a lamppost. So back we went to the hospital. They decided to fly me out on an ordinary airliner. The Intensive-Care doctor made them put me in first class on an inflatable stretcher that took up six seats. But the other passengers complained, so they moved me to the back of the plane in economy. The flight took twenty hours. I had two heart attacks.'

Dr Desmouches's little blue rabbits were real veterans.

And they were randy rabbits too. After supper, they'd park their wheelchairs around my bed.

'Hey, Léo, how do you manage with all your girlfriends?'

'If they don't get jealous, they must be slags, mustn't they?'

'Would you screw a paraplegic girl?'

Their curiosity was just an excuse. They'd barely been there five minutes when one of my girls turned up. At Garches the grapevine worked pretty efficiently: the girl had been spotted in the car park; Freddy Cut-Cut had whistled to Filou the Spider, who sped off to tell Vizirette, who got Max Two Wheels and Bernie the Anvil, who rounded up Stan the Seagull, Medhi Couscous and DJ Sarcelles, and so on.

'Hey, Léo, introduce us to the young lady.'

40

Kerpape

I never should have come here, to this land of the bedridden.

Ploemeur, in Morbihan. It's like a song by Laurent Voulzy: there's sea, sun, sand, guys windsurfing, topless girls spreading suntan cream over their breasts, parents in swimsuits dancing to Luis Mariano. But I'm trapped. It's my own fault. I wanted to see the Atlantic, breathe sea air, get a suntan, swim . . . and get better, not die a little more.

Kerpape – the most famous rehab centre in Europe. It's one of the places where they train monkeys to be helpers for people who are completely paralysed. They've set up a showflat with a bedroom, sitting room, kitchen and bathroom, and people from all over the world come and watch a marmoset and a young paralysed woman interacting. Cute and attentive, the animal climbs on to shelves, tables, washbasins, always returning to the knees of its mistress, who sits motionless in her wheelchair.

On her signal, the little domesticated monkey opens the fridge, heats things up in the microwave, grabs a fork or a toothbrush, switches on the TV, runs the bath, picks up the phone, turns on the toaster, cuts off the alarm – and tears out the poor defenceless invalid's eyes and tongue. They cancel the programme: too expensive, too lengthy, too risky, too dangerous. There are guide dogs for the blind, dolphins with healing powers and pigeons that carry messages, but there always comes a time when even the most devoted guinea pig can't replace human intelligence and reverts to the wild. In a wheelchair you're weak, vulnerable, restricted; there's always a kerb that's too high, a doorway that's too narrow, a slope that's too steep, to thwart your attempts at independence.

As I found out when I took the plane from Paris to Lorient. There's no point in asking to go to the toilet during the flight. The corridor's impassable and the staff are rarely qualified to carry you on their back the length of the aircraft, which is being shaken by air pockets, and get you, undamaged, into a tiny dark cubicle and balance your floppy great body on a loo that was designed for the backside of a pygmy.

Luckily, the flight lasted only sixty minutes.

As I stared out of the window, I remembered my trips with Alizée to the West Indies, Morocco, the United States. We made love anywhere, even in the plane over the Bermuda Triangle! 'The past is dead, Léo. You've got to turn the page, get a change of scene, head into the unknown, naked.' It was six months since my accident and my condition had scarcely improved, though I could now push my wheelchair laboriously using the heels of my hands. Joel, the occupational therapist at Garches, had made me some special leather gloves to protect my numb palms.

When I arrived at Kerpape, they put me in a bed and wheeled me to the dining room. I'd studied the ways of ancient Rome and as my imperial bed was pushed by my slaves over the vinyl, rather than marble, floors of my new palace, I looked forward to my first Breton orgy. I pictured a room large enough for twenty beds on wheels parked in a circle. Lying on our side, we'd be served by slaves in filmy white tunics, to the sound of harps and Egyptian drums.

I was the only person lying down, in the midst of an army of electric wheelchairs. Everyone ate in silence at tables of eight and studiously ignored me. Me, Tetraplexus Caesar Imperator! I asked a nurse about the misunderstanding. 'I may be paralysed but, as far as I know, tetraplegia isn't contagious. So why've I been quarantined?'

'You'll have to stay in bed until you get a wheelchair.'

'And when will I get a wheelchair?'

'You'll have to speak to Mrs Sibylle le Quellec, who deals with admissions. We weren't to know you wouldn't be bringing a chair of your own.'

'But I haven't got a chair of my own!'

'Fine, sir, but you're the one who's paralysed. If all the patients arrived without equipment, where would we be?'

Once dessert had been served and swallowed, everyone headed back to their rooms with a great humming of electric wheelchairs and clattering of crutches and artificial limbs. At the dining room door there was a big traffic jam, with nobody moving. It was just like a motorway on a Sunday night as everybody rushed home. I had to wait for the place to empty before my flying carpet was moved out.

I was alone in my room. The telephone hadn't yet been connected or the TV plugged in. Towards the end of the afternoon, after a long nap, I spotted an auxiliary in the corridor. I asked if there was any chance I might see Mrs le Quellec and sort out all these little problems.

'You'll have to hurry,' the young woman answered. 'She'll be leaving the office in ten minutes!'

‘So where’s her office?’

‘On the ground floor, right next to the library.’

‘Could you take me there?’

‘Oh, it’s easy, you can’t miss it. Turn right as soon as you come out of the lift. Don’t take the lift by the pool though. It’s not working. Use the one by the bursar’s office.’

And she left.

41

Canteen

The next morning, everything was sorted out. As Gwenaelle, an auxiliary, was setting up the trolley for my breakfast, I noticed a wheelchair waiting for me outside the bathroom. Funny, at Kerpape people were pushed around in bed and wheelchairs moved around on their own at night!

My doctor was, like Gwenaelle, a Breton. He reminded me of Crocodile Dundee. He really didn't look like a doctor. Tanned, with tousled hair, he looked like a bit of a boozer and was always teasing me. If I'd met him a few months earlier, I'd have been sure he was a charlatan, a crook in a white coat. Dr Dundee was in favour of using the minimum of drugs – I fully agreed – and when he went through my prescription, he crossed off the tranquilliser that I took to help me sleep at night.

'You'll soon learn to be as independent as possible,' he told me. 'But you haven't chosen a good time to be here. Kerpape is very quiet in August.'

In summer, while most of the physios were on holiday, the patient population increased. Most of the fully paralysed tetraplegics lived at home during the year but were left stranded when the holidays came. They had no choice but to be admitted to medical centres. Kerpape was Club Med for the severely disabled.

I'd come for a month, but by my second day I already wanted to leave. Meals were an intolerable ordeal. I'd never before sensed so much grief and loneliness, so many wounds, so much desperate anger. We were all shut up inside our own personal dramas and rare attempts at communication came to nothing. Luckily for us, there were helpers to supervise, feed the most incapacitated and make fascinating conversation: 'Would anyone like their bread dunked in their soup?' or 'Would you like to eat your cheese now or take it back to your room?'

There were four distinct groups at the tables, and there was no question of moving to another.

Sporty paraplegics occupied the first table. They were by far the most lively and the most radical, and obviously familiar enough with the place to present a united front against outsiders.

The older patients on crutches were mostly people in their fifties or over, with light to medium injuries. They'd had operations to their hips, collarbones, thighbones or feet, and were as cheerful and excited as schoolkids on holiday. Indeed, in this topsy-turvy world, they had something to be cheerful about: they, the old, were up on their feet, running about like rabbits, while the young sat rotting in wheelchairs.

Then there were the tetraplegics who couldn't move much at all. Some guided their wheelchairs using a joystick under their chin. They were totally dependent on others, often young – between eighteen and thirty – and the only sound they made came from the hum of their electric wheelchairs.

Finally, there were the new arrivals, with all kinds of

medical conditions and of varying ages. Recently injured, they had ended up at Kerpape in an attempt to escape isolation, rather than with any hope of regaining their independence.

I was one of them – outraged by my fate, furious at finding myself in this Kafkaesque canteen, depressed by the zombies and well-meaning helpers around me, terrified of what the future held. We exchanged smiles occasionally but the person facing you was the enemy, a cracked mirror reflecting your own decline.

Seeing them in their tracksuits, chewing their mince with shallot sauce, my heart clenched and I was desperate for a way out. I looked out through the bay window at the summer, at the coast beneath the blazing blue sky.

In Cuba the year before, Marco, Alain, Gérard and me had gone diving off the coast of the Isla de la Juventud, fished for crayfish and skydived from 8000 feet. How to forget the mountains of Pinar del Rio, the ochre walls of Trinidad, the big salsa bands of Havana and nights in the arms of Belem, my tropical brown-skinned girl with a pert bottom?

What had happened to me?

42

Moïsa

I was soon getting Dr Strangelove to re-prescribe tranquillisers for my night-time anxieties and morbid thoughts. But then a phone call from my father helped to calm me.

'Only three more weeks, son. You can get through it, I know you can. Go and swim, sit in the sun. You're better off there in Brittany than in your room in Garches. You're through the worst now, so don't worry. We're thinking of you. Your mother's going to send you some books and parcels to keep you going. Here she is, I'll pass you over to her. Be brave, son, don't give up.'

'Darling, how are you?'

I couldn't answer straight away because of the lump in my throat.

I felt as if I'd reverted back to being the anxious boy of my childhood, who had to be comforted, protected, encouraged. I desperately needed my parents now – I, who had cut the umbilical cord long ago. My accident had brought us close again. Our ties were more than the branches of a family tree, which we thought of only at weddings, births, deaths and anniversaries. A member of the tribe was in danger and the family tom-tom sounded the alarm, summoning brothers, sisters, cousins, uncles, sons-in-law, godfathers and godmothers from the four corners of the land.

That evening my phone rang constantly. Survival has no price. Whether someone gives you their time or sends you a cheque, that's love. And that night, after nine long-distance phone conversations, I fell asleep greatly comforted.

I was woken at eight the next morning. Washed, dressed, and with hair combed, I pushed myself, as best I could, to the Olympic-size pool. In the changing rooms, two auxiliaries lay me on a bunk and changed me into my swimming trunks. They sat me in a plastic, waterproof wheelchair and pushed me to the side of the pool. There, they put me on a kind of remote-controlled camp bed which lowered you into the water.

Moïsa, a pretty brunette of around twenty, with olive skin and green cat-like eyes, supervised the operation and caught me as I entered the water. Wearing a pleasingly tight black swimsuit which showed off her ravishing figure, she was ready to give me thirty-five minutes of her youth and beauty. I didn't care that she was only a student physio. Her mother was Breton and her father Jewish. When I saw her smile, I knew at last why I had come to Brittany. It was wonderful to fall into the arms of a half-naked stranger and rub against her in tropically-warm water. *Kolé séré, nous té ké cadencé . . .*

Moïsa asked me the standard questions: when did I have my accident, what level was my injury, how did my body react to ambient temperature and to water, how well could I float, how long could I hold my breath underwater and what equipment did I need in addition to my big water-baby swimsuit – board, rubber ring, flippers, goggles, float, swimming cap? I answered her questions as precisely as a naval frogman about to go on a deep-sea mission. I too would have liked to bombard her with questions: 'Moïsa, do you love me?' Instead, I just asked for a pair of goggles and two floats.

A few minutes later, we were facing each other, in a half-embrace. Equipped with my goggles, I let myself slide down her body, my hands gripping hers. The view underwater was excellent. I dived down past her smooth firm breasts and found myself only inches away from her pussy. Standing with her back arched, Moïsa was unaware of what was going on underwater. I was in heaven. After a couple of minutes she made me surface and asked me to float on my back. I hesitated. She thought I was scared, but I didn't want to scare her with my ill-timed erection. So she let me paddle in the shallow end and told me to try the breaststroke. I did a few strokes, sank, did another few strokes, sank again, only just being missed by an idiot paraplegic who was doing laps of the pool in a canoe and showing off in front of my darling Moïsa.

'Regis, would you mind paddling elsewhere?' asked Moïsa.

Yeah, get lost! I wasn't going to let some legless guy get between me and the object of my affections. Before I got out of the pool, I had time to swim behind Moïsa and follow her at a distance like a pilot fish. She had a narrow waist and firm buttocks that didn't wobble when she kicked her feet. I left reluctantly, determined to repeat the experience as soon as possible.

In the water, I was free, I felt good, and I was in love. All essential to a man like me!

43

Serial physio

In the afternoons, I went to see Mr le Goff. He was a strange man. Short and bald, with round glasses, he was the very image of a pen-pusher: self-effacing, industrious, punctual and polite. He answered my questions with a 'yes', a 'no', or a mumble that put an end to the conversation when it had only just begun. In a whole month, I learnt only three things about him: he lived with his mother, he liked gardening, and he had no intention of letting any woman disturb his peaceful life. At 4 p.m. on the dot, like a civil servant, he exchanged his white coat for a cardigan and went home. As I watched the stocky figure make its way around the sports field, I noticed his square shoulders and his powerful, gnarled forearms and wondered whether, beneath the exterior of a contented little man, there didn't lurk the serial killer of Finistère.

As I found him intriguing and our sessions were terribly tedious, I decided to try and flush out the psychopath in the physiotherapist. I lay on my back staring at the ceiling and monologued as if I were alone, in the grip of an obsession. I spoke about a woman, without specifying her age. I called her, predictably, Malicia. Little by little, session by session, I fleshed out my tale with scabrous details and paranoid threats. Malicia, as I described her, was a depraved, insatiable, scheming woman whose sole aim was to do me harm. The more silent Mr le Goff remained, the more sordid my descriptions became of this angel of darkness, who used her beauty and intelligence to torture men's hearts and mine in particular.

'Ah, Mr le Goff, if you only knew how much I loved that woman!'

He didn't bat an eyelid. The next day, I added the final touch. How could I get rid of Malicia without arousing suspicion? I reviewed the possibilities: fire, poison, drowning, electric shock, strangulation. After a long silence, I asked him straight out, 'What would you use if you were me, Mr le Goff? Cyanide?'

He mumbled, shaking his head. 'No woman, no problem!'

'I absolutely agree, Mr le Goff. In fact, I have an idea.'

And off I went again on my crazy, wild fabrications, surprised that, even when I went too far, the physio never once appeared worried about my mental health or notified any of the medical staff.

'Tell me, Mr le Goff, how much d'you think a hired assassin would cost?' I asked innocently, expecting him to tell me to get lost. But he didn't! If I'd told him I wanted to murder my own mother, he would probably still have nodded and said: 'No woman, no problem!'

I was keeping my mind and my imagination busy, but I realised, as the weeks went by, that loneliness, boredom, madness lay in wait every minute. I felt like a schizophrenic prisoner of a world of which I wanted no part.

44

Tadpole and canard

At lunchtime there was a parcel waiting for me in the canteen. Inside I found a Ralph Lauren polo shirt, magazines, sweets, a bottle of Armani aftershave and a note from a stranger, Isabelle Canard, known as Zaza:

> Léo,
>
> I heard about your accident a few months ago. I'm a little shy and, as we've never actually met, I was hesitant about getting in touch until now. I'm in Brittany at the moment and I'd like to invite you to my house one weekend. If you agree, I'll come to Kerpape next Friday and kidnap you for a couple of days.
>
> Love, Zaza.

I was worried. I hadn't been out in the world on my own yet. And for good reason. I had to be lifted into my chair, washed, dressed, fed, given my pills, got into bed and, above all, helped with catheterisation, the major problem of the wheelchair-occupying class – how to empty one's bladder. Catheterisation is an intimate, tricky, painful ritual which you perform, like a heroin addict shooting up, in a quiet corner. You have to retire to a private place five to eight times in every twenty-four hours in order to stick a lubricated catheter up your prick, through the sphincter into the bladder, to drain the urine, taking all sorts of hygienic precautions so as to avoid infection.

On Friday morning I handed in my permission slip at the outings office. When Zaza and her gang arrived, I realised I knew a lot of them by sight. We immediately launched into reminiscences of our heroic partying: Caca's Club, the Evening of the Seven Deadly Sins, the Sluts' Ball, the Night of Endless Torment, the Party of the Clans . . .

Mrs le Quellec had packed my bag. Terrified at the thought of being without medical assistance for two whole days, I checked the contents like an anxious child going away to summer camp. Briefed by the nurse, Zaza assured me that everything would be fine and that she wasn't in the habit of abandoning her invalid friends in motorway lay-bys.

During the course of that weekend, as Zaza and her friends drove me around Brittany, I rediscovered how exhilarating such freedom and companionship can be. Hélène and Olivier took my chair out of the boot and, without arguing, tried to follow the instructions for re-assembling it in the right order: the folding back, ergonomic cushion, wheels, footrest. Meanwhile, Niko and Thierry extracted my sixty kilos from the passenger seat. Once I was in my wheelchair, I had to watch out for slopes because any lapse in concentration could prove fatal. At one point I forgot to block the wheels, thinking that someone was pushing me along the tarmac. I suddenly started gathering speed and realised to my horror that I'd been chatting to a non-existent pilot for the last couple of minutes. Shrieks and a stampede ensued, with the bloke who could run fastest stopping me at the edge of the cliff.

Zaza had a fit. 'Guys, are you crazy? My little tadpole almost died of fright!'

That evening for dinner, we had a platter of seafood. I realised, as I tried to tackle wobbly oysters, slippery mussels and unpeelable prawns with my frozen hands, that I'd ordered greedily without thinking. I made a terrible mess; a one-armed chimp could have done better. Zaza, with motherly authority, spent half her dinner feeding me.

'Eat, little tadpole! Sea, seagulls, mussels – it's all good for your morale!'

I was experiencing the unexpected and providence. I couldn't endure everything alone, and such chance meetings made my burden feel lighter. It was also good to know that, even if I was nothing like the carefree boy of old, my personality hadn't been completely extinguished. Life was forcing me to make new efforts, gain new insights, be humble. I didn't have a monopoly on suffering. As we chatted and reminisced, I found out about the tragic destinies of some of the people we knew. Heroin had done plenty of damage. So had AIDS.

About ten years earlier, Niko, François, myself and several others had spent a weekend in Guétary. I had a very precise image of that holiday – a photo that I stuck in an album. One detail came to mind: everyone was wearing sunglasses and t-shirts despite the leaden sky. Niko told me that even then they were all off their heads, hooked on the needle. Grouped in front of a low wall on the Basque coast, the little gang fooled around for the camera, unaware that four of them would soon be dead – in a motorbike accident, from an overdose, AIDS, suicide. Of the rest, now, François was in remission; Niko had escaped the virus, but he still wasn't clean and he went on one detox after another; and I was dragging my carcass around in a wheelchair. Zaza listened in silence. Beyond the jetty, the sun was sinking, colouring the fishermen's nets and the sail of a boat returning to port a deep ochre.

On the Sunday night, the whole gang took me back to Kerpape. It was very late and the centre was deserted and silent, but we were full of energy. The sun and sea air had done me good. As Niko wheeled me back in the darkness to my room, he got a fit of the giggles when he caught sight of ten electric wheelchairs parked in the corridor. The pilot lights on the rechargeable batteries were blinking like Christmas lights. The beasts were getting high on electricity, while their owners, stuffed full of sleeping pills, dreamt they were playing leapfrog.

'Hey, Léo, ever had a go in one of these?'

'Not yet, but I expect the time'll come.'

'Let's have a little ride,' suggested Zaza.

'Yeah, but . . .'

And off we went, in single file along the corridors of Tetraland, a little band of Parisians racing at full speed in the darkness. Kerpape by night! Hair all over the place, eyes stinging from the salt air, we cut each other up trying to get into the lead. Our night-time escapade would probably get me into trouble, but I didn't care. We were waking the dead!

At this rate, thanks to Zaza and her cowboys, my stay in Brittany wouldn't be so bad after all. At this rate, maybe an electric wheelchair . . .

Well, it was something to look forward to in my old age.

45

Sabine

I sensed her circling like a sheepdog around a stray sheep. In big circles at first, then smaller ones, until she came to a stop in front of my wheelchair. She didn't hold out her hand. A veteran of the world of disability, she could tell at first glance the extent of my paralysis and she didn't want to make me feel awkward. Sabine had also realised immediately that I was new to this game.

We were in the big gymnasium at Kerpape watching wheelchair basketball. The wheelchairs dashed about, tyres screeching, leaving skid marks on the court, crashing into one another at the basket ends with a deafening sound of clashing metal. There were able-bodied players as well as disabled ones, and every half hour they stood up to stretch their legs. That was my dream, to stand up and walk!

'Would you like to play?' Sabine asked me.

I looked at her and shook my head.

'Have you just arrived?'

A paraplegic in her forties and a sports instructor, she was there on a visit. She knew the place well, greeting everyone, giving tips to the wheelchair ping-pong players.

She must have sensed my distress – I made no effort to hide it anyway. And she noticed my antiquated wheelchair. Next to the Formula One Turbos of the basketball players, it looked like a clapped-out panzer tank.

'Are you going to get your own wheelchair soon?'

Sabine forced me into a conversation and, though the state of my wheelchair was the least of my worries, I thought I might as well ask for her advice.

'I mean,' I said, 'you can't imagine a sitting room without armchairs, a dining room without a table or a table without a stool. Whatever you do in life, you have to sit your arse down at some point, don't you?' I supposed I'd get used to it in time but, for now, I found it intolerable having to sit all the time.

'You know,' said Sabine, 'when you come to buy your chair, choose something you really like. Make sure you get a model that's light, fast and comfortable, but have fun with the look. They do gorgeous colours now: bottle green, bright red, metallic grey. They're fantastic! If you wear sports clothes, choose a colour to match. Or if you wear jeans, get a lovely lavender blue. Really! When I see kids having fun on their skateboards or rollerskates or mountain bikes, I think, it's exactly the same for us. We're all on wheels! Just you wait, when you're in the shop and you see yourself in the mirror sitting in your brand new chair, you'll be thrilled!' She paused, before adding cheerfully: 'What do you think?'

I stared at her and opened my mouth but no sound came out. Everything around me went into slow motion. Even the players' shouting gradually faded. It was as if someone was inside my brain, reducing the volume and field of vision. And right in front of me, standing out from the haze, was this woman's smiling face. Something violent, traumatic, was paralysing any possible exchange. My subconscious shut down my hearing and power of speech. What did she want from me? How long had she been stuck in that wheelchair? How much suffering had she endured that she believed for an instant her muddle-headed theories? Well, she'd picked the wrong guy.

I knew the world of snow and watersports like the back of my hand. As a child of the Basque coast, I was crazy about surfing and sailing. Not to mention skiing, snowboarding, rock-climbing. Reaching snowy peaks, silent icy summits – it was a way of witnessing the divine.

What were you singing, Sabine, if not the sad lament of a woman in shackles? Of what heroic cavalcade were you telling me, sitting there on your poor little horse on wheels?

Being in a wheelchair isn't a game. Tetraplegia isn't a hobby. It's a life disfigured, a slowing-down just before death.

46

Navigation

Rather than getting high on drugs, I preferred going to the pool and chasing after Moïsa. For a week now I'd been swimming without a float, but I kept my goggles. My slender siren wore many different swimsuits, revealing more or less of her breasts, her stomach, her bottom. She inflamed my senses. I knew every one of her curves by heart. She was my joy but she was also, increasingly, the cause of my suffering. Away from the pool, my beauty didn't give me a second glance.

One evening, as I was hanging around at the entrance to the centre, I saw a guy of around twenty come to get her on his motorbike. They kissed on the mouth. She climbed on to the machine, hitching up her skirt and pressing her hips against his. I watched them head away to freedom, the picture of perfect young love. I was in torment and filled with gloomy thoughts. 'Take that, tadpole!'

I imagined Moïsa's supple, tanned body, naked beneath the sheets, and her sensual, childlike pout as she watched her biker undress. I knew that he'd take her in his arms, that she'd slide under him and open her thighs. He'd push gently into her slit and set their rhythm, their breath as one. She'd look at him through half-closed eyes until the pleasure made her lose control, throwing her into a furious convulsion that made her moan and cry out. She'd catch her breath, then, hands gripping her lover's hips, set a new pace with her pelvis, and he would start up again with even more energy for an extra round of pleasure.

I couldn't bear to think about it. Their youth made me sick. Tomorrow, like a rejected, jealous old lover, I'd be in a sulk with her when I got to the pool. But tomorrow, she'd be happy. Tomorrow would be the same as today: dealing with a poor fool getting an eyeful underwater and making his own private porn film.

Thankfully, my holiday in Brittany was coming to an end. At Kerpape I'd learnt to swim, live outside hospital, survive in a canteen, steal electric wheelchairs, and to steer clear of rehab centres.

The afternoons seemed to last forever. All activities stopped at 4 p.m. You got a terrible desolate feeling as you watched the physios and occupational therapists change out of their uniforms to go home.

'See you tomorrow,' they'd call cheerfully to all us poor sods thinking anxiously of the hours to kill before supper.

Sometimes, when I got back to my room I'd find a surprise waiting for me: Fredo and Thibaut, two musician friends on tour in the area, strumming their guitars on the terrace; Herma, a singer who was playing at the Celtic festival in Lorient, bringing me her new CD; Jean Eudes, an old school friend, turning up with his wife and six children; Zaza, come to take me out to dinner; Mickey and Thierry dragging me off for a boat trip.

This last prospect, though tempting, terrified me. My disability had given me new phobias: the sea, fire, crowds. When Thierry had suggested the trip two days earlier, I'd been keen. 'Great idea! You know, I can swim on my own now!'

'That's great. We can take you out to sea.'

'Er . . . out to sea? Where?'

'The Gulf of Morbihan. Don't worry, it's calm out there.'

'Hmm . . . yeah . . . are you sure?'

I slept fitfully that night. OK, I could float, but that was in a pool heated to 29°C under the watchful eye of a *Baywatch* babe in a red bikini. It was quite another matter to face icy water in a gale force 8 with ten-foot waves, madmen on jet-skis, hungry moray eels, KGB frogmen, paranoid seagulls . . . I trusted Thierry: he worked in advertising, had five children, collected ancient books. But what exactly did he know about sailing? Did he have a fully certified sailing permit? What would he do if the boat started sinking and I fell overboard, knowing that first he had to look after his five children, his wife, his mother-in-law, his dog and the young Irish au pair for whom he was responsible? It would be the *Titanic* all over again.

I mentioned it to my landlady, Mrs le Quellec. She listened, and nodded as she packed my bag. 'It's your last weekend. Make the most of it!'

My last? What did she mean? That I'd be heading back to Paris in a body bag? Was she in on the plot?

'If you change your mind,' she added, 'we're organising a canoeing trip on Saturday. We'll be having a picnic on the beach.'

I was done for. My childhood friend was proposing a remake of *The Raft of Medusa* and now this old madwoman wanted to load me and her limbless wonders on to floating suppositories that capsized at the slightest breath of wind. If I was going to drown, I'd rather it was among friends.

I got on to Thierry's boat eventually, but we never left dock. Mickey, Zaza and my brother installed me by the outboard motor, beside the helm. Sitting in my wheelchair, surrounded by picnic baskets and squawking brats, I savoured the pleasures of stationary sailing.

Delightful. From my precarious perch, while Mickey and Louis struggled to start up the idiot-craft, I felt a growing serenity. I was happy at sea after all, I was happy in water, I was happy surrounded by my friends. If my paralysis was going to stretch on indefinitely, I'd organise my new life around those things. I needed sun; tetraplegics suffer from the cold – in addition to enforced immobility (and low blood pressure, like the old and athletes), their thermoregulatory function is impaired. Keeping warm also depends on the circulation and therefore on moving the body. When you're on your feet, whether you're out for a stroll or a long-distance run, the heel strikes the ground, sending blood back up to the heart. This constant, automatic motion regulates the temperature inside the human body and gives alarms signals – sweating, shivering, getting goosebumps, teeth chattering. In the invalid sitting in a wheelchair, this network is disrupted. He has to watch out for sudden changes in temperature and take protective measures, such as putting on a hat, sunglasses, fleece or cagoule.

So I wanted sun, temperate seas (26°C minimum), a boat to take trips in, a heated swimming pool (full of girls) and lots of friends.

I had a year to sort things out and find the house of my dreams. Soon I'd be receiving a letter:

Dear Léo,

I have the perfect house for you. It's above the little village of Lumio, in Upper Corsica, and the view is magnificent. The only problem is you'd have to share my bed, because my room is the only one on the ground floor. Also, I must confess that I always sleep in the nude. I hope that doesn't bother you. Waiting for you impatiently.

All my love, Laetitia Casta.

The boat wouldn't start, so we set off by car with the whole retinue for a beach Thierry knew. As the wheelchair got stuck in the sand, several different methods of lifting and carrying were tried:

- four people carry the wheelchair (20 kilos) + tetra (60 kilos) = 80 kilos;
- two people link arms on which the tetra sits, enthroned. 60 kilos ÷ 2 = 30 kilos;
- one person grabs the tetra under the arms, another grabs him under the knees, as if carrying a bag of dirty washing = 60 swaying kilos;
- one person carries the tetra like a young bride: 60 kilos + 1 slipped disc = 1 month off work;
- one person says to the tetra: 'We've had enough. Sort yourself out,' while the other kicks the tetra in the gut. 'If you want to have a swim, you can crawl over the sand!';
- one person shuts the tetra in the car with the dog.

It was Zaza who found the answer: a piggyback. They lifted me on to Thierry's back, I put my arms around his neck and off we went. A paralysed body is heavy and difficult to manoeuvre; an adult's leg can weigh between ten and twenty kilos; the head, six kilos; a full stomach, ten kilos; an empty stomach . . . Well, there's no such thing.

Thierry carried me to the water's edge. His children,

running ahead of us, were giving me dirty looks, especially the youngest one, who was still a toddler. 'What's that big lazybones who still sits in a pushchair doing trying to strangle Daddy from behind?'

Zaza had brought me a deckchair. I lay in the chair catching my breath, while the kids, supervised by Joanna, the au pair, put on their swimsuits and got out their buckets and spades. Mickey, Louis and Zaza ran into the sea. Thierry went to enquire about hiring a windsurfing board. His wife, Marie, lay on a towel reading *Marie Claire*. I observed the beach scenes, taking over in my imagination the male bodies playing frisbee or volleyball, or lurking at the water's edge in search of young women desperate for company. The sound of children and their anxious or irritated mothers shouting, of the lifeguard blowing his whistle, of the waves lapping on the shore, and the smell of chips, all wafted to me on the wind. I made a mental note to myself, 'Next time, remember to bring books, binoculars, a Thai masseuse and a Range Rover.'

I was experiencing summer at a distance, as a spectator. Like Dirk Bogarde in *Death in Venice*, except that I was the age of Tadzio's older brother. But later, when Thierry threw me into the water and I swam out to sea, I changed my mind.

Joanna took the little one to paddle by the water's edge. Very gently, she splashed water on his head, his shoulders, his tummy. I could imagine the child's silky skin under her fingers. He submitted, docile. He could have been my son. I made another mental note, 'Think of having a baby,' as I admired the au pair's firm curves.

47

Couples

Back at Garches, I was given a room with two beds. Life there went on as before. There had been an intake of new residents, mostly young, injured on motorbikes – August's sad harvest. It's too hot in summer to wear a helmet. The slightest fall or crash can be fatal; a body without protection explodes, breaks, burns on the tarmac. There were also divers who'd surfaced too fast; surfers who'd been struck by a wave that was too powerful; lunatics who'd dived into empty swimming pools; climbers who'd plunged into a void; and botched suicide attempts.

Dr Desmouches came to say hello. He was just back from his holiday and looked tanned and relaxed. Without catching his breath, he was off on another tour of duty: eleven months looking after around a hundred patients. I admired his devotion. And what a huge task he faced: patients, bewildered parents, pessimistic prognoses, hopes, disappointments.

'So how was Kerpape?' he asked.

I told him about my Breton escapade.

'It's good to have done it,' he said. 'But let me tell you something: those people in wheelchairs that you found sad and resigned, they were probably like that before their accident. People don't change as much as all that.'

'I'll let you know in a few months.'

'By the way, are you going to physio this afternoon? I've got a group of policemen visiting the department for a campaign on road-traffic accident prevention. It'd be good if you could tell them your story. You don't have to, of course.'

At the door, he turned. 'How many months is it now since your accident?'

'Seven.'

'Have you tried intracavernous injections yet?'

'And what would they be, Herr Doktor?'

'Injections into your prick to make you ejaculate. Are you planning to have children?'

'Not right now. I've got to have lunch. But later, if Hélène is agreeable . . .'

Sylvia, Mickey and Zaza came to take me to the cafeteria terrace. The weather was lovely and I felt like getting out of the hospital, playing hooky. Mickey announced that he was organising a barbecue in my honour at his house.

'Surprise! There'll be lots of people.'

He'd arranged to borrow the special vehicle that the hospital lent out to patients' families for outings.

'I've spoken to your doctor,' said Zaza. 'You can spend weekends out of hospital now.' And she handed me the keys to her house in Versailles.

'The place is yours. My parents are away for a year, you can move in when you like. We can have dinner parties, even during the week.'

Now that I was going to be let out of hospital, I had to find a nest, rebuild my life.

'Look, it's Darius.'

There was my older brother, with his open smile;

tenacious, meticulous, ever-efficient Darius. As he opened his bag I glimpsed all the folders inside, labelled with my name and different headings: hospital, bank, insurance, Social Security, Cotorep (Commission for Career Guidance and Professional Placement), Paris City Council.

'I've been slogging on your behalf, little brother. Quite an assault course. Enough to make you want to bash your head against the wall.'

'Thank you so much, beloved brother.'

'Oh, stop it. You'd do the same for me.'

'You must be joking! I've always hated hospitals and paperwork.'

Darius smiled. 'For your trips at the weekend, you're entitled to an ambulance. It'll come to fetch you on a Friday around six and bring you back on Sunday evening. You're also entitled to a visit from a nurse twice a day.'

Someone came up behind me and put their hands over my eyes. It was Hélène, my physio.

'So, Léo, you're back. You've improved, I hope?'

'Not a bit, my dear. Without you, my body has no meaning.'

'So you missed me, did you?'

She sat down at our table and ordered a coffee. 'I've got a new patient, Adelaide, a head trauma case. Twenty-two. She's just arrived from New York. She was knocked over by a taxi. She was in a coma for three weeks. We have to keep an eye on her – she has no inhibitions at all! During physio this morning, Medhi got her going and she started undressing. I arrived just in time! Her boyfriend still comes to visit her. For the time being . . .'

Garches wasn't simply a meeting place for the physically wrecked, it was an emotional crossroads for couples and parents. Often, when someone who was engaged or married ended up in a wheelchair, they rejected their partner.

Young men couldn't bear their partner to see them when they were so physically diminished and sexually less powerful, or even impotent. Both partners needed huge amounts of courage to deal with the situation.

Hélène had shown me a copy of research carried out over the last ten years into couples where one partner was able-bodied and the other disabled. It was more likely that a single man in a wheelchair would get married, than a woman in a wheelchair. Able-bodied men were reluctant to take on a woman with dead legs and a barren belly. Whereas the survey showed that for a great majority of women it seemed natural to devote themselves to an injured man. After all, it's women who push the prams and the shopping trolleys. Lastly, women married to paraplegics felt safe, their partner's disability guaranteeing them enduring fidelity.

The medical staff and psychologists at Garches were on the front line and they had to answer questions that were painful but legitimate: will I be able to have children? How will this affect my relationship, my sex life with my partner? Will I be able to do a decent job of bringing up my kids, protecting them? Will they be ashamed of me?

In this dramatic context, a person was revealed in all their strength, and their weakness: 'For better, for worse . . .'

But you never imagine the worse.

48

Lapsus linguae

One afternoon, just as Hélène had stood me in the verticaliser, Aunt Laurence made an entrance that attracted a great deal of attention in the physio department. She was wearing a bright yellow suit with matching hat, tights and shoes. She looked like a giant banana. She'd left Amadeus, her poodle, in the car. He was a stuck-up little thing who had something against wheelchairs. Whenever he saw one, he went up to the wheel, cocked his leg and gave it a good shower.

'Hello, darling,' she said and kissed me at my perch. 'I've just got back from Lourdes. It was a wonderful pilgrimage!' Then, lowering her voice, she added: 'You know, I met some lovely young paraplegic girls there. One of them gave me her card. A remarkable young lady. She drives her own car and is an executive with AOL. Would you like me to have you both round for dinner?'

'I'll have to check my diary. I'm pretty tied up at the moment.'

Shit! My aunt was trying to set me up with a cripple! I could picture it: we'd get married at Saint-Eustache and produce loads of little brats in wheelchairs; in the afternoon we'd wheel round the supermarket in convoy, then back at home we'd park our chairs, in order of diminishing size, in our specially adapted garage.

'So, what are your plans?' Aunt Laurence asked brightly.

Good question. For the time being I was housed, fed and connected (I had an answerphone in my room). My love life was non-existent, not counting the disabled hussy my aunt wanted to palm off on me. And I was pretty sure Father Christmas was going to bring me a fantastic present: my very own, brand new wheelchair. Apart from that, maybe I could attempt suicide, as a break in the routine?

Aunt Laurence's face lit up. 'You know, I was watching the Michel Drucker Show the other night and it made me think – if you want to carry on with your music, look at Gilbert Montagné – he's blind and his handicap hasn't stopped him playing the piano. Why shouldn't you do the same?'

'I'd love to, Auntie, but I'd have to gouge out my eyes. And I can't use my hands anymore.'

'Oh.'

Aunt Laurence, queen of the quiche lorraine – she'd brought me some in a Tupperware box – looked disappointed.

'You won't forget to give me back the container, will you?'

A little later, I was sharing the quiche with my new room-mate, Mr Verdier, a paraplegic in his fifties, when the phone rang: it was Xavier Pollet, a guy from my past. I hadn't heard from him in over five years.

'So, Léo, I hear you're a tetra now? Shit, that's bad luck! By the way, did you ever meet my cousin Edouard?'

What the fuck did I care about his cousin Edouard?

'Yes, of course,' I said. 'Really nice bloke.'

'You know, he had an accident too, in 1989. He was a tetraplegic for three years.'

My heart started beating faster. 'Three years? And he got better?'

'No, he did himself in – drink, prescription drugs, heroin, the lot. He couldn't take it any more, poor sod. So how about you? Can you move anything?'

'Yeah, mainly my dick! It does the twist.'

'You can get a hard-on?'

'Oh yes, I ejaculate! I get it everywhere.'

'Good old Léo. You haven't changed a bit.'

I'd had to get used to gaffes, slips of the tongue, things left unsaid; to forced smiles and treacheries of language that could be as brutal as any diagnosis; but mainly, to the passing of time.

I was surprised, not by my endurance of misfortune, philosophical resignation, serene indifference to the occasionally ludicrous behaviour of my contemporaries, but to the yawning chasm in my soul that grew a little wider every day.

I was facing a great void, but my only strategy was not to ask myself any questions. There was an unknown factor in this paradoxical equation: before my accident I'd always had faith in the future, yet sought to escape the present in compulsive activities which somehow never fully satisfied me. Today, annihilated, I no longer expected anything from life. All that remained was the crazy hope of getting back my legs, my hands. Nothing else mattered. Stripped of everything, I no longer overloaded my soul with trivial upsets, because I'd identified the source of my torment, my anger, my frustration.

Today, I knew the cause of my suffering.

49

Tetramobile

Mickey was as solemn as a judge at the wheel of the tetramobile. The van was quite a sight. It was a prototype and looked like a combination of three types of vehicle: the police van, for its cell-like qualities; the horsebox, for its narrow height and method of securing its occupant; and the submersible, for its extra large windows and panoramic views. The big rear cabin could accommodate even the most imposing of electric wheelchairs. The driver could keep an eye on his passenger through the glass partition and the wheelchair was held in place with a system of tracks and straps.

I was glad Mickey lived near the hospital. At red lights, drivers gaped at me as I sat, an unjustly condemned man in my electric chair, exposed to stares through those wretched large windows. But I didn't bear a grudge and blessed them with a magnanimous sign of the cross. Mickey sat hunched at the wheel and kept under 35 kph. Our snail-like pace got on quite a few drivers' nerves and despite the blue and white sign – 'Severely Disabled Person on board' – they drove right up our arse and swerved trying to overtake, honking their horn.

My friends were all waiting, lined up on the pavement singing: 'For he's a jolly good fellow, for he's a jolly good fellow . . .' Mickey leapt out, brandishing the tetramobile's remote control; the back door opened, and the folding ramp slid out and sank to the ground. Sylvia, Caroline, Vanille and Dagmar, who'd never been into bondage, undid the straps fastening me to the wheelchair and securing the chair to the metal floor. My female escort then unloaded me. Ambroisine, who always had her camera with her, got all the girls to climb inside the van and press themselves up against the windows.

'Come on, girls, be nice,' said Richard. 'Take off a few clothes! It'll make Léo's day!'

Mickey pushed a few bottoms and closed the door on a dozen hysterical hens. He got back in the van and drove his 'Harem Peep-Show Circus' around the block. En route he passed a few suburban ladies who looked shocked by his white-slave-trade caravan. Mickey noticed several fathers smiling lustfully and he wished he'd put a sign on the back saying: 'You can laugh, but your daughter might be inside.'

When Louis and Mickey got me back to the hospital at around midnight, the nurse told them off. 'He was meant to be back by seven. Really, boys, this isn't good enough!'

'Don't be cross, Marie-Jeanne, it was my first outing.'

'Come on, bed!'

They undressed me and when I was naked, Marie-Jeanne gave a shriek: 'My God! What have you done?'

Now it was me who had problems with my bodywork: I had a red mark on my coccyx. Stage one of a pressure sore.

'I suppose Léo hasn't been moved all day, so his bottom is suffering the consequences. We'll have to lie him on his front all week, until the mark disappears. Well done, boys!'

That night I lay on my side waiting to fall asleep, watching the little Virgin of Nazareth glowing in the dark above the bed. Though our friendship was in its infancy, I always made sure to ask for her protection during our evening tête-à-têtes. My friends took care of my emotional well-being, the nurses looked after my body, and I did the best I could with the rest. There was so much spiritual turmoil that I had to repress, to keep under control, if I didn't want to fall into an abyss of questions without answers, but I sensed that such existential conflicts would inform both my successes and my failures. Hope isn't an end in itself, simply the driving force.

Mr Verdier, my room-mate, was snoring in the other bed. He was far away from home, from his garden and from his wife, who was too scared to come to see him. The man loved the soil, trees, flowers. The day before, a visitor had brought him some cherry tartlets. He'd looked at the red, shiny fruits and burst into tears.

Later, I asked him whether it was the unexpected visit that had upset him.

'No,' he said. 'It was the cherries.' And he added, gazing sadly at the tartlets lined up on the table, untouched: 'I fell from a cherry tree.'

The gardener had ended up as a vegetable.

50

Fellini

Et gratte, gratte, gratte, sur ta mandoline, mon petit bambino . . . Dalida's voice came from the loudspeaker, the volume turned up to maximum. Dominique, the auxiliary, worked the remote control for the hoist. I left dry land and was lifted out over the water.

On Tuesdays and Thursdays I splashed around in the pool which was edged with green plastic plants and heated to 28°C all year round. Behind the window, Hélène watched me being immersed and made faces at me, doing a perfect imitation of a Parkinson's patient. Françoise, the *Baywatch* babe, was on duty by the pool, supervising entries and exits. Every three weeks, she checked the bacteria levels of the water. What with the elderly patients who 'leaked' in it, the kids who pissed in it and the filthy pigs who spat in it, they had to monitor our aquatic paradise closely so that it didn't turn into a septic tank teeming with infectious germs, and have to be closed.

A strange pair used the pool at the same times as me: an old woman and a monster. In the changing room, while Dominique, the auxiliary, was changing me into my swimming trunks, I asked him about the Felliniesque duo.

'Jean Benoît and Mirabelle? They're husband and wife. She's at least twice his age. While he's in the pool, she knits scarves for him and takes care of the soundtrack. She only plays easy-listening stuff, like you get on *Radio Nostalgie*. I once tried to put on one of my cassettes – Jean Benoît almost throttled me!'

Except on Wednesdays when it was reserved for sick children, the pool could be used by outsiders like Stone Benoît and Charden Mirabelle, the visitors from the fifth dimension, the living dead from Frankenstein city. 'Tell me who, who, who will make me forget?' sang Mike Brandt, trying to make me forget that I was perched in a fucking remote-controlled basket, instead of sunning myself on a ski lift above the slopes of Méribel, my tongue entwined in that of a Gwendoline mark two. Meanwhile, Jean Benoît, the amphibian, flapped his flipper and stared at me with his single bulging eye. He puffed like a harpooned seal, a few sparse hairs sticking up from his dented trepanned head. Ill-proportioned, humpbacked, with an atrophied arm, he swam in circles, a bit like a remote-controlled model boat with a jammed rudder. The gentle lapping of the water together with the ghastly music lulled him.

Françoise was in the pool, ready to catch me. 'Léo, wait for the hoist to . . .' she warned sternly.

Too late. I'd flung myself into the void as if from a diving board, and landed in the steaming water, splashing an amused Dominique by the side of the pool. Jumping in like this was one of the few things that made me feel exhilarated. It was the only voluntary momentum I could impart to my leaden body; I swung my head forward, and the rest followed.

'Max is free . . . some say they've even seen him fly.'

Jean Benoît was in trouble. My sudden leap into the

water had caused a mini tidal wave that had made the hemiplegic toad lose his precarious balance. He was now swallowing water. There was a great big tadpole on his territory! Françoise grabbed him under the arms and dragged him to the side of the pool. 'Calm down, Jean Benoît, everything's alright now.'

I swam off, to reassure him. Unable to speak, he made little plaintive grunts as Dominique hoisted him out of the pool. He was the size of a twelve-year-old child. One of his legs was shrivelled and without a foot, the other one was drawn up towards his hip, and couldn't bear weight. Mirabelle sat in her deckchair knitting, smiling to herself. She was swaying in time to the music and hadn't noticed that her other half had almost drowned.

She got up, packed up the disco, and went to help her little man in the changing room. Silence at last. That kind of music had once made me smile but now, in hospital, I found those popular 'lite' tunes unbearable. Their jauntiness and banality seemed to highlight the pathos of my situation, the end of all my plans. The great music to which I aspired had turned its back on me. I'd sunk really low, my brain was feeding on filth. This pair, these songs – the whole thing was sordid. I was taking everything head on and becoming incapable of any detachment.

Later, as Dominique was drying me and changing me back into my clothes, he admitted: 'I was just kidding, before. Little Jean Benoît . . . well, the old woman, she's his mother, not his wife. Can you imagine it? I mean, the two of them in bed together?'

The thing that struck me most was that I had actually believed him. I'd seen so much unhappiness that nothing surprised me any more. And anyway, I was in the same boat. At that very moment, someone somewhere in Paris was probably saying, 'Can you imagine? Poor Léo, stuck in that wheelchair! How awful! If I was him, I'd shoot myself. I hear he doesn't want to see anyone. Not surprising, is it?'

Suffering doesn't make you noble. It just hacks at your heart and drains you of your blood, your innocence, your intelligence.

The beautiful people are outside. In here there's only sadness, misery and shame.

51

Morning

During my romantic years, I found mornings conducive to love. I adored warm languorous embraces at dawn. But sometimes my girlfriend would thwart my amorous plans by rushing to the bathroom to get ready for work. So then I would drag myself to the kitchen, make a lemon-grapefruit-orange-rum combo in the blender, following an old recipe invented by the Empress Josephine, and, a few minutes later, invigorated by the vitamin-rich mix, turn up in the bathroom.

'Darling, can I get in the shower with you?'

'I can wash myself, Léo! Will you never leave me alone?'

'Please . . .'

'Listen, I'm already late.'

'Please . . .'

'Out of the way!'

It was best to give in. I would potter around the flat, witnessing the metamorphosis: body lotion, clean knickers and bra, shiny new tights, kitten heels, jacket, lipstick, eye-liner (with the little mime show in the mirror: 'Could put on more, but not too much or I'll look like a tart'), a spray of scent and a quick brush of the hair. Wow!

This ritual drove me wild. It was a striptease in reverse. I'd wait by the front door, ready to nab the beauty. She would struggle and curse, but if by chance I found a chink in her armour, then how my senses were assailed. All the clean new clothes, the freshness, the scent, were released, crushed, unbuttoned and moistened with bodily fluids and the ravages of desire . . . And afterwards, what a mess!

From the window, I could then watch my girl running down the street and hailing a taxi. Full of male pride, I'd consider how, inside her warm belly, a little of me, of my seed, would be with her for the rest of the day, in a wild, frantic bid for survival.

On the other hand, sometimes all I got was a slap and a slammed door. 'Out of the way, Léo! And I won't be round this evening, I'm going out for dinner.'

So I didn't always have the last word.

Every morning, around 8 a.m., before the auxiliary opened the shutters and brought me breakfast, I thought of my sleeping girlfriends, of lovemaking in the early morning. What had become of them? Who were they making love to now? Had they forgotten me?

I lay on my side with a cushion placed between my knees to prevent pressure sores. I tried to retreat back into sleep by hiding under the sheets and convincing myself that the pains racking my stiffened body belonged to the land of my dreams; that everything would go back to normal. Gwendoline would ring at the door, I'd go to open it, and she'd come back to bed with me. She'd slip naked under the covers, climb on top of me and press herself against my hips, my chest, my mouth; I'd feel her fresh young skin, her perfect, invigorating energy.

Instead, at the hour the milkman called, I now got a finger up my bottom. The nurse or, if not, Roger – a rather primitive auxiliary – would surprise me with a suppository. Delightful way to start the day. Was there a limit to the negation of the self, the loss of privacy, the relinquishing of all modesty?

Well, I still had my dignity. Even with my arse on show.

52

The footprints in the sand

I'd hardly heard from Antoine, my younger brother. He couldn't understand what was happening to me. He lived alone in Lyon and, on the rare occasions when he'd come to see me, I'd sensed he was uneasy, overcome by the situation.

Perhaps he was too emotional, too fragile, too shocked? Things would sort themselves out in time, when I got out of here. He wasn't the only one to be put off by hospitals, and I wasn't offended. Apart from a few brief visits to congratulate women friends who'd had babies, I had myself, for years, avoided the waiting rooms of medical centres, the corridors of casualty departments and the air-conditioned rooms of clinics.

At the beginning of December, as I was finishing lunch, Darius and Louis came and sat on either side of the bed. Even before they spoke, I knew something terrible had happened. Darius took my hand.

'Antoine . . . has had an accident. Last night. He's in Intensive Care in Lyon. Mum and Dad are with him. We don't know much, only that it's serious.'

'What happened?'

'He fell from a third floor window. They think he took some pills and lost consciousness. A neighbour heard a noise outside and saw him lying in the courtyard. The ambulance came pretty quickly.'

'I've spoken to his doctor,' said Louis. 'He smashed up his lungs when he hit the ground. And he has multiple fractures. I'm going to see him this weekend. It's pretty bad.'

I looked at Darius. 'Are you thinking what I'm thinking?'

'Yes. Misfortunes always come in threes.'

'Shit, so who's next?'

My brother and I had both had the same thought: that for some inexplicable reason our family was jinxed. It was terrible for our parents – two children struck down. 'Somebody up there doesn't like us,' Senator Ted Fitzgerald Kennedy had said after the tragic deaths of Joe Junior, John and Bob.

The saying that disasters always come in threes was confirmed a couple of days later. While driving home, my other sister, Marie-Antoinette, skidded on a patch of ice and spun off the road. She was praying and quietly calling on heaven to spare her when the firemen cut open her mangled car door and they found her calm and unscathed. 'Thank you, St Christopher!' she exclaimed, straightening her clothes and looking at her watch. Blast! She was going to be late to the Conservatoire where she was due to give some lessons.

We'd had a lucky escape. I needed to be with my loved ones. I got permission from the hospital to spend Christmas with my family in Poitiers and took the TGV, escorted by Camille, her husband Fred, Louis, Darius, his wife and their four children.

The whole tribe was there – vulnerable, anxious, but

closer than ever. My mother was the most distressed. It seemed to hurt her more than it did me to see me trapped in a wheelchair, sitting forlornly at the keyboard of a silent piano. Cheeky smiling photos from happier times stood on the sideboard in the sitting room. Ever since we'd been kids, the five of us Champ' brothers had always shown off in front of the camera, striking poses like a university sports team, moronic rock group or paranoid special forces commando unit. There had always been some competition and physical rivalry between us. The only area in which my brothers conceded defeat was the conquest of girls. It was as if I'd been the sole recipient of the family libido.

My parents let me have their room as it was the only one on the ground floor. Twice a day we phoned Lyon for news of Antoine. His condition was critical. He had been well and truly defenestrated. Members of the family took turns by his bedside. Louis and I planned to go and visit him the following day. My father was an incredible source of strength to us all. A quiet, tenacious man, he had long ago accepted that no life was immune to tragedy. Having lived through the war years, he was ready to deal with adversity. We now realised that as we'd grown up, these attitudes had become imprinted on us, imperceptibly, like dormant cells ready to be activated.

On the road to Lyon, we tried to think of reasons for Antoine's desperate act. I thought of romantic upsets, of an insidious accumulation of setbacks and disappointments. My brother was an intense being, acutely, even morbidly sensitive, and his tendency to judge others too severely had distanced him from his peers. He had never gone in for small talk or worldly posturing. He must have felt rejected and perhaps his isolation had gradually led to nervous depression. It was highly likely that my accident had been a triggering factor: I was the focus of attention for the entire family. Antoine must have thought that he couldn't help, that the others were looking after me just fine, and that it was better if he kept out of the family turmoil. He was his own harshest critic.

At the René-Wildeck hospital in Lyon, we were shown to the waiting room for Intensive Care. Unlike at Garches, it was in the basement. The pallid fluorescent lighting emphasised the timeless isolation of the patients. A young doctor recognised Louis and hurried off to fetch Antoine's medical notes. After he'd given us a rundown of our brother's condition, he asked what had happened to me. He listened, nodding sadly, as if to say, 'In the smashed-up family, give me the brother, the younger brother and a wild card just in case.' For the time being, he gave us his assessment: 'Your brother suffered a severe blow to the ribcage with bilateral pulmonary contusions, massive alveolar haemorrhaging, multiple secondary infections and heart failure. Needless to say, it was touch and go for a fortnight. We had to drain all the fluid in his lungs in order to facilitate the O_2–CO_2 exchange. There's a risk of serious after-effects as a result of part of the alveoli being destroyed. For the time being we're draining his lungs and trying to prevent infections, until he's ready – though it's still much too soon – to come off the artificial respirator and start breathing on his own.'

Louis slipped on a green gown and the doctor took him to Antoine's bedside. I stayed behind with Fred, my brother-in-law. He lit a cigarette. I hadn't smoked for eight months. I asked him for a drag and greedily inhaled a dose of nicotine. I felt dizzy for a few seconds. I needed something to help me cope with being back in Intensive Care. As I'd looked at my younger brother with a tracheotomy, stuck full of tubes, it was myself I was seeing.

I left the hospital groggy: I didn't know who I was, what I was doing, or where I was going. On the way home, Louis said only: 'Hey, it's Christmas Eve . . .'

It was a total disaster, that's what it was.

Charles had arrived unexpectedly and after Christmas Mass I confessed my despair to him.

'Perhaps you shouldn't try to bear the burden alone. You must let go, and trust in providence.'

'Very funny, Charles! Where was providence the day of my accident?'

'Perhaps it's what stopped you dying . . .'

'And now, with what's just happened to Antoine, maybe we should take out a subscription . . .'

But Charles was like my father. Unshakeable.

'Do you know the parable of the footprints in the sand?' he asked me. 'A man is walking along the shore with his guardian angel. The sky is blue, the sea is calm, the sand is soft beneath their feet. The future seems bright and, as they walk along side by side, they leave footprints behind them in the sand. But suddenly the weather turns bad, the sky darkens, the sea starts to rage. The man hunches, enduring the storm. He's alone now. He collapses at the other end of the beach and, glancing back at the way he's come, he sees only his own trail of footsteps. He looks up at the sky, calls his guardian angel and berates him: "Where were you? Why did you abandon me when I most needed you? When we were together, we were walking side by side, but now, as far back as I look, all I can see are my own footsteps, my solitude." The guardian angel takes the man's hands. "Those footsteps that you see are mine. During that journey, when you thought you were alone, I was carrying you."'

The eternal struggle between the visible and the invisible. Tragedy profoundly affects human nature. I tended to believe it did so for the worse. But how could one overlook solidarity, compassion, or those beautiful souls who caught you just when you thought it was all over? I had faith in my fellow man. Even at the edge of the abyss, I would never give in to a pessimistic view of the world.

I'd never intended to follow such a path, but if I was to be that man on the beach, then I had to continue on my way.

53

Soraya

The ambulance was waiting for me at the Gare Montparnasse. It was parked in the space reserved for fire engines, opposite platform 1. I hated having to lie on a stretcher, but the regulations were firm. In the time it took for the paramedic and driver to open the back doors and slide me inside the ambulance, I glimpsed people's inquisitive, frightened, prying stares. I hated arousing such morbid curiosity. I hated reading rude comments on their lips. My eyes were wide open but they still thought me deaf, impervious, dead.

'Did he try to commit suicide? Did he jump under a train?'

'A drug addict. There are loads of them round here . . .'

I could have spat in their faces, although sometimes, a sincere, sympathetic, fleeting smile was enough to erase my anger at being tied up and stuffed into a van. I felt I'd never escape the cycle – hospital, transfer to ambulance, transfer to wheelchair.

'Are we going to Garches then?' asked George, turning the key in the ignition.

'Change of plans! D'you know the Avenue de Malakoff?'

I'd decided not to go back to hospital until the beginning of January. In the meantime, Soraya called me at my parents' in Poitiers to ask if I'd like to spend New Year with her and her family. My other friends were all away. There was no question of me staying at Raymond-Poincaré over New Year, but I'd been so thrown by Antoine's accident that I hadn't thought to arrange anything.

Soraya had come into my life through a physicist friend, Grishka Brijatov. A true visionary when it came to atoms and particles, Grishka was convinced that the nerve networks of the spinal cord would soon hold no secrets for scientists and that I would – he was definite – be back on my feet before spring! He mixed with scientists, researchers, geneticists and laboratory mice, and assured me that he was kept up to date on an hourly basis with all the spectacular advances taking place in the world of science. I couldn't imagine how he could possibly have such speedy access to all these confidential reports since he owned neither mobile phone, computer, fax or Palm Pilot, his telephone had been cut off and he didn't even know how his television worked. But none of this mattered, since he got all his information first-hand!

'How on earth does he know all this?' I asked Soraya, while Grishka stood on the stool in my room and tried to hypnotise a fly on the fluorescent light.

'I think he reads the papers . . .'

With his infectious enthusiasm, intellectual fervour and algebraic formulas, he really made me believe that I would be part of the last convoy of tetraplegics of the century.

'Absolutely no doubt about it!' said Grishka, laughing, as if I'd asked if it was possible to cure athlete's foot.

Wouldn't it be fantastic if the dream came true? No

more paralysed people, no more wheelchairs, no more miracles and no more pilgrimages to Lourdes or Fatima! But what chaos too. If all the cripples of the world got their legs back, all hell would break loose, especially over in America! Christopher Reeve would be back in action filming *Superman IV: the Return of the Electric Robot*, and the 50,000 veterans of Vietnam, Cambodia, Lebanon and the Gulf rotting in their desert-storm camouflage-green wheelchairs, would get their revenge at last.

'Soon,' my Grishka assured me, 'tetraplegia will be no more serious than the common cold!'

So, best to steer clear of open windows and cold draughts.

One evening in November, Soraya and Grishka came to visit me in hospital around midnight. Soraya sat on my bed, smiling, gentle, sensual, exotic. She was half Croatian, half Moroccan and spoke fluent Mandarin and Arabic – she'd spent three years working in Hong Kong. She'd just moved back to Paris. Tactfully, she helped me do things, anticipating my needs. By following the direction of my gaze, she understood what I wanted – a glass of water, the cuff I used for eating, a book, or to have my position changed.

Tall, voluptuous, her dark hair cut short like Isabella Rossellini's, she had olive skin, high cheekbones, almond eyes and full lips framing perfectly white teeth. I wasn't sure if I was in love with her, but I was certainly charmed. She lived with her mother and her brother, Medhi, in a flat on the Avenue de Malakoff. She'd found me a nurse and let me use her room, while she slept in her mother's room. We had some good times together, and this first love affair taught me two things: I could still be attractive to women; and I must under no circumstances involve my partner in my daily care (dressing, washing, catheterising) at the risk of taking the magic out of any intimate relationship.

Over the New Year, with Soraya I re-entered the Parisian social scene of parties and dinners. I discovered a tedious obstacle course of narrow lifts, staircases that could only be negotiated with the help of four people, and high-risk return journeys at dawn, when I had to trust in the devotion of friends under the influence of alcohol or illicit substances. A momentary lapse of concentration, crazy bit of improvisation, or poor hand-hold and a fall was certain.

I still found it excruciatingly uncomfortable to sit in the wheelchair for long periods. As soon as I arrived at my destination I asked two friends to sit me on a sofa. Your average civilian then couldn't tell that I was a tetra-flowerpot. People came, sat down, moved away; and a succession of women friends kept me supplied with alcohol, cigarettes, plates of pasta or cheese, coffee and kisses.

Tom, a chic rasta, son of the Jamaican ambassador, sat and talked to me until late into the night. He smoked joint after joint and chattered away in English about guitar duels between Peter Tosh and Bob Marley. The advantage of the dope was that it attracted plenty of the other guests and made them open up, even if it did fog their brains. Babeth, a friend I hadn't seen for about five years, asked me between tokes what I was up to these days.

'I've been at Garches for about nine months.'

'Oh? So you don't live in town any more? Have you got a house there?'

'No, no, I'm at the Raymond-Poincaré Hospital.'

'So you're studying medicine now?'

'No, I'm a patient there. I had an accident. My hands and legs are paralysed.' And I added in English to Tom, who was lighting another joint: 'I am tetraplegic!'

'What the hell are you on about?' Babeth laughed, keeping an eye on the spliff as it was passed around.

'You can believe what you like, but really I can't stand up.'

'Hey, nor can I, I've smoked too much.'

'What about my hands? Can't you see my hands?'

I waggled my numb mitts under her nose, but it was no use. In the old days, Babeth knew me as a bit of a clown, and to her that's what I still was.

'OK, move over, I'll show you,' I said.

I swung my upper body into the void. Soraya, standing chatting a little distance away, suddenly saw me lying on the floor in a cloud of smoke. She leapt to my rescue. Nobody was moving, brains were functioning in slow motion. I looked quite comfortable. But, as I continued to lie there unable to get up, it became clear to all that this was neither an overdose nor a piece of Living Theater improv.

'Léo, what's going on? Were you feeling dizzy? Give me a hand, you lot.'

While Babeth and Tom watched in amazement, I was lifted and gently placed back on the sofa. Soraya propped me up on cushions and, reassured, left me with my new friends.

'Yeah, man, you're a master,' Tom congratulated me. 'A yogi man.'

'You haven't improved with age,' remarked Babeth.

Around 5 a.m. Tom got up to leave and gave me a long hug. To him I was a sage, capable of sitting motionless for hours.

Out on the fourth-floor landing, I was getting impatient. Lost in the middle of about twenty guests all kissing one another goodbye, I wanted only one thing: to be back at home in bed. The lift had been overtaxed that evening and it had given up the ghost. Where had my bearers got to? They were staggering about, still clasping bottles. Trying to raise my voice above the din, I called out to Eric, Henri, Patrice, then Richard to come and help me down the stairs, but they didn't hear. In my wheelchair, I was a hundred and twenty centimetres tall, in other words the height of a little boy of nine. Nobody paid me any attention. Soraya, a little distance away, was getting chatted up by a tall blond guy. It was exasperating.

Suddenly, the crowd parted and a rather sturdy-looking young woman I didn't know grabbed the handles of my wheelchair and turned it round. I now had my back to the stairs. 'Don't worry. I'm used to this. My cousin's paraplegic,' she said.

She tilted back the chair and set off downstairs with the wheels bouncing on the narrow, polished steps and me being thrown from side to side. I tried to concentrate on keeping my balance, and not giving in to panic. I could see the noisy, merry group following us. My pilot speeded up, not even stopping on the landings. I suggested a pause but, deaf or intoxicated, she took no notice, dragging me on an infernal helter-skelter ride. Mute with terror, I tried to signal with panic-stricken eyes to the troupe coming down behind me. Too late, we'd soon left them way behind.

Soraya was already downstairs, outside the concierge's office. She wanted to go on to a club, Les Bains, and suggested to her friends that they drop me off at her place on the way. A big strapping lad lifted me into his car. During the operation, I got his booze-and fag-redolent breath full in the face. I thought back to a time now gone, recalling all the girls I had kissed at the end of a party. It wasn't the smell of the man's breath itself that troubled me, as much as the things it conjured up. I counted all the outrages my body imposed on me:

- I had to let Soraya go and have fun without me, and risk losing her a little bit more;
- I could feel my porter's muscles beneath his jacket and I mourned my lost youth;
- I had to draw a line under my past as a rogue, with its endless round of parties and surprises at dawn;
- All I wanted now was to sleep alone in a big bed with an ergonomic mattress after swallowing a sleeping pill and donning an eye-mask – dead sexy!

One morning, Soraya brought me my coffee. She opened the blinds, put on a CD and slid into bed with me. Sun streamed through the window, filling the room. I stroked her cheek, then slid my arm down her neck to her shoulder. She stopped me.

'Darling . . . Can we speak frankly?'

She didn't look up. I put my fingers on her lips. Shh, don't say anything. You took me into your home, your family, your heart. You made me laugh, you soothed my pain, you held me by the hand.

I'm not a rejected or disheartened lover, I'm just learning.

54

Rocking rolling chair

Darius was driving fast. The shop closed at lunchtime.

'D'you get nervous when you're in a car now?' he asked Léo.

'No, but I always look in the rear-view mirror at red lights and stop signs. I've heard too many stories of people being slammed into from behind by drunks.'

When an accident causes a major disability, the resulting situation is quite different depending on whether you're the victim, person responsible or, worse still, killer driver. In Léo's case, it was the fault of 'bad luck' and it was also 'his fault'. But there were some cripples who'd caused the death of their passenger, friend, spouse or child through careless driving, thus adding eternal guilt to their suffering.

For those who'd been knocked down by a drunken or dangerous driver, it was often impossible to forgive their assailant. How can you not hate the person who's maimed you, smashed you to pieces, turned your life upside down? Nothing can lessen that kind of suffering, resentment, bitterness. However much victims are paid in compensation – and insurance companies only cough up for absolutely irrefutable claims – they're haunted for ever more by the way their life is divided into three eras: before the accident, the day of the accident, and after the accident.

At night, in the darkness and silence as he waited to fall asleep, Léo probed the depths of his soul. These were the only times he found any inner peace. In the city everyone was asleep, which made them all equals. The only difference was the metallic presence crouching by his window. Moonlight glinted off it but did nothing to soften its sharp angles. His wheelchair. He looked at it with horror.

Mr Gilbert Mollet, representative and salesman at Speed and Comfort 2000, however, had an entirely different view. In the shop window in the Rue Émile-Zola, he displayed his latest models: the Speed 300, Pulsy Stability, Koschek Usa, and the famous Tekno V8 Interceptor that was on the covers of all the specialist magazines: *Tetra Magazine*, *Handicap Info*, *Chair and Leisure*, *Polio Weekly*, *Living on Valium*.

'This model's been a huge success. If you take one, we can give you a special price,' said Gilbert, wiping the fluorescent yellow frame of the electric wheelchair with the back of his hand.

'We discussed manual chairs on the phone,' Darius reminded him.

'Wait, let me take a look at the order book.'

Léo watched the rosy-cheeked salesman as he twiddled his moustache, took out his handkerchief and mopped his sweaty forehead.

'What was the name again?' he asked, flicking through his files.

'Champollon. My brother and I and his physio, Hélène Levasseur, had a meeting with you at Garches.'

'Ah, Hélène . . . I'm very fond of little Hélène,' wittered the man.

Darius came to find Léo, who was looking around the shop. He put his hand on his shoulder and asked, 'You OK?' His brother answered with a smile. They both knew that D-Day had arrived. It was a weird day to get through and included the signing of an 18,000-franc cheque. Social Security reimbursed 3500 francs.

'Tell that idiot that my wheelchair's over here. Look, it's still in the box, in bits. It's going to take ages to assemble.'

'Are we still going out for lunch?' asked Darius.

'Yeah. We'll have to come back anyway if I want to get my wheels today. I think Mr Speed 2000 is in a hurry to go for his lunch break.'

'It's like getting the car back from the garage. They never have it ready when they say they will.'

'Don't worry bro', I've got all the time in the world, but I'm sorry to be taking up so much of yours.'

Darius shook his head and turned back to the salesman, who was still rifling through his papers. 'Mr Mollet, our wheelchair's over here.'

Léo slipped away. He'd spotted a door leading into a big store room. He wheeled himself in and discovered the cave of Ali Tetra and his Forty Thieves on Wheels. There were about a hundred wheelchairs inside, from infant size to racing trikes. There were also rigid shells mounted on skis, and chairs with angled wheels that turned at the flick of a wrist – the kind used for wheelchair tennis, basketball, ping-pong, rock 'n' roll, chasing chicks. On the walls, posters with spectacular photos extolled the virtues of different makes. The Americans were the best when it came to sporting exploits and independence – 'Just do it!' The Californian magazine, *Spokes & Roll*, with a circulation of 250,000, was the bible of the disabled urban warrior, always on the lookout for new products and prototypes on land, sea or in the air. Keep on rocking, like in the good old days in Vietnam.

The posters were an extravaganza of colour and idyllic landscapes: a paraplegic on his bi-ski cut through powdery snow, leaning over like a slalom skier; a climber strapped into a mountaineering chair abseiled down a rock face; a dark tanned hunk prepared, despite his restricted mobility, to take off at the controls of his twin-engined Cessna. He was wearing a flying jacket and checking his flight plan. He was off to fuck the sky, while a tart with a blow-dried mane, silicone-filled tits and tight jeans showed off her nice arse and watched admiringly. The guy looked a bit like John John Kennedy. Less upright, but more alive.

The final poster showed a middle-aged guy in a baseball cap sitting in a speedboat, holding a fishing rod, against the backdrop of a turquoise sea. He was smiling and showing a newly caught tuna to the camera. He looked happy, but while he was off tormenting fish, his wife was probably shagging her tennis instructor.

'Not enough chicks,' thought Léo, staring at the posters. Where were the sexy paraplegic girls? He remembered an issue of *Playboy* in 1982 in which, over three pages, a model, Ellen Stohl, aged twenty-five, had posed naked, lying on a bed. There was no way of telling that this young woman with a perfect figure had paralysed legs. Wheelchair-bound after a car accident, she'd asked her boyfriend to photograph her and send the pictures to Hugh Heffner. The Bunnies' boss had immediately sent over his personal helicopter and his best photographer. The photos had caused a stir in the media and made Ellen a star for the summer. She'd broken a taboo and aroused the anger of puritan America.

'What? An invalid posing naked in a porn magazine?'

'And to think that at this very moment guys are jerking off to pictures of a cripple!'

'If paraplegics want to get laid now, they should do it in private, not in the papers!'

Léo stopped in front of a little multicoloured wheelchair. So as to hide the wheels the manufacturer had devised plastic covers decorated with cartoon characters. One handle was the shape of a duck's head, the other a giraffe's. But there was something horribly dishonest about this garish Walt Disney wheelchair. Parents would give their kid this magic pushchair that gleamed like a new toy car from Toys R Us. But the little darling would soon realise that he'd been tricked, and he'd want to kill Father Christmas.

'Ah, there you are, we've been looking for you!' said Gilbert Mollet, rubbing his hands. 'So, what do you think of my garage?'

'Wonderful. What a space!'

'We only finished painting it last Monday.'

'Do you know where my brother is?'

'Yes. He'll be back in a minute. He's supervising the assembly of your wheelchair. We're terribly busy at the moment.'

'That means business is good.'

'Fantastic! And we only started up in September.'

'Excuse me, Mr Moffet, I'm having second thoughts . . .'

'It's Mollet, but please, call me Gilbert.'

Léo looked embarrassed. Since his wheelchair 'test drives' on the private circuit at Garches, he'd been wondering if he'd made the right choice. True, he had been seduced by the manoeuvrability and fluid styling of the Olympus, a chair with an adjustable back, but now he was worried his independence might be limited once he was away from the smooth floors of the hospital. Perhaps a motorised chair would make life easier. Gilbert frowned – the order form had been signed, there was no going back. Even in an electric wheelchair.

'There is one solution,' said Mollet. 'You could always purchase a second . . .'

'. . . wheelchair. The Tekno V8 Interceptor, for instance?'

'Of course! But it all depends on your funds, because that model costs around 50,000 francs.'

'Oh, that's no problem!'

Gilbert rubbed his hands. 'Don't move, I'll go and get one.'

All three of them were now in wheelchairs. Darius was sitting patiently in the old cart that had carried his brother for the past nine months. Léo was driving the V8 around the shop. And Gilbert was testing the balance of the brand new Olympus. Mr Mollet had spent hours at specialist shows and medical equipment exhibitions waiting for customers, so he'd had plenty of time to practise. He was an expert at wheelies, getting up steps, and doing skids, jumps and turns. As in skateboarding there were a dozen or so manoeuvres that were obligatory for any self-respecting paraplegic.

But Gilbert Mollet wasn't paraplegic, he was just doing an impression of a paraplegic. He was very good at pretending to have paralysed legs; his performance was very realistic. But Léo wasn't pretending; and he had no career plan. When you didn't have the use of your hands your choice was pretty limited. At least paraplegics could apply for jobs as taxi drivers or TV presenters.

Léo suddenly came careering from the other end of the shop and crashed into the Olympus, which fell over backwards. Mollet hurt himself but did not, unfortunately, sever his spinal cord. Léo apologised and completed his loop.

'These buggers certainly go fast, they're pretty nifty. What colours do they come in?'

Mr Mollet was grimacing with pain on the floor. But the customer is always right. 'They do them in red, and in green . . .'

'Racing green, like a Jaguar!'

Mr Mollet didn't dare give the Severely Disabled Person a rollicking for fear of jeopardising the sale – Darius hadn't handed over the cheque yet. Léo finished his turn in the electric wheelchair, scraping walls, furniture and a couple of other wheelchairs.

'Could you put one aside for me?' he asked Mr Speed 2000 as he was being lifted into his new wheelchair.

Gilbert gave him a free gift, consisting of a puncture repair kit with two inner tubes, some rubber repair patches, glue, a pump and an Allen key. He took the cheque and walked the brothers to their car.

'Are you really planning to buy that other chair?' asked Darius.

Léo had no idea. He just wanted to have fun. It was the first time he'd had a new vehicle. In the old days, he'd always driven second-hand motorbikes or old bangers from the 70s.

In the old days, above all, he'd liked to play the hard guy.

55

Clara

She'd stuck photos from magazines, and covers of *Vogue*, *Elle*, *Harper's Bazaar*, *Biba*, on the wall behind her bed. She'd been injured at T5, somewhere on the motorway to Clermond-Ferrand, a month after her twenty-second birthday. Clara was blonde, sexy, flirtatious, and she never missed a chance to open her blouse and show off her lingerie and voluptuous bosom. She had a boyfriend who came to visit her but, in the corridor leading to my room, she always kept an eye out for good-looking male visitors.

'Your friends look nice. Really charming.'

Clara loved life, men, women, love and fashion and, as it was only three months since her accident, she was still hopeful of getting her legs back. I tickled her toes while she lifted weights on the physio table.

'Did you feel that, there?'

'Course I did. You touched my right foot.'

Clara was lying. I'd touched the empty sock lying beside her foot. We were all lying. It was impossible to cheat at sensory tests, even if the brain continued to make imaginary – imagined – connections. The living half of the body took over for the inert half, turning the negative into positive. If I stroked my 'insensitive' thigh with my 'sensitive' hand, I experienced a phantom feeling that had more to do with seeing the action than any actual sensation on the skin. I touch, therefore I feel. An outside event was all that was required to remind the patient that the body was simply a vulnerable envelope of flesh.

There was a little gang of young paraplegics who liked to experiment with physical resistance to pain – sometimes their own pain, but mostly the pain of others. They called themselves the Scissor Gang. The Scissor Gang didn't do anything they hadn't tried out on themselves. Their rallying sign was crossing their index and middle finger. They charged at full speed along the corridors in the physio department, the cafeteria, and around the hospital buildings. They'd start a conversation, distract you and, without you noticing, cut through your clothing and slice off a piece of flesh, always aiming at the dead, numb lower limbs. Their victims didn't feel a thing. They hid knives, razorblades, sharp pointed objects in their many pockets, and set off again as soon as the crime was committed. A few hours later, or maybe even at bedtime, the nurse would discover a gashed calf, or a bleeding ankle, or a knee deliberately burnt by a cigarette or cigarette lighter.

They liked to play with fire and metal. They placed drawing pins or small nails on the cushions of unoccupied wheelchairs. When the unwary owner, who couldn't feel his bottom, went back to his chair, he didn't realise that there was a sharp point sticking into his arse. Sometimes, victims only just avoided getting a pressure sore.

This kind of self-mutilation, scarring, ritual tattooing – also practised by prisoners, gangs, bikers and certain tribes of Africa, the Amazon and India – evoked the isolation, the precarious nature of daily life and psychological violence, as well as the physical challenges these boys faced. They were modern-day warriors martyred in metal disasters.

Two expressions obsessed me: 'Feeling good about yourself', and 'A healthy mind in a healthy body'. Tetraplegia isn't an illness, it's simply learning how to manage a heavy, inert body and the loss of sensation, of gentle intimacy, of muscular relaxation. Every session on the physio mat at Garches helped me to understand my new body, to try it out and improve it, to live with it as best I could.

Hélène tested me. She lay me on my back, or my front and I shut my eyes.

'Your leg, is it bent or straight? Your ankle, flexed or extended?'

'And your grandmother, does she ride a bike?'

'Come on, Léo, we've got to work.'

'Leave it, Hélène, I don't feel like it today.'

She could tell from my tone whether it was simply a whim, momentary laziness, a bad case of the blues, or cold anger. But she never left it, she always pushed me. I needed a really good reason to miss a session.

We were so close. No other woman had warmed my bones in the last ten months. There was a sensual complicity between us, a chemistry – the kind couples have – that was beyond words and physical therapy. The blue physio mat was the width of a double bed. I lay in the middle, and Hélène took off her sandals and crawled across it, a tender, enigmatic smile on her lips. Sometimes, she pretended to be a lion devouring an unwary backpacker. 'Come here, my little one.'

'You don't look at all tetraplegic,' she said to me one day when I was on the mat.

I was regaining strength. My shoulder muscles had bulked up and I was better at keeping myself upright. I still lost my balance sometimes but Hélène would always catch me. I could feel her strength, her energy, her firm soft skin. She'd lay her head on my shoulder. She was my mistress. We talked about her children, about love, the sea, travel. My imagination ran wild. She would have followed me down snowy slopes, into the ocean waves or along winding Pyrenean paths. We would have drunk mulled wine at roadside inns, pinched cows' arses at the festival in Bayonne and danced flamenco in bars in Fuenterrabia. I would have taken her into the big lounge of the Hotel du Palais in Biarritz at dawn, sat at the piano and played her a Cole Porter song: 'Every time you say goodbye . . . I die a little . . .' I die a little.

I would rather have my body broken into a thousand pieces than my heart. Bones can be fused, muscles repaired, flesh stitched; organs can be transplanted, blood replaced; plaster casts, bandages and splints can be applied, drips inserted; time does the rest. I'd seen living mummies lying in bed with weights suspended from their limbs. Six months later these patients would be getting around in wheelchairs, then shuffling about on crutches. One morning they'd be gone. Some of them came back to visit their physios and I could see the gleam of triumph in their eyes, the fierce pleasure of returning as tourists. I wasn't envious of their happiness. We were all survivors, we were all on the side of the living. Not on the side of the 8500 killed on the roads each year.

Clara was full of hope. There was the stuff she knew, what she thought she knew, what we knew, and what she didn't know. The junior doctors talked, the physios talked, the nurses talked, the parents talked. She wasn't aware of it but I knew some of her medical history. I assumed she knew some of mine. Like an old family secret, the truth was kept from us for as long as possible; we all had a skeleton in the cupboard. Clara thought she was only temporarily paraplegic. She was still a woman who liked to please, tease and attract men. She did her face, her hair, her nails, wore jewellery, and took care over her clothes. She picked a stylish wheelchair.

Mickey, my most faithful visitor, often stopped by her room. I could hear them laughing and joking. Mickey arrived one evening looking very smart. 'I'm taking Clara out to dinner.'

He took her to a restaurant in Versailles, then back to his place on the second floor with no lift. No problem, he carried her up, like a young bride. They lay down on the bed to engage in the preliminaries. No problem, Clara was good at flirting. She was wearing a long, button-through denim dress. Mickey uncovered her breasts as if opening a present. He left her bra on, testing his desire and patience. Her breasts were two domes spilling out of the cups. He was running his tongue over them when she freed them. They intensified their efforts and attentions towards each other. They each wanted to surpass themselves, but without overdoing the raunchiness. Mickey was being gentle but he didn't want to offend her by being too careful. He was there to arouse her, not play the humanitarian.

Clara was confused by all the new things happening, anxious at the thought that he would soon lift up her legs and enter her. She tried to identify the areas that were still sensitive. From the navel down, the feeling in all her lower erogenous zones was hazy; she could only tell what was happening by sight. She breathed faster as she became excited, but she felt self-conscious about moaning. Before, sex had made her scream with pleasure quite naturally, increasing her lovers' ardour. This was the first time she'd made love since her accident. She had no intention of faking an orgasm or talking dirty.

When he parted her legs with his, she bit her lip so as not to cry. Her legs felt separate from the rest of her. Nowadays even in bed she wore tights and, over them, ski pants. Mickey became heavier on top of her. Clara didn't take her eyes off him. She knew he had entered her when he threw back his head and started thrusting with his hips. She thought of the time she lost her virginity, with an impatient, clumsy boy who made no effort to give her any pleasure. Her brain was no longer connected to her lower abdomen. Mickey slowed down and she felt suddenly afraid. Did she get as wet as she used to? Did he no longer feel like it? He was catching his breath. She could feel that he still had an erection. She saw him move up towards her face and she took him in her mouth. Like before.

'The most difficult bit,' Mickey told me later, 'was taking her back. While we were making love, I had to hold up her legs. That's about twenty pounds on each shoulder. Afterwards, I helped her put her clothes on and I carried her, and then the wheelchair, down to the car. We drove to the hospital, and she asked me to help her get into bed. It was 5 a.m. by the time I got home. I was thinking of what I'd say to my friends. "Yeah, guys, I'm going out with a paraplegic girl and . . . no problem!"'

Mickey saw Clara again often before she left hospital. He followed all the stages as she lost her hopes of recovery. One day, she tore the pictures off her walls and sent her dresses back to her mother's house. She was going back home to Avignon. He took her to the Gare de Lyon and helped her get on the train. It was Easter. Behind the window of the compartment, Clara winked at Mickey if a handsome guy walked along the platform, and he did the same if he saw a pretty girl.

The whistle blew, the doors were slammed shut. Mickey walked with the train as it gently gathered speed. Clara waved. She blew a cloud of mist on the window and wrote a couple of words, back-to-front so that Mickey could read them: ‘Goodbye youth’.

The day before had been her twenty-third birthday.

56

Intracavernous

I had never paid for sex. I suppose I had to start some time. Darius explained that when I came out of hospital, I would be classed as LTD – Long-Term Disabled. I translated this as 'Limp Tired Dick'. I'd intended to save my pennies, but I was going to have to fork out if I wanted to have an orgasm. In order to get a decent erection and ejaculate fertile sperm, I'd have to inject the little guy just before engaging in intercourse.

When Doctor Desmouches suggested I try Cavergex intracavernous injections (130 francs a shot) and a Handjoy, a Swedish make of vibrator (3500 francs) or Viagra (140 francs a tablet), I congratulated myself on having had a busy sex life before the accident because, from now on, a roll in the hay was going to cost me between 120 and 150 francs a time. The price of a blow job in the Bois de Boulogne or a crappy trick in Pigalle with Madame Irma. If I wanted the beautiful Slav with blonde tresses and long legs who looked like a Barbie doll arousing my libido, I'd have to save up penny by penny. It was a scandal. They really didn't want tetraplegics to reproduce, just like under the Nazis when Mengele sterilised the retarded. Nice one, Ministry of Health!

Lunchtime was the best time to try out an intracavernous injection. Ejaculation wasn't guaranteed and there was a risk of retrograde ejaculation when, instead of coming out of the urethra, the sperm went the wrong way and ended up in the bladder. There was also the possibility that the chemical injected might cause a very long and painful erection. I therefore had to keep all afternoon free in case it took time for the swelling to subside. I didn't want to turn up at physio or swimming with my prick sticking up between my legs. An uninhibited head trauma case might jump on top of me and rape me. I could well imagine the fruits of such a union. I sometimes got a hard-on when I was working on the mat with Hélène. Was it involuntary? We'd just laugh about it. She'd leave me for ten minutes while Alexander returned sadly to his flaccid state.

Desmouches came by at midday, with Marie-Jeanne.

'Doc, I've had twenty years of satisfying lovemaking, voluptuous conquests and flamboyant mistresses! Now look what I've been reduced to. *Mamma, que tristeza*!' I grumbled.

'I've asked Cécile to come along too.'

'Who's she? I don't know her! Another one of those stuck-up students in glasses, with a crew cut and drooping tits . . .'

'Are we going to do this injection or not?'

'Oh, just leave me to die. Stick a needle in my heart, Doctor. Let's get it over with.'

Someone knocked at the door. Marie-Jeanne went to open it.

'Come in, Cécile, but I'm afraid you're wasting your time. Mr Champollon is in a bad mood.'

'Nonsense, Marie-Jeanne! Go ahead and inject me. If

scientific advances require guinea pigs, then I'm happy to come . . . er . . . forward.'

Which college was Cécile from? The carioca school in Copacabana? She had olive skin, almond eyes, strawberry-red lips, a slim lively body and shapely tanned legs, not to mention full breasts that strained the poppers of her white coat. Was she part of a programme for getting limp dicks going? Desmouches took her aside and explained the different protocols in the treatment of spinal injuries. She had arrived at just the right moment. My sexuality had to be rehabilitated too, and now that Cécile was standing a couple of feet away from my prick, I was ready for take-off. My nervous breakdown could wait.

Desmouches decided to start with an injection of ten milligrams. The needle was very fine and it had to be inserted into the upper part of the penis. The chemical, Cavergex, took effect in twenty minutes.

Desmouches explained the role of the vibrator. Its distinctive feature was an excrescence – a circular plate the size of a mini CD that vibrated as it turned. The rhythm, set by the electric motor, stimulated the penis until it ejaculated. The vibrator was more effective than a hand, mouth or vagina. It was simply placed at the base of the glans. You had to hold on tight – a difficult task for a tetra – because the strong centrifugal force made the device jump out of your hands. Marie-Jeanne helped me. Cécile didn't. The miniature Frisbee had to be moved up and down without reducing the pressure. My prick was growing under the effects of the drug. I hadn't ejaculated in ten months, having taken a vow of chastity just before being admitted to Intensive Care. My body was shaking as if I were having an epileptic fit, I was in agony. Through half-closed eyes I watched Cécile, who stood transfixed, staring strangely at my prick. She seemed fascinated by its increasing size and by the wild spectacle of my jerking limbs. I'd lost my taste for fellatio and masochism.

'Please, Marie-Jeanne, can we stop?'

I pulled myself together. Desmouches had disappeared. Cécile sat on the bed and took my blood pressure.

'Have you got a headache?'

'Yes, darling. Not tonight, I've got a migraine. I'm so sorry.'

She touched my burning forehead.

'That's normal. It often happens the first time.'

The first time? What was this silly little virgin on about? A year earlier I'd have screwed her without a second thought on the bonnet of her car! Instead, I was reduced to hiding my impotence by pulling the sheet across my naked body. Cécile looked at her watch. 'Oh, it's one o'clock. I've got to go to lunch.'

No question of this young lady skipping her meal, or jumping on top of me for that matter. I'd have to get on with it on my own. At least Marie-Jeanne was sympathetic. She was holding my hand. 'D'you want an aspirin?'

I nodded. She went out, leaving the door open. My penis still hadn't gone down. I stroked it. The sensation was vague, as if I were wearing a couple of condoms. But I had to follow its example and rise up – like a worthy standard, it was showing me the path to redemption. It was standing, straight as an arrow, while my body lay flaccid.

'I have to make love again. I've got to get the motor going, however many injections it takes,' I said to myself, slapping my penis against my belly. I liked the sound it made, like the brief dull thudding of a tom-tom. A sound of love. The symphony of bodies. How I missed it! The cries, moans, panting, pleading; brutal or controlled entry.

I'd have to invent a new score, write some new music.

My speaking voice sounded the same but what about my singing? As in love, everything came from the belly, but my abdominal muscles were out of action. I tried a few singing exercises but the notes petered out as soon as I tried to go up the scale.

I could no longer sing, no longer play the piano, no longer write music.

My soul emitted only darkness and silence. Could anyone hear it?

57

Yes-Yes

St Tetraplegic, pray for those of us who seek your help.

I cursed the accident and never tired of drawing up a checklist of my physical and psychological decline. My stay in hospital was dragging on with no end in sight. From a neurological point of view, there was no change, except I now got goosebumps at the slightest draught. It was lucky I slept alone, because I wet the bed. Daily catheterising caused urinary infections and therefore leakages. A nurse would stick a Penilex – a kind of adhesive sheath attached to a bag – on to my penis. And the nervous breakdown I'd been warned about . . . well, it still hadn't happened. Things were getting desperate.

My new room-mate, 'Yes-Yes', alias Slimane Abdellatif, munched crisps all night and nicked my saucisson as soon as my back was turned.

'Slim, you mustn't eat my sausage! It's pork, it's against your religion. I'm going to tell your sister!'

He'd just give me a big smile and point at the dry sausage hanging by my window. 'Yes, yes. Good . . . eat . . . me . . . lamb . . . very nice . . .'

'It's not lamb, Slim, it's PORK!'

'Yes . . . yes . . . lamb . . .'

Slimane had had a stroke at the age of twenty-six. It had happened in the middle of the street while he was broadcasting a TV news report. Now he couldn't remember which channel he worked for. When Dr Desmouches asked him about it, Slim became a talking TV remote. 'Yes, yes . . . TF1 . . . TF2 . . . TF3 . . . France 4 . . . Antenne 5 . . . Canal 6, M7, M8, M16 . . .'

'M16? Isn't that Israeli TV?'

He always answered, 'Yes, yes.' He got around in his wheelchair excruciatingly slowly. His twisted body leaning back, he moved at a snail's pace, his hands gripping the wheels: three little pushes forward, one push back. You could hear him coming, his wheels squeaking on the lino. Sometimes he'd stop for half an hour, or an hour, in front of an awkward obstacle or the lift. He went into a kind of trance, staring at the ceiling, while urine trickled down his leg and formed a foul-smelling puddle on the floor.

Once a cheeky kid in a wheelchair came up behind him. 'Slim, you pisser, move your arse!' As Slim didn't budge, the boy gave him a push, propelling both chairs into the goods lift.

His big dark eyes expressed constant surprise, but sometimes you could see a veil suddenly descend, reducing him to a blank. Of all the injuries, the most frightening are those affecting the brain. The patient loses all independence and, outside hospital, requires constant supervision.

Slimane had six sisters. All very demanding, all expecting BEI (Big Emotional Involvement). They kept a close eye on his food, his medication, his treatment, his clothes. They didn't trust the nurses. Latefa, the most attractive one, came to visit him the most often. She couldn't bear to see her young brother so physically diminished. At first, she gave me black looks, then suddenly she started asking me strange questions: 'Are you Jewish?' 'That nurse, did you hear her calling my brother a "dirty Arab"?' 'Does Slimane smoke? Do you?' 'Do you think he's well looked after? As well as the others are? As well as you are?'

I wondered what could have made her so paranoid, so suspicious of the medical staff. I imagined she must have been given the brush-off on numerous occasions by the various government departments where she'd taken her brother's medical file; had to spend hours waiting in corridors and offices; and heard unkind remarks and contradictory diagnoses that she didn't understand but didn't dare ask to have explained.

Latefa supported the whole family. During the week she worked as a correspondent for a Canadian newspaper and at weekends she was a waitress in a Chinese restaurant. Eventually, we started to have more pleasant conversations and we became friends. One evening, she arrived wearing jeans with her hair loose. I noticed her golden skin, her young girl's body, jet-black eyes, the fine straps on her top, her white teeth. She knew I was attracted to her.

'You're stunning, Latefa. Why don't we get married?'

'I'm engaged,' she said, crossing her arms.

'I'm not the jealous type!'

'But I am. You have too many women around you!'

'That's my Eastern side. You know the Arab proverb, "He who is not satisfied at his father's table will never be satisfied".'

'You're an unfaithful liar, like all men.'

'You know, that hurts, even if it's true.'

She'd put me in my place. Tears stung my eyes, ran down my cheeks. We were alone in the room. Latefa went to close the door. She came over to my bed and put her arms around me. I let her. She kissed my neck, then found my lips, my tongue. After a long kiss, her mouth lingered over my face, my forehead, my cheeks. She ran her tongue over my eyelids, tasted the salt of my grief, followed the damp trail left by the tears. She stroked my hair, my chest, my stomach. I knew not to try anything that might spoil this gift of tenderness. Her body was sacred, untouchable. Her long, soft black curls coiled around my inert hands, giving off a scent of vanilla and cinnamon. She lay her legs beside mine, pushed back the sheet and pressed herself against me. Her hand found my penis and, eyes closed, she leant towards it. But suddenly she sat up and I thought she was having second thoughts, feeling guilty or ashamed.

'If you want to please me, promise me you'll protect Slimane,' she whispered in my ear.

Then she took me in her mouth. I substituted mental excitement for the physical sensation. It was my mind to which Latefa was giving a blow job. My climax seemed to come from very far away, hers was gathering pace. I could see her pelvis shuddering, her leg wrapped around mine, in a simulation of the sexual act. As in my teenage days when girls kept their trousers on during such encounters in case their willpower failed, imagination intensified the physical sensations.

'I'd like to see you again, but outside hospital,' she said, tidying her hair.

At the door she winked, and mouthed her brother's name to remind me of my promise. I wondered if Latefa could predict the future.

The Scissor Gang was circling around Slim. They'd managed to get hold of spare keys for the swimming-pool area on the ground floor. They planned to take Slim on a little jaunt and throw him in the pool. Who would get him out? Not them, that was for sure.

I had a word with Yuka, a young Bosnian from

Sarajevo. Before joining the Scissor Gang, he'd been part, aged fourteen, of the first special forces unit defending the city from the Serbs, because small, fearless kids like him could get through enemy lines by crawling along sewers and hiding in underground pipes. They waited till nightfall, slipped on dark clothing, blackened their faces and disappeared into the bowels of the city, their backpacks crammed with explosives. They located the houses of Serb snipers and blew them up. Working in groups of four, they got back at dawn to report on their missions to their commanding officers. These children of war were taking huge risks, unaware that one of them, whose mother was Serb, had denounced them. They fell one after another in horrific ambushes, trapped in tunnels they knew by heart. The sewers of Sarajevo became their grave.

Yuka was the only survivor. He wanted to carry on, to avenge his comrades, but his commanding officer convinced him not to. Two days after he was forced to resign, as he walked to the old post office a rocket exploded behind him and peppered his back and legs with burning metal fragments. The war was over for him. He was crippled at sixteen. He was airlifted to France and had an operation in Lyon, before being transferred to Garches.

'Yuka, why have you got it in for poor Slim? He can't defend himself.'

'I've got nothing against him. But chucking him in the pool might liven him up a bit.'

'You really think so?'

'Yeah. Either that or he'll end up a vegetable.'

'Or drown?'

'No, I've never let a guy down.'

Survival. It was a major preoccupation, and took the form of hierarchies and tests. The strong made decisions for the weak. Without the protection of family, or the intervention of teachers, social workers or organisations fighting their corner, who would help these kids? Growing up was hard enough when you were standing on two legs, but at least you could run away if you got into trouble.

The day Mathurin went home, after nine months in hospital, he held a farewell party in his room. Tetraplegic as a result of a car accident, he could move only his head and had to be strapped into an electric wheelchair. Originally from Martinique, he got his mother and sisters to prepare some Creole sausages, a light punch and a fish dish called a Colombo. Dr Desmouches and all the nurses and auxiliaries dropped in for a drink, and all of Vidal Wing was invited.

In the corridor I saw Ben Koski, the leader of the Scissor Gang, plotting with his cronies.

'Aren't you coming for a drink, Ben?'

He shot me a black look and with a flick of the wrist spun round and shot off, taking all his mates on wheels with him. I stared after him, wondering why he was pissed off. By the nurses' desk, he turned abruptly and reared up on his back wheels, as if challenging me.

'Hey, Léo!' he yelled. 'When my grandfather left Buchenwald, he didn't throw a cocktail party!'

58

Psychosis

I'd always said no, but today I'd changed my mind. The in-house psychologist, Catherine Lacour, didn't hide her surprise. Employed part-time by the hospital she was kept busy, even though she didn't suit everybody – too posh for some, too bossy for the kids, too dim in the physios' opinion, too old and decrepit for the Scissor Gang, too hard on women, too sympathetic to men. I often saw her in the corridors looking for one of her depressed or suicidal patients.

'Mr Martinez, you wanted to see me?'

'Ah, yes, Mrs Lacour, I'm feeling really dreadful!'

'Come along, follow me!'

And she rubbed her hands ('A client at last!'). She always had a student trailing after her, a spotty guy with glasses doing work experience, or a plump hippie chick chewing her pen.

'How about three-thirty on Wednesday, Mr Champollon?'

'Er, could you make that a quarter to four? I'm going out for lunch.'

*

The session took place in my room. I would have preferred psychoanalysis, I mean, I was used to lying down. There were three of us: me, Catherine and Charlotte, her new student. It was because of Charlotte that I'd changed my mind. If I had to have tea, it might as well be with Nicole Kidman, even if she did have a chaperone. Blue eyes, a mad tumble of red curls that she tried hard to tame, and milky white skin as immaculate as spring snow. Lacour must have briefed her. 'Charlotte, you're not to intervene. You're here simply to observe!'

I recounted my most recent dream. 'I was driving fast along a B road. My passenger had pulled up her skirt, I was pretty turned on and my hand was wandering. I let go of the wheel and the car swerved off the road. Black hole. I was in Intensive Care, I couldn't move. A doctor with a rabbit's head and big ears came in and said, "My friend, it's open season!" Then he picked up a carrot and bit into it with a terrifying crunch. The carrot . . . was my big toe. But I hadn't felt a thing.'

Lacour nodded, waiting for me to go on. Charlotte sat beside her, staring at the photos on the wall behind me.

'That's all. Ah, no, I was forgetting – I always have trouble getting to sleep at night. I reproach myself for being too weak, too resigned. With all that's happened to me, if I was a normal bloke I'd have it in for the whole world. I'd want to throw myself out of a window or slit my wrists, but I don't have the courage to do it. I'm a coward. I've messed up everything in my life – my career, my relationships, even my accident. If I'd been any good at anything, I'd be dead, wouldn't I?'

The shrink stroked her chin, doubtfully. I thought of all the confidences she must have gathered, analysed, decoded and filed in her notes since she'd been working at Garches. Charlotte uncrossed her legs. I caught her eye.

'If you had the choice, which would you prefer? To spend the rest of your life in a wheelchair, go blind, spend five years in prison, be HIV positive, get a mental illness, or have acid thrown in your face?' I asked her.

'Mr Champollon, I don't understand your comparisons. Let's talk about you instead,' Madame Lacour cut in.

'I thought that was what I was doing.'

'In that case, explain what you mean.'

'Well, which would you rather lose? Your mobility, your sight, your freedom, your health, your mind or your looks?'

Catherine Lacour straightened and shifted on her stool.

'It's best to accept yourself as you are, despite the terrible thing that's happened to you. There's no going back. In your case, you're in a period of mourning. Mourning for your body. But you'll develop other senses, discover new skills . . .'

'Reformat the disk, is that it? I don't know much about computers, I'm more into electronics – the guitar, the piano. But without my hands, well, I'm stuffed.'

'I know, I've had lots of patients who were musicians, or performers. But your imagination has no limits. You can find other ways to express your creativity.'

She took out a notebook, a pen and a packet of mints. 'Would you like one?' she asked, turning her back to her student. 'They're peppermint.'

'Thank you. I'd forgotten, bad breath is a terrible affliction too, quite beyond the pale. Mind you, I haven't got anyone to kiss . . .'

Catherine opened her notebook and scribbled a date. 'Do you take any tranquillisers? Any sedatives?'

She wouldn't have asked if she'd read my medical file. On the other hand, perhaps she was discreetly introducing the subject of soft drugs; there was a memo going round the hospital about the trafficking of hash and grass. Perhaps she was leading the investigation. I was way ahead of her.

'I don't smoke joints. And I've given up cigarettes, cocaine, medicines. They stuff me with drugs for my muscle spasms and bladder and neurological problems as it is,' I said.

'Are you in a lot of pain?'

I was amused by the possible double meaning of the question. Stupid woman! I sneaked a look at her student.

She was there as a visitor, fully dressed, stylish, while I was naked. I answered: 'Physically, yes. My body's sending me messages all the time: what's going on? Why has the machine stopped? And what about pleasure? Why can't I feel anything any more? What's going to happen to me?'

I stared at Charlotte and repeated: 'What's going to happen to me, eh?'

She was beautiful, indifferent, bored. In the afternoon she'd go home and tell her boyfriend about her day. Her skin was white and smooth. I bet she went to the beauty salon once a month to have her pretty little triangle of pubic hair waxed. I was sure she was wearing a G-string. She twiddled with a rebellious red curl, pulling it straight, smoothing it between her lips before letting it ping back, then going on to another strand. I could imagine her doing the same with blokes, driving them crazy. She looked like a real little bitch. Maybe if I heard her voice I'd get a different impression. I imagined it as velvety, sensual, fragile, but she remained mute. I was starting to get silly.

Catherine tried another tack. 'Have you cried since you've been in hospital?'

'I think my situation is pathetic enough without me bursting into tears.'

'It would make you feel better to let things out . . .'

'But there's nothing to let out.'

'I'm sure there is.'

'Please, get out.'

I looked down. I had nothing more to say. Lacour didn't turn a hair. I sensed that she was looking for a counter-attack. Not to upset me, but to prove to herself that she could defuse the situation.

'So why did you want to see me?' she asked.

'It's not you I'm interested in, it's her! Your student, the deaf and dumb one . . .'

'But I'm not dumb!'

'She speaks, at last!'

'Charlotte is a student, she's not authorised to . . .'

'Next time, take her to the zoo. No need for qualifications, peanuts will do.'

'You're not thinking about what you're saying! You're speaking and . . .'

'I say whatever I like! Go on, *ciao*, bye bye, *arrivederci*.'

The two women got up. Lacour put her stool away under the table. She gestured to Charlotte to leave the room.

'Mr Champollon, I . . .'

'People call me Léo. It's been nice chatting to you. Now go away, I've got a headache.'

Catherine Lacour shut the door behind her extremely gently, as if it were the hatch of a time bomb. I listened to the sound of her footsteps as she walked away, heels clicking on the lino.

On the subject of zoos, I remembered a story I'd heard. A couple is standing in front of the gorilla's cage. The bloke tells his girlfriend to get her tits out and stroke them to get the ape excited. The girl takes off her bra and the animal starts to get worked up behind the bars. The girl moves closer and lifts up her skirt. The gorilla roars and pounds its chest. It wants the female. The bloke eggs on his girlfriend: 'Go on, take off your knickers, show him your bum, your pussy, have a wank!' The girl complies and throws her panties at King Kong, who rips them to shreds and sticks a big hairy arm through the bars, trying to grab her. She keeps her distance.

I forget how it ends.

I've got a headache.

59

Amputation

I mostly stayed in at weekends. Zaza gave me her room on the second floor. Mickey slept across the landing. In the evenings we had spaghetti parties in front of the fire. When it was bedtime, Mickey picked me up and carried me to bed. There was a constant stream of visitors, old faithfuls as well as new friends and even a few figures from the past, like François-Jean Bastier, an old classmate. How had he got my number?

'I bumped into your sister, Camille, at a petrol station. We often went to parties together when we were kids. I recognised her straight away!'

François-Jean insisted on coming to see me, but I wasn't too keen. I'd always tried to avoid him at school. We'd called him 'the big lump' and put sugar in the tank of his moped. He loved messing about with engines.

'I can take a moped apart with my eyes closed . . .'

While me and Mickey were chasing girls, he spent weekends in his garage tinkering with his two-seater moped. Seeing him again years later, I had misgivings. He seemed just the same, only now he had a car. 'I can take a 2CV engine apart with my eyes closed . . .'

But I soon changed my mind about him. He was sturdy and eager to help. I used to find his gauche amiability irritating, but now his patience with me made me realise that he was kind and well-meaning. He suggested we go for a drive in the Vallée de Chevreuse and stop at a restaurant for lunch. Mickey left us to it, after showing him how to fold the wheelchair and transfer me, and check that all my pills, orthopaedic cuffs and catheterising equipment were in the backpack, together with a thick woolly jumper and my credit card. 'Like kit inspection in the army,' he joked.

I liked car journeys. I felt a bit like a Labrador travelling with its master, sitting on the front seat and sticking its muzzle out of the window. The wind went up my nose, whipped my face, ruffled my hair. A ray of sun and I was happy. We were driving through the countryside at medium speed on a B road. I'd been through this before.

'This is a nice trip, isn't it?'

'It's funny, it feels like a dramatic reconstruction. Let's just try not to swerve off the road.'

'D'you still think about your accident?'

'I'll think about it for the rest of my life. There'll always be a narrow country road stretching ahead of me with the sun dipping behind the trees.'

'Does it upset you?'

'What difference does it make?'

'You know what Nietzsche said: "What doesn't kill you makes you strong".'

'I prefer what his nephew Maximus said: "What doesn't kill you makes you dead".'

'He said that?'

'Yeah. The same happened to him as to Primo Levi. He survived deportation and then, a few years later, he hanged himself.'

François-Jean bought me lunch. I looked on while he cut up my meat. He had a great *joie de vivre* that was contagious. To him everything was possible, fluid, solvable; I wasn't stuck in a wheelchair but on a constant upward path, and if my life had taken this turn, there had to be a good reason for it. I ended up believing him. My fate as a paralysed man need obsess me no more than my anxiety about the future had in the old days. The radical novelty of my situation put an end to any angst about my 'self'. Now, I lived in the present, existed in a state of psychological neutrality, flatness. No joy, no sadness, no desire, no suffering, no plans, no frustrations. Of course I was dying to get better, to regain the use of my body, but I tucked the thought away in a corner of my mind, like a man does of his teenage dreams of travelling the world.

During coffee, François-Jean asked me if I'd like to hear something funny. 'You know, last year when I lost my job and Christine broke off our engagement, I found out I had testicular cancer. They removed the testicle and replaced it with a plastic prosthesis.'

'A bit much all at once, wasn't it?'

'No, it woke me up. My life was crap.'

'Still, pretty heavy.'

'Well, I was pretty stupid! I had a shitty job, a boring girlfriend, useless family, and friends who came nowhere near me when I was in hospital. No, it was an incredible opportunity!'

He glanced up at the ceiling. 'It comes from up there . . .'

After his illness, François-Jean had shut himself up in his flat for a month. His only link with the outside world was the Internet. He wanted to share his experience with others. At first, he visited cancer, medical research and support-group websites.

'It was around that time that I heard about your accident. I'd just come out of hospital and had no wish to go back. I still didn't feel strong enough to visit you, but I thought about you all the time. One evening, I typed "spinal cord", "tetraplegia" and "paralysis" into a search engine. Most of the information was from the US. I found a site for people in wheelchairs, mainly amputees and I got in touch with a Californian girl called Priscilla. There was an immediate connection between us and we started emailing twice a day. One night, she asked me if I thought I could fall in love with a woman in a wheelchair. Frankly, I had no idea, but I assumed this was something that concerned her closely, so I said yes. She answered with another question: "What about a girl with both legs amputated?" That was a bit difficult to answer, so I turned the question round: "Are you asking me because you've had both legs amputated?" But I'd got it all wrong. She was normal, with two legs. Her life was like any girl's her age, except she didn't have a husband or boyfriend.'

'So she was looking for a bloke?'

'No, a surgeon.'

'To marry?'

'No. You'll never guess why.'

I listed all the plastic-surgery procedures Californian bimbos went for – facelifts, nose jobs, eyelid tucks, cheek remodelling, dimples, chin reshaping, lip jobs, boob jobs, liposuction, electrolysis, hair implants? François-Jean shook his head: no, no and no again. This was just the opposite. The dream she'd had since she was a child was to have both her legs cut off at mid-thigh! At weekends she rented a wheelchair to get in some practice.

'Have you heard of apotemnophilia?'

Apparently, there were people on this earth who were in perfect health but got themselves admitted to hospital to have their bodies changed. These were people who suffered because they weren't suffering.

Across the Atlantic, Priscilla – Silicon Valley single girl – sat at her computer sending out SOS's to all four corners of the world. Fate and the Internet had put her in touch with a Frenchman whose brush with death meant he could hear anything, understand anything. Even the unimaginable, even Priscilla's insane quest.

Other than the priests and numerous shrinks she'd been seeing since adolescence, she'd never told anyone of her feelings. How could she explain that her legs didn't feel like a part of her, but like a monstrous, cruel deformity that prevented her from being happy. In order to achieve her aim, she'd planned the amputation of her lower limbs down to the last detail. Ideally she wanted the operation done legally, but she was quite prepared to do it herself (by lying on tracks, shooting herself in the legs, etc.) or to resort to some shady butcher over the border in Mexico.

'Hers isn't an isolated case,' François-Jean told me. 'And she knows that some people who've had illegal operations have died under the anaesthetic or from gangrene.'

'Is that kind of operation legal in America?'

'In certain states it is. But it's not easy to get it done.'

First, she had to prove that she was of sound mind and get the written agreement of two reputable psychiatrists to present to a surgeon. A British doctor had agreed to perform the operation at a clinic in London, but an unfavourable report from one of the psychiatrists had brought everything to a halt. Perhaps he'd sensed that Priscilla had always been extremely lonely because nobody had ever taken any interest in her. Infirmity seemed like the only way to attract attention and find her Prince Charming. She was so obsessed by her dream of being disabled that she couldn't see the other side of the coin: that men would reject her even more violently. Sooner or later, Priscilla would regret what she'd done and have a nervous breakdown. Then would anyone be able to stop her taking her own life?

'But François-Jean, don't you think it's simply that she hates what she looks like and that if a man fell madly in love with her tomorrow everything would be all right?'

'No, I think she really believes that shc'll never meet anyone who'll love her as long as she has her legs.'

'Shit! By the way, have you got a photo of her?'

What surprised me weren't the extravagant obsessions and phobias of some Americans, but my friend's support of Priscilla's cause. I didn't think he'd been wrong to tell me, it was just that asking a tetraplegic what he thought of someone who, more than anything, wanted to have both legs amputated, summed up the folly of the world.

'Here you are,' said François-Jean, handing me a photo, 'meet Priscilla.'

He twisted his napkin while I stared at a full-length colour JPEG photo, signed priscillajohnston@basket-ball.com.

'She's got it all wrong, your Pamela Anderson. It's her head she should have cut off, not her legs.'

60

Operation Ejaculation

For his second intracavernous injection, Léo, who hated defeat, left nothing to chance. Calling on his professional experience of organising events, he planned this production down to the last detail – the time, the place, the duration, the means and the budget. He lined up his technical assistants, allocated key roles, and even allowed for unforeseen occurrences, to make sure that nothing derailed the project.

Soon Operation 'Ejaculation at Garches' was ready and, if all went well, by 3 p.m. on Wednesday 12 May, he'd have filled a plastic phial with millions of sperm, which FedEx would convey in all haste to the lab. He'd set Mickey two tasks: to find him a VCR and to borrow a few good porn films from Patrice S. On D-Day, Johnny, the auxiliary, would switch on the VCR and tape the remote to the bedpost in case Léo wanted to fast forward, and Marie-Jeanne would give him the injection, set the video and switch on the vibrator before decamping. She was to come back as soon as Léo rang for her, to collect the precious package.

He'd be alone in his room. The injection took twenty

minutes to take effect. The film lasted an hour. The vibrator could run for thirty minutes before it needed recharging, so he had a limited time to climb the coconut tree, taking the build-up into account: waiting for the Cavergex to kick in and revving up his engine as he watched Pussy Love and her friend Tamilla Climax hitch-hiking around Beverly Hills and being ravished by the young Duke of Finger-My-Fanny in the back of his limousine. By the time the trio got to the car-wash to be greeted by Samantha Sweetlips, the pump attendant and the mechanic, Tracy Missdeepfuck, Léo would have to get a move on and discharge his seminal fluid.

Mickey had turned up at around 9 p.m. the night before, smiling conspiratorially. From a plastic bag he produced two old copies of *Penthouse*, which he'd bought in a junk shop in Versailles. Annoyed, Léo explained that he couldn't turn the pages and handle the vibrator at the same time; he needed both hands, a VCR and some good videos. Mickey apologised – he hadn't given the matter enough thought. He was working the following day, so he'd have to sort things out that evening. Mickey's mother lived only two hundred metres from the hospital, so Léo suggested he go and borrow her video recorder and rent some films from the local video shop.

Mrs Saferis, Mickey's mother, always went to bed at 8 p.m. after double-locking every door and window in the house. Mickey slipped into the garden and let himself into the house through the garage, to which he had a key. Inside, he was attacked by Nounouta, the fox terrier, who hadn't recognised him. The dog tore his trousers and woke his mother. Mickey kicked the mutt and rushed into the sitting room, calling out, 'Only me, Mum!' and unplugging the VCR. But it was too late. She was furious: it was a disgrace, a son burgling his own mother in the middle of the night and torturing a poor animal that was only doing its duty.

Later, at the videoclub, Mickey called Léo several times on his mobile because he couldn't decide between *Big Girls' Dorm* or *Barbecue at Hilary and Monica's*. Luckily, the manager knew his catalogue by heart; he explained the plot and casting of *Suspenders at Matignon* to Mickey, who relayed it to Léo over the phone. By midnight, everything was sorted out. Léo could sleep soundly.

At 2 p.m. the following day, after a light lunch, Léo had a needle stuck in his prick. Just as the opening shots of *Hot Love in the Kremlin* appeared on screen, the vibrator jumped out of his hands and fell under the bed. He rang for Marie-Jeanne. There was a knock at the door and he said, 'Come in', only to find himself face to face with a Chanel suit and Hermès scarf: Louise Capucine Jouvelin was paying him a surprise visit!

She threw her arms around Léo's neck and, twisting her scarf around her wrists, she proceeded to berate herself for several minutes. She beat her chest and said how guilty she felt for not coming sooner; she hadn't felt brave enough – she was terrified of hospitals and her new job kept her very busy. But mainly she hadn't visited because she'd had to take her 306 Baccarat back to the garage three times (the mechanic was a crook!).

Louise Capucine was hugging Léo tightly when she felt something vibrating against her shoe. She bent down and picked up the vibrator. Léo managed to get a good look at her arse and thighs. Had they fucked in the past? Definitely flirted, but anything more? He pulled up the sheet because the drug was starting to make his prick itch. He wondered how he could stop the video. Louise Capucine, now sitting on the remote, didn't know what to do with the buzzing turquoise appliance that she was holding against her stomach. She asked Léo what it was for. He explained that it was both to stimulate and relax his muscles. She said she could do with one too, because when she went jogging with Jean Villeneuve ('You know, my best friend, he was at INSEAD?') she felt stiff all over the next day. Léo told her how to turn it off. The humming stopped, only to be replaced by loud sucking noises as the Russian lady spy gave her oral report to Boris, thc KGB boss, and his henchmen who were penetrating her.

Louise Capucine stared open-mouthed at the screen for several minutes, until Léo asked her to turn off the TV because he had something important to tell her. She was docile and compliant. Removing her brightly-coloured jacket ('It's always so hot in hospitals, isn't it?'), she assured him again that she felt really guilty for having neglected him and that, from now on, he could count on her 100 per cent, especially as she'd realised, since Daddy's death last year, how important it was to tell one's nearest and dearest how much one loved them while they were still alive.

Léo made her move right up close and recounted in detail the tragedy that had befallen him – the painful journey of a young man who was mourning the loss of his body and resisting the daily urge to swallow pills, stick his fingers down his throat or chuck himself out of a ground-floor window.

Louise Capucine discreetly wiped away a tear and again threw herself into Léo's arms. He took the opportunity to massage her hair, back, waist and legs, while explaining that medical science was making huge advances and that she'd arrived at just the right time because they were, at that very moment, testing out a treatment on him that would drastically improve his quality of life, in particular his sex life.

Louise Capucine said this was really good news. As she was offering her help and boundless affection ('I've got so much love to give, you know'), Léo told her of his wish to become a father and watch a little one grow up and bring joy into his sad life. He explained to the young woman snuggling up to him, as he guided her hand under the sheet, that a painful injection had caused his *corpus cavernosum* to swell and that they ALL (Dr Desmouches, the consultant, the junior doctors and the nurses, as well as his family and friends) hoped that it would lead to ejaculation.

Louise Capucine jumped when she realised that her fingers had been placed round Léo's prick. He set the rhythm for her, as he continued to recount his tale of woe. She pretended nothing was happening (luckily, everything was hidden under the sheet) but, as she held forth on the advantages of her new job ('Only five stops on the Metro') and her engagement ('Amaury de Senlis, a brilliant and considerate man'), she realised that she was half-lying on the bed, her skirt was riding up, her knickers were showing, her blouse was unbuttoned, a tongue was exploring her breasts, and a hand was sliding inside her tights. She protested but Léo, whose penis was still growing, begged her not to let him down, to take him in her mouth and finish him off.

Louise Capucine refused ('Why . . . Why me?') but jerked him off all the more energetically so that he'd forgive her. Léo, whose body was jumping about, threw off the sheet and, gripping her breasts, forced her to maintain a more even rhythm and asked her to please shut up (she was telling him about her new flat in Levallois with a garage and maid's room) so that he could concentrate. She complied and, as she could no longer talk, the frenzy of the embrace aroused her and she ended up spreading her legs ('Please don't ladder my tights, they're new!').

His last image before he ejaculated was of her beautiful face, messy hair (her ponytail had come undone), flushed cheeks and neck, and her beautiful eyes staring astounded at his tumescent member, her crimson lips forming a fellatory O. The eruption was violent and convulsive.

Ever the good sport, Louise Capucine didn't let go immediately, although she gave him a little miffed pout when she discovered that her sleeve and Rolex watch had been coated with sticky, odorous gametes. She got up off the bed and sighed when she saw the full extent of the damage: Léo *had* laddered her tights, crumpled her skirt, snapped one of her bra straps and left big lovebites all over her neck. ('But I'm meant to be meeting Granny at Angelina's.')

Before she left, she asked Léo where she should send the wedding invitation – to the hospital or to his parents' house? Just a small cocktail party, followed by a dinner for their nearest and dearest. Two hundred guests, at the Villa Beauséjour, the house of her great-aunt, Marthe Volvic (whose grandfather had discovered the spring). There'd be dancing afterwards . . .

'I'll be there,' said Léo. 'And, Louise Capucine, how about a fuck afterwards?'

61

Insurance

Darius arranged for Dr Klinkert, the doctor appointed by the insurer, to come to the hospital to assess my level of disability. He entered the room armed with his little hammer.

'What about your hands – anything? Your legs – anything? And your . . .?'

'My prick? Zilch. Nothing's moving, doctor.'

He wrote: 'Condition stationary eleven months from accident. Another examination to be carried out before the end of the year.'

Darius had got me my Severely Disabled Person's orange card, for people 'unable or virtually unable to walk' (how true!). Darius told me that I was already being paid 1230 francs a month in disability allowance. Once I left hospital, I'd get another 4000 francs, the personal care allowance, but I still had no idea how I was going to pay for a full-time carer. There was also the unfortunate proviso that 'all sums received in personal care allowance are to be repaid in full upon the death of the recipient from his personal account or estate.

If I lived another twenty years, that was 20 years × 12

months × 4000 francs. I'd have to pay out a sum of 960,000 francs upon my demise. The loss of my hands and legs was going to prove very expensive. Not to mention if I wanted to make love. If, during the course of those twenty years, I wanted to have intercourse once a week, that was 4 intracavernous injections a month at 140 francs = 560 francs, multiplied by 12 months × 20 years. I'd have to cough up 134,400 francs for my sex life.

Until the dawn of my last breath, the total sum spent would be in the region of a million francs. 1,840,800 francs to be precise. Over twenty years, that was equivalent to 5000 francs a month, in other words the amount of the two allowances the state had paid me since my accident. So it would recoup its expenses.

At this rate, I was going to have to take drastic measures: I'd have to get back on my feet right away, or marry a rich heiress, or refuse the poisoned chalice and head down to the ANPE to apply for a job. But as what? A guinea pig for a pharmaceutical company; driving a taxi with voice controls; a limbless TV newsreader; a human heating pad; a food chewer. A flower pot?

At Garches, there was a volunteer legal adviser who helped you with claims for compensation and looked through your insurance policy, recommending a lawyer if he thought you needed one. In the case of an accident at work, the victim received a substantial payment which kept him safe financially for the rest of his days. But there were fewer options for those who smashed themselves up all on their own, who were found to be responsible and didn't have comprehensive insurance.

As they would do if they were in prison, the inmates at Garches exchanged good tips, including the numbers of the best lawyers. During the course of my inquiries one name seemed to crop up all the time: Marsilla & Co.

Marsilla's answer was prompt: he wasn't interested. He recommended a colleague, who also turned me down when he found out that Marsilla had rejected my case. My situation was all too banal: third-party insurance, no mutual insurance, 100 per cent client responsibility. Lucky I hadn't maimed or decapitated Gwendoline. What would I have done then, and what would I have said to her parents? That I'd lost my head that day and they'd lost their daughter? What value do you set on a life?

During a physio session, I was sympathising with Jerome, a lawyer who'd had Guillain Barré's syndrome, a virus that strikes at random, affecting the nerve centres. It can develop into total paralysis, so that the patient has to be admitted immediately to Intensive Care and put on a respirator. Luckily, the disease is curable. Within a few months, most patients recover their movement and suffer no after-effects.

Jerome had been in hospital five months and could now, at last, walk without the help of a wheelchair or a physio. But, mysteriously, his neurological recovery was, so far, incomplete: he still couldn't move his arms. They swung uselessly at his sides, he couldn't dress or feed himself, or go to the toilet on his own.

It was driving him out of his mind. He couldn't stand being an angry, embittered, misanthropic cripple. He refused to go home at weekends, even though his wife was very caring and they employed a nurse. His pride condemned him to be isolated and reclusive. The doctors challenged him on this, but they couldn't make him change his mind. Only his business partner, Philippe, managed to shake him out of his torpor. I saw them sitting on the terrace outside the cafeteria together and witnessed the transformation. With files spread out in front of him and his colleague firing questions at him, Jerome once more became killer lawyer at the Paris bar, cold steel glinting in his blue eyes. His brain was sparking, finding solutions. Forced into making an effort, he became a man again.

When I mentioned Marsilla, he laughed. 'Everybody knows him. His office handles about a hundred disability cases a year and, as he's always dealing with the same insurance companies, he's become their best rep, the king of the all-inclusive deal. He turns up and suggests an overall sum for his ten clients: "So, if we give three million for him, two million for him and five for him, spread over three years . . ." and so on. Same story everywhere: "Ah, Mr Marsilla, nice to see you. And what have you got for us today?" He makes such big savings for those bastards, I bet he gets commission!'

He paused. Philippe lit him a cigarette. He offered me one, but I refused. I'd kicked the habit since the accident. Booze, dope, coke – all that was 'before'. I wasn't healthy enough for it now.

'So how's your insurance claim going?' Jerome asked.

'Fine! I just have to find a dog . . .'

If I followed Albert Zimmer's advice, I'd get a fortune. 'You just need a dog,' he assured me. And he'd already found the dog's owner. Florence, thirty-ish, sexy and sporty, she looked like a woman of the world with a subtle hint of venal provocation, and she knew exactly the effect she had on men.

'Your mate told me you like beautiful women,' Albert had said over the phone. 'You won't be disappointed.'

I arranged to meet Florence and Albert at the restaurant in the Parc de Saint-Cloud. Amaury Blanchard, a musician friend, had recommended Albert. With a useless right arm as a result of a braquial plexus lesion, Albert was a medical adviser in court cases, an alcoholic and occasional heroin user.

'But I only snort it, I can't stand injections, or junkies for that matter! They're too sad. And you can't make a toast over a syringe, can you?'

We had lunch on the terrace. I'd ordered the terrine of wild boar and Florence was cutting it up for me. She was having avocado with prawns while Albert was on his second whisky and Coke, washed down with Saint Emilion. In his pinstripe double-breasted suit, he looked like Joe Pesci in *Goodfellas*.

'This is how your accident happened,' he said. 'You were driving happily through the countryside. Florence was walking her dog. The stupid animal ran out into the road just as you came by. You swerved to avoid it and bam! You ended up in a ditch, paralysed, and the rest of it. With a high degree of impairment, you can count on around twelve million, with fifteen per cent for me. We just have to get our story straight, make sure we're singing from the same hymn sheet, OK?'

'What about Gwendoline?'

'Who the hell is Gwendoline?'

'She was with me in the car.'

'She saw the dog too, didn't she?'

'She's in New York.'

'How much does she want?'

'I have no idea.'

'Slip her a hundred grand and that should do it. She'll keep her mouth shut.'

Albert ordered a bottle of Château Pétrus and we drank a toast. 'To the twelve million!'

'To fortune, love . . .'

I looked Florence in the eyes. She held my gaze as she drained her glass. She'd taken off her hound's-tooth check jacket to reveal a see-through silk blouse. I stared at her chest. I was truly obsessed with breasts. Air-bag syndrome perhaps? I could have really done with some the day of the accident.

Albert got up to go to the toilet. He staggered and bumped into a waiter.

'Have you known him long?' I asked Florence.

'Forever. I married his brother.'

'Lucky him. You're a very beautiful woman.'

'You're sweet.'

'Tell me, do you always dress like that or is it part of the plan?'

'What plan?'

'The story with the dog . . .'

'Oh no. We went to a wedding this morning. Albert likes it when I look nice.'

'So do I.'

'Yes, I'd noticed, you don't keep your eyes in your pocket.'

'No, I've been keeping them on your breasts, and your mouth too. It's a good sign. Means I'm getting better. Having said that . . .'

'Yes?'

'If you could just undo one more button, you'd make me really happy.'

'This one?'

And Florence slipped her hand inside her blouse.

Albert came back to the table. 'Hello lovebirds, how's the flirting going? Watch out, young man, my brother's the jealous type. Just kidding! Florence can do what she likes.'

They drove me back to Garches. Albert was nodding off at the wheel. In the main drive leading to the hospital entrance, he only just missed crashing into a guy in a wheelchair. 'Where does that idiot think he is?' he yelled.

'At Garches,' said Florence.

She slipped her mobile number in my pocket. Before they left, Albert said: 'Call me next week and have an envelope ready with 5000 francs. For the dog.'

'You're going to pay a dog?'

'No, cretin, I'm going to buy one! Have you seen my sister-in-law? We can't give her a mangy mongrel.'

'What about a Labrador?'

'Yes, something friendly and obedient.'

Florence kissed me goodbye on the side of my mouth.

I'd had a good day: a Mafioso had bought me lunch at a restaurant, I'd met a sex bomb who'd showed me her tits, and I'd won twelve million francs and a Labrador.

Think I'll just keep the girl.

62

Clinical director

That evening, it was party time at Sylvia's in the Rue de l'Université – a Chinese takeaway for the stomach, Massive Attack for the ears, and three pin-ups for the eyes. The flat was bathed in candlelight. As well as Sylvia herself, there was her sixteen-year-old cousin, Garance, and Vanille, one of my exes. While one set out the food, the other two danced on my bed, rubbing against my legs. The doorbell rang. Garance jumped into my wheelchair and headed for the door. You didn't often see paraplegics in such short skirts.

'Yes, he's here, come in. Léo, someone for you!' yelled Lolita, coming back into the sitting room.

It was François-Jean. The man really loved me! How had he found out where I was?

'I was at a petrol station . . .'

'When you bumped into my sister?'

'Did she tell you?'

Camille was indefatigable. She, Ambroisine, Darius and Henri had mobilised all my friends and set up a fund that would help me when I got out of hospital. It was over a year since the accident and I had to give some thought to my new life. The prospect terrified me.

Darius and I had had a meeting with Véronique, the clinical director. I'd always hoped that on leaving Garches, I'd leave the tetraplegia behind too. At first, we considered a specially equipped flat in a building in the XXe arrondissement, funded by the Order of Malta. Newly built, it consisted of thirty units for seriously ill or disabled people. There was twenty-four hour medical care, and a head doctor and physios were available during the day. I went to see the place and met the psychologist there, a young tetraplegic woman who was completely independent. She drove a car, travelled by plane, did her own shopping, cooking and washing up, and washed and dressed herself! How did she manage without her hands?

I passed the new residents of the home in the corridors, most of them in electric wheelchairs. By the time I left, I knew one thing for certain: I never wanted to set foot in a wheelchair city ever again. But I had to find a place to live. Camille put the word round: 'Léo is looking for a smart little ground-floor flat with room for a live-in carer, a cook, a butler, a Brazilian nurse, a chauffeur, a personal secretary, two mistresses and a dog.'

Véronique, the clinical director, sat on my bed. She and Darius set an approximate leaving date. I wasn't being thrown out exactly but, in the twelve months that I'd been loafing about in hospital, another 987 people (80 per cent of them under 30) had smashed themselves up on the roads. Sometimes at night, I could hear their wheelchairs squeaking in the corridors. They hung about outside my door, chanting, 'The room, give us the room!'

My clinical director had a very nice face, with great skin and a lovely smile, all of which must come in handy when you spend your time breaking bad news. It was a striking contrast, unless you've seen a lot of Martin Scorcese films. The more vicious the killer, the more politely he talks to his victim: 'Rizzotto, I'm going to tear out your eyes and balls and stick them up your ass, but you won't feel a thing because before I'll cut off your tongue and stick your little dick down your throat! And your hands, let me think . . . How 'bout we dip them in acid?'

Véronique never raised her voice. Even when she was giving bad news, nothing in her demeanour changed. Only her hands betrayed her. She started gesticulating, her long, slender fingers tracing invisible arabesques. As she waved her arms, she stirred the air in front of me like a fan. Except that you can switch off a fan. Véronique only switched off when she fell asleep. During the day, she saw patients, diagnosed, prescribed, reassured, sent them packing.

And she sent me packing in my brother's presence. We would soon have to go our separate ways and before we parted, certain things had to be said. I knew I was paralysed, but nobody ever actually spoke about it. I knew my future was uncertain, but not to what extent. It wasn't my illness itself they treated, only the consequences.

'You get cold because you've got poor circulation. Your circulation is poor because your heart isn't pumping as hard. You can't exert yourself physically because you can't move your body much. You can't move much so you've got low blood pressure. This means you take a long time to get warm, so lie down and take an aspirin.'

As I was being treated, I thought I was being cured. And if I was cured, that meant I could leave.

Like the matador swinging his cape in the final stages of a bullfight, my lady-doctor performed her *veronica* and prepared to plant the sword. I lowered my head. Darius listened. She addressed him, looking him straight in the eye so as to avoid looking at me.

'It's important that Léopold prepares to accept living with his handicap even if, at the moment, he's not aware of all the difficulties that lie ahead. His injury was very serious and he will probably never regain the use of his legs and hands. He's going to have to come to terms with the fact that he'll always be in a wheelchair and dependent on others.'

Darius nodded. He had faith in me, in my friends, in our family. Even though I was there with my brother, at that moment I didn't feel like anybody's brother. I was the idiot who'd completely fucked up his own life and who I hated more than anyone else in the world. The lovely Véronique gave me her loveliest smile.

'When you first leave hospital, you may get depressed. But don't worry, it's normal, you'll need time to adjust. Then you'll start to enjoy your new life and when you come back for your check-ups . . .'

'Check-ups?' asked Darius.

'Yes, urological tests, skin checks, and various other things. They'll only require short spells in hospital, but they're vital. Prevention is better than cure!'

I was certainly prevented. But cured? Definitely not.

In a month's time I'd be escaping Garches. The last time I'd left hospital was thirty-seven years earlier, a week after my birth. At the time, I was already lying down and couldn't move much. I was already a tetra!

63

Sheep

'You sure it's a good idea?'

'She's OK with it. She's expecting me.'

François-Jean was going to California to meet Priscilla and try to make her change her mind.

'If I don't do it, I'll never forgive myself. D'you know the parable of the shepherd?'

'Can't say I do.'

'A shepherd is herding his sheep one evening when he notices that a ewe is missing. He leaves the rest of the flock and sets off into the mountains to find the ewe before it's too late. He searches all night and finds it at dawn. It's weak and injured, so he carries it back to his hut to take care of it . . .'

'And?'

'The end.'

Sylvia, Garance and Vanille listened in silence, eating their Chinese food. We were all on the bed, except for François-Jean, who was sitting cross-legged on the floor.

'That was nice of the shepherd,' I said, to keep my friend happy.

'No, it was stupid.'

'Why?' asked Garance. 'He's doing his job, he cares about his animals.'

'Have you ever talked to a shepherd?' enquired our philosopher.

'I've slept with one,' joked Sylvia. 'A Greek shepherd boy.'

'A shepherd would never leave his whole flock to go and rescue a single ewe. It would be stupid. There are wolves around at night. Better to wait till morning, or forget about it. Better to look after the ninety-nine other sheep and sacrifice the one that got lost.'

'And yet, the idiot still goes looking for it.'

'Yeah, and he finds it and, as it's knackered, he carries it back. D'you know how much a ewe weighs? They're really heavy.'

'I bet he ends up roasting it on a spit . . .'

Amused, I glanced at the girls, their faces bathed in candlelight. Vanille had snuggled up to me and was stroking my hand. We were going to sleep together that night.

'It doesn't make sense,' François-Jean went on, 'except, it's a parable. So what's it really about?'

Garance was frowning. 'Come on, tell us!'

François-Jean got up, strode across the room and tapped the table superstitiously, before coming back to stand by the bed.

'Am I prepared to sacrifice everything to go and save another person? My time, my money, my health, my flock? What am I willing to do to save a lost sheep? How much of her despair can I take in order to comfort her? If a beggar holds out his hand in the street I slip him a coin, but what about someone whose life is in danger? There's no greater proof of love than total self-sacrifice. Otherwise, you may as well settle for any old emotional or social compromise.'

He was thinking of Priscilla. I was thinking of my idol, the famous singer. We'd known each other for fifteen years and had worked together. He sang at benefit concerts for the homeless, for Ethiopia, for Armenia, for children with AIDS, for illegal immigrant workers, for the Téléthon. The stricken called to him and off he went in his glittery costume. I saw him in the papers, in videos, on TV. The only time I saw him in my hospital room *was* on TV; he was looking good. Darius phoned him several times and Camille wrote to him, but he never answered. He must have preferred me making him laugh, introducing girls to him, us going to apocalyptic parties together. The famous singer was used to looking me in the eye, not to looking down and seeing me on the ground, sick and defeated.

Meanwhile, I had three women around me. That afternoon, we went for a walk down the Boulevard Saint-Germain. We passed the Flore, where I'd met Gwendoline. A couple was sitting kissing at 'our' table. I saw familiar faces. Some didn't recognise me or pretended not to. Their gazes slid over me. It was painful. 'No, it can't be him, he wouldn't go out in public in that state.'

Sylvia reminded me about a walk we had taken in the Jardins du Luxembourg a few weeks before my accident. By the big pond, we'd seen a mother pushing her son in a wheelchair. The young man looked cadaverous and was staring vacantly into space. His lifeless body shook as he was wheeled over the gravel, his head lolled. I'd squeezed Sylvia's hand. 'If that ever happened to me, I'd shoot myself, without hesitation.'

'Did I say that?'

Sylvia leaned towards me. 'Yes, my darling. So what shall we do today, chuck you in the Seine?'

'Yeah, but let's have dinner first!'

We'd planned it all – the Chinese food, the music, the candles – but not François-Jean and his tales of sheep.

'You need to re-read the gospels, Léo!'

'Just in time – I've cancelled all my magazine subscriptions.'

François-Jean came and sat on the bed. In the candlelit sitting room the girls were dancing to a compilation from Les Bains Club. I watched them moving their hips. They brushed against one another, held hands, put their arms around one another's waist.

'They're lovely,' my friend whispered in my ear. 'Which one is your girlfriend?'

'I don't know. I'm waiting. Like in your parable. I've got lost and I'm waiting for someone to rescue me. But hey, we've got all night!'

'Léo, I wanted to talk to you about something else. You're a musician. I'd like you to do me a favour. It's about my niece.' François-Jean explained that his older sister had recently come back from Brazil, where she'd been living for the past fifteen years with her husband and three children. They'd only just moved to Paris and they were finding it hard, especially the kids, who were used to the sun, sea and laid-back atmosphere of Rio.

'So where are they living?' I asked my good Samaritan.

'In the XIIIth arrondissement, by the Porte d'Italie.'

'Right, they've gone from Copacabana to Hong Kong on the Seine.'

'The move's been particularly difficult for Manon.'

His sister's eldest daughter was bunking off school. She'd moved to a new school in the middle of term. When she wasn't skipping classes she locked herself in her room and listened to Vinicius de Moraes.

'You see,' said François-Jean, 'over there, as well as her schoolwork, Manon was taking samba, steel drum and bossa nova lessons. Not to mention the beach and all her childhood friends she's had to leave behind. My sister's worried she's going to do something stupid.'

'How old is this kid?'

'Seventeen. She's in her final year at school, but she's almost certainly going to fail her baccalaureate.'

Life was hard for exiled beach girls.

'I'd like you to meet her,' he added, 'to talk to her. You could make music together, couldn't you?'

Dubious, I said nothing. I could certainly talk to her, but make music? Whenever I saw a pianist or guitarist on TV, my sense of failure was unbearable. I could still write music using a computer, but I'd left computer music and electronic machines behind long ago. They were just props. Music came from my head, my heart, my vocal cords and my hands. It was pure feeling. Acoustic to the tips of my fingers. I'd been 'unplugged' too soon.

Couldn't François-Jean see how helpless I was? What kind of music did he think I could make for his niece, with my hoarse voice, my frozen hands, my creativity reduced to ashes?

'OK, no problem,' I lied. 'Tell your Manon to ring me. I'll give her one of my guitars. I don't need them any more.'

I was on the scrap heap. A professional 'ex'. Alizée's ex, ex-walker, ex-musician, ex-fornicator . . .

64

Gadgets

The hospital offered Léo some leaving presents. A device for his willy, another for his bladder, and an operation to his forearms and hands. Fitting the gadgets also involved major operations, requiring weeks in hospital and lots of tests and check-ups. He'd have two remote controls: one for the willy device, and the other for a little receptacle in his tummy, the 'Lioresal pump'. In the first operation, to make up for the lack of movement in his hands, the surgeon could restore some grip between thumb and index finger by taking a tendon from his triceps and inserting it in his hand, grafting it on to the wrist tendon.

'Does it hurt?' Léo asked the doctor.

'A bit. You'd have to take things slowly at first, but it would make you more independent. It's like the string of a bow. The tendon will stretch but, if it's not properly exercised, it can snap!'

'Then what?'

'We re-open the forearm and stick the tendons back together!'

'Sounds gruesome. Anything else on offer?'

With the willy device, you got automatically controlled

hard-ons and peeing. All the nerves to the bladder were severed and replaced with miniature circuitry. You pressed the ON button and the little guy stood up or let out a stream of piss; you pressed OFF and he went back in his cage. You had to make sure you didn't lose the remote control and the batteries had to be changed every two months. The operation couldn't be reversed.

'Does it hurt?' asked Léo anxiously.

'A bit, and post-op recovery takes time: three months. With a foreign object under your skin, you have to take it slowly!'

'Yeah, the guy who thinks he can screw around as much as he likes had better not overheat the remote. Bad news if it short-circuits!'

Lioresal relaxed muscular contractions or 'spasms', which could be as violent as an epileptic fit. It's a mistake to think that the paralysed limbs of a tetraplegic are always limp or flaccid. Your legs can shoot out suddenly and unexpectedly, with the force of a footballer striking the ball, and if a man has the misfortune to be standing in front of you, he can get a nasty kick in the balls. People with the most spasms take Lioresal in pill form. Up to twelve a day. Léo was against using drugs to mask symptoms. The body became accustomed to medication and the dose always had to be increased. The spasms caused him discomfort, but at least his muscles were moving, dancing the twist: they were having fun.

The doctor wasn't trying to sway Léo, he was simply offering him something that might improve his physical condition. 'The Lioresal pump is connected to the spinal canal. The receptacle is refilled every three months via a subcutaneous injection. The pump then injects into the cord the precise dose required to keep the muscles relaxed.'

'Like an epidural?'

'That's right. It reduces nerve pain too.'

Léo consulted his friend Pierre Lambaye, a psychiatrist and psychoanalyst who was writing a paper on the tortures of the modern world and the different forms of incarceration and alienation inflicted on the body in car, train or plane accidents.

'Man always wants to go faster, further, higher. He takes more and more risks, smashes himself up, ends up in a terrible state but survives thanks to modern medicine. Roads have replaced the battlefields, duels and tournaments of the Middle Ages.'

Gladiator of the B roads, Léo was in a lot of pain, but Pierre had a solution: 'Smoke dope and go swimming!'

Léo was OK with the swimming but he was scared that smoking dope would bring all his unhappiness to the surface, instead of relaxing him. Escape through opiates wasn't the answer. After the high, he'd find himself still stuck in a wheelchair, with a big black cloud over his head. It wouldn't even have to start raining to make him cry.

Léo never wanted to set foot in hospital again. Fourteen months was more than enough. These gadgets seemed risky and unnecessary. Léo's only advantage was that he was the tetra, the medical researcher wasn't. He himself knew best what he needed. He couldn't bear the thought of being opened up and having devices put inside him. He already had some plastic holding his cervical vertebrae together.

The die was cast. Unless there was a miracle or spectacular advance in medical science, Léo was preparing himself for a long, stationary cavalcade. He was sure his cells were rewriting his programming, reorganising themselves according to the physiological and molecular changes in his body. Léo now listened to what his body was telling him, and it was telling him it wanted to be left alone. It had had enough.

He didn't sleep much during his last night in hospital. The clock said 3 a.m. He rang the bell and asked Victoire, the nurse on night duty, for a glass of water.

'So you're leaving us tomorrow? Have you got all your things ready?'

'Yeah. How about a kiss goodbye?'

'Night night, Léo. Good luck!'

His friends had found him a large ground-floor flat near the Porte de Saint-Cloud. There was a big Quiksilver sports bag beside his wheelchair. Stupid bag. Brand new and stuffed to bursting point, it sat there impatiently as though it was heading off on a long holiday in the sun with stopovers in the cities of light: New York, 'Frisco, Rio, Havana, Cairo . . .

'Idiot,' Léo yelled at the bag, 'haven't you read the itinerary?'

Garches, Saint-Cloud, Suresnes, Bois de Boulogne, Porte d'Auteuil, Boulevard Murat . . . What a crappy journey.

65

Moving in

Léo left Garches as discreetly as he had arrived, hidden in an ambulance. Hélène, his physio, came to kiss him goodbye. He held her hand while the nurse put his bag in the ambulance. Hélène's hand was warm, soft. Léo was going to miss her. He held her hand against his cheek as best he could and covered it in kisses. A big kiss on the lips would have been more appropriate: he'd asked her to marry him and she'd said yes.

'As soon as I can walk again, I'll come back for you.'

'If you walk again, I'll leave you,' she answered.

The ambulance door closed on that promise. Léo switched on his Walkman. His friend, Nilda Fernandez, wished him good luck: '*Où que l'on aille . . . nos fiançailles? Fuerte, fuerte y con la muerte voy a hacerte una canción . . .*'

He stared at the bright blue June sky through the windscreen. At traffic lights at the Porte d'Auteuil, he saw students revising for exams on café terraces. Skirts were getting shorter, bodies were getting ready for summer. There was a scent of sex and *la dolce vita* in the air. Couples showed off, pelvis to pelvis on their mopeds.

Léo was exploring his new apartment. He'd been given a special electrically-operated double bed – the back could be lifted and the mattress raised to over one metre fifty from the floor, a magic carpet on which to get laid. Darius and Louis put up shelves while Camille and Sylvia unpacked boxes, and Ambroisine and Garance hung up clothes.

Léo was stunned, his brain was overloading. Seeing all his things, his photos, clothes, pictures spewing from their packing cases, was like having a bad trip. Too much of his past, too many memories.

'Hey, Darius, what's this?' There were some lizardskin cowboy boots, a pair of shredded jeans and a bloody combat jacket in one of the boxes. The jacket had been cut with scissors. In between the Special Forces badge and the Vietnam insignia sewn on the shoulder, there was a name tag: Sgt Elliot J. Kacere. Léo had bought the jacket in a New York army surplus store. He'd been wearing it the day of the accident.

'It's stuff the police gave me in a plastic bag. I thought I'd thrown it out,' said Darius.

There were big brown stains on the camouflage fabric. Léo didn't realise he'd lost so much blood. He thought of the soldier, the young sergeant wandering in the Vietnamese jungle. Had he died there? Léo believed that the souls of the dead, both good and bad, floated among the living. Some of them haunted houses, places, so why not a uniform? He was quite prepared to believe that the jacket might have brought him bad luck. It had seen blood, death, mud, horror.

'Chuck that crap in the bin,' pleaded Léo.

Darius took the box out into the courtyard. 'I'm sorry, I should have thought of it earlier,' he apologised.

'It's me who should have thought of it earlier,' said his brother. 'You should never wear dead men's clothes.'

He went on exploring his new territory, with neither joy nor curiosity. This wasn't a reunion, it was torture. The most humiliating finds were his flight cases with his synths and guitars, waiting to set off on tour. The show must go on . . . the damned show. He circled them, feeling like being sick, or setting fire to them. There was the extra-flat red leather case for his favourite guitar, the one he'd bought himself for his sixteenth birthday, a 1957 Fender Stratocaster. She had a sound that rooted you to the spot. A powerful riff à la Dick Dale, hero of surf music. When Léo used to run his plectrum along the six strings, playing with his right palm on the vibrato bar, it was a pure rock 'n' roll moment. Wrapped in red velvet, she was waiting for someone to wake her. But it wouldn't be him.

Léo thought of old family pianos, forgotten in a corner, disguised as furniture. One day, the tuner would arrive with his tool kit and tuning fork, replacing worn-out strings, chipped dampers, adjusting the pedal mechanism and, finally, striking a chord on the ebony and ivory keys. The piano would come back to life after its long sleep. Léo remembered how a woman had once cried in his arms after they made love. She'd been without a man for two years. Bereavement had dulled her body, extinguished her desire.

Women, music, instruments – ties with the past. He just wanted to be free of them all; they were as cumbersome as the boxes, packing cases and suitcases now being opened, explored, unpacked, put away. If Léo had known how painful this was going to be, he'd have told Darius to leave everything in storage. He'd have moved in with only new stuff, and made do with the bare minimum – a bed, table, chairs.

In the room next door, they had no idea what was going on. To them it was simply moving day, not a funeral. The telephone started ringing. It was hidden under piles of boxes in the hall so nobody could find it. But the person at the other end of the line was persistent.

'OK, OK, we're coming!'

Camille picked up the phone. 'Hello? Yes, hang on, I'll pass him over.'

Léo was surprised: so people already knew he'd moved?

'Could I speak to Mr Champollon?' asked an anxious voice.

'Champollon senior or junior?'

He found it annoying to have a woman call him 'Mr Champollon'. It was bad enough being an invalid, if he was old now too . . . There was a silence at the other end of the line which he made no effort to fill.

'My uncle, François-Jean, said I should phone. I hope I'm not disturbing you.'

Manon, the Brazilian girl. Léo wanted to cut the conversation short, but he caught sight of his guitars lined up against the wall and he remembered his promise.

'Ah, yes, you're into music? Actually, I've just moved into my new place. Everything's still packed up. Would you mind ringing back in a few days? I'll have more time.'

She apologised effusively and was about to hang up but Léo sensed she was sad, despondent, as if she'd been disappointed so often. She probably wouldn't ring back. He said quickly, 'How d'you get around? By metro?' Léo used the informal 'tu' instead of 'vous'.

'I've got rollerblades, otherwise I borrow my brother's scooter. What about you?'

'Oh, I wheel about, otherwise I take a taxi.'

'You can't drive?'

She must have thought he meant a skateboard. Léo realised she didn't know anything about him – the hospital, the wheelchair. François-Jean must simply have given her his phone number. ('He's a musician friend. You should meet him, he's a nice guy.')

When she talked about music and the guitar and asked Léo to give her lessons, he didn't react. The whole thing was ludicrous. His hands were useless – was a beginner going to be the one to get his neglected guitars out of their cases? From his first lessons in classical guitar in Pau, to the Parisian rock scene – had he come all this way just to end up here?

'You know, I love singing, but I'm pretty useless at playing!' admitted Manon. 'I can do the samba and I'm not bad on the congas, but don't expect me to play you any Antonio Carlos Jobim.'

'Do you sing in Brazilian?'

'I do lots of things in Brazilian,' she said, with a burst of laughter that took him by surprise. 'I dream in it, I speak it, I dance in it. I even kiss in Brazilian! You know, when I lived over there all I ever wore were micro-shorts and a bikini top. It was cool! If I wasn't in the water, I was on the beach, and if the weather was bad, I was at my dance class! You get the idea. Daddy called me his *pichadenuda*.'

'*Pichadenuda*?'

'Yes, it means "open air creature", well, "naked"! Needless to say, I've had a lot of trouble getting used to proper clothes since we've been back in Paris! Lucky it's summer now! Right, when shall we meet up?'

Léo found her amusing. He'd been expecting a dopey self-conscious teenager, but she sounded lively, curious, enthusiastic. They arranged to meet the following Saturday.

He'd only just hung up when the doorbell rang. Reinforcements were arriving: Mickey, Henri, Ludovic, Patrice and Richard.

'Is this the office of tetra assistance?'

'This is cool. Now, thanks to you, I've got the perfect excuse for getting away from my wife and kids!'

'Yeah, at last we've got a place to party!'

Léo had now become the ideal alibi for his married friends who were looking for a bit of freedom: 'Yes, darling, Léo is really down in the dumps! I've got to go and cheer him up, or I'm scared he'll do something stupid! Don't wait up . . .'

The girls were giggling in his room. They'd found a bunch of polaroids. 'Wow, take a look at those knickers!'

'Hey, I know her! Léo, come and look!'

They were sitting in a circle, passing round the photos. 'You're a filthy pig,' remarked Garance. 'Who's this Playmate?'

'Wait, you haven't seen the video . . .'

She waved a picture of a platinum blonde caressing herself in the bath at him. Garance couldn't understand why the girl had kept on her high heels, stockings and see-through top.

'The idiot's ruining her clothes . . .'

'It's meant to be erotic, sweetie. And anyway it just turned out like that.'

'That's quite enough. You shouldn't be looking at this kind of thing,' Sylvia said to Garance. Garance pretended to head for the bathroom. 'If I find the bath, I'm happy for someone to take a picture of me!' She licked her lips and wiggled her bottom.

'Come on, girls, there's work to do!' yelled Darius, emerging from the wardrobe, hammer in hand. The girls scattered.

'Where are the others?'

The boys were sitting in the kitchen, reading comics: *Corto Maltese*, *Torpedo*, *Rank Xerox*.

'Hey, guys, grow up!' A big row ensued. The girls complained that, as usual, it was them doing all the work. The boys moaned that they were starving, it was late and Sylvia had forgotten to fill up the fridge. Camille leapt to her defence: 'OK, so Sylvia forgot the food, but shouldn't someone have remembered the fridge?'

Shit, there was a cooker, a microwave, a table, plates . . . But no fridge.

Léo moved about in the midst of all the noise, looking for somewhere to have a little rest. At least in hospital he got some peace and quiet. People were calm, spoke quietly, and you always got dinner on time. Here, it was chaos, Little Italy, a campsite, a kids' playground.

66

Dancing queen

The clock radio pulls me from sleep: 8.30 a.m., the news on Europe 1. I fling off the duvet which lands at the end of the bed. I sit up and count to ten. My circulation re-adapts to a vertical position.

I feel the parquet beneath my feet; I love wood. My soles sink into the floor like the roots of an oak. One day, I'll become dust again, I'll lie under a bed of dead leaves. Or maybe I'll be buried at sea off the Basque coast. I think of water, waves . . . Quick, into the shower! I stop as I pass the bathroom mirror. Apart from my spiky hair and the dark rings under my eyes, I look just as I did at twenty. I'm now twenty years older. My shoulders are broader, and the triangle formed by my biceps, triceps and pecs is sharply defined. My stomach is flat; I've got the waist, the posture of a toreador and an arse like a black man, of which I'm very proud.

Every morning, I thank my parents and their forebears: warriors, émigrés, Basques, natives of the Bearn, sailors, victims of the guillotine, Prussians, Silesians, diplomats, generals under Napoleon, rebels, lost officers, aristocrats, legionnaires, intellectual women, mothers of large families, widows, music critics, journalists, painters and musicians. I've got all that on my hard disk. And often, by chance, these mysterious particles of my genealogy are awakened in my blood.

Why am I so at ease in the depths of a forest, or lost in scrubland, or tossed by huge waves? Why do I love deserts, prayer, silence, music, ambushes, danger, brotherhood, sacrifice, children and all the women of the world? Why do I love luxury hotels, seedy bars, igloos, teepees, the Apache, the Masai and Scandinavian air hostesses? Why do I die a little every time I like a girl or a baby gurgles in my arms? Why do I cry? Why am I always asking 'why'?

Water jets from the shower over my body. I turn the control to blue – a stream of cold, and I'm under a waterfall in the jungle in Borneo. I shiver. Red, and I'm in a jacuzzi with Virginie Ledoyen. A towel round my waist, a quick comb of the hair, and I head for the sitting room. It's music time. I dawdle, choosing the ideal track. I open the window. The sun is shining, fresh air fills my lungs. I hover in front of my sound system. Sun + cold + good mood = winter sports = energy = Sweden = ABBA = 'Dancing Queen'!

A cup of coffee later and I go to brush my teeth (I've never understood why people clean their teeth *before* breakfast). In front of the wardrobe, I can't decide whether to go for comfort – jeans, sweater, trainers – or a classic look – black suit and polo shirt, black suede shoes. What day is it? Thursday? What's on the agenda? Drop in at Staccato Studios and listen to my band's latest mixes, at 6 p.m. meet Gabrielle Mankoven at the Hemingway Bar in the Ritz and take her swimming (it's my third date with this green-eyed brunette and the prospect of seeing her in a bikini is driving me crazy), drive her back to her place around 8, stop off at home to get changed, and grab my keyboard and guitar for our gig this evening at the Café de la Danse. Sound checks at 9 p.m., dinner at the venue, the gig at 10.30. Gabrielle will be there, in the front row. Will she come home with me afterwards? If she does, I know exactly what I will and won't be doing to her; we've already discussed it.

She'll lie down on the sofa, on her tummy. I'll light candles and incense, and put on a CD called *Ocean Surf Relaxing*, New Age music combining sounds of running water with marimbas, *bamboo tren* and celestial choirs. I'll remove her bra and glance at my watch: forty minutes for a massage and, just before, a joint. I open a bottle of Balinese essential oil, brush the hair from her nape and kneel over her, straddling her thighs. She keeps her tights on. She isn't wearing knickers. Her white buttocks look very beautiful through the shiny lycra. They remind me of the rounded plastic behind of a giant doll with the pussy hidden or not drawn in, like the schoolgirls in Japanese Manga comics. The elastic waistband marks the boundary between territory offered and territory yet to be conquered. Eroticism is that which is forbidden.

My fingers slide over her silky skin. Relaxed, she shuts her eyes and puts her thumb in her mouth. She's a child again. Slow caresses, gentle at first, then harder, as her flesh stretches and burns under the pressure of my hands. Her breasts quiver; she becomes a woman once more. Her skin shines in the tropical light. I pause. She waits. I pour a few drops of the Eastern oil into my palm, and spread it over her skin. She smiles, then frowns when I grab her tightly by the waist.

I move up her sides, to the edge of her breasts. She buries her face in her arms and sighs. She's hot, me too. I take off my shirt. I come back to her waist and she turns on to her side, compliant, offering me her stomach and the curve of her right breast, which I cup in my hand. She changes position and offers up the other breast, the left. It's a tacit, almost motionless sequence; a complicity between her skin and my fingers, a sensual, erogenous journey, in steps and stages. I get off her legs. When am I going to remove her tights? She must be getting impatient. I've been on top of her for forty minutes now. We haven't kissed and she hasn't touched my body. She keeps her eyes shut, she acquiesces.

Suddenly, she gets up and heads towards the bedroom. I assume she is slipping under the duvet. I follow her in the dark, removing my jeans and underpants, and slipping on the tights she's dropped on the floor. I put out my hands, I can't see a thing. I bump my knees against the bed.

'Let's take a walk in the woods while the wolf isn't around . . .'

Gabrielle is there, lying on her stomach. I stroke her lower back, buttocks, thighs, calves, feet. My hand slides back up between her legs. She parts them, letting me in. This is the moment I've been waiting for since we met. I don't yet know the taste of her mouth, her tongue, and even less the warmth of her sex. It's there, a couple of inches from my face. My hair is long and lashes her like a bunch of wild herbs.

The clock radio alarm comes on: 8.30 a.m., the news on Europe 1. My legs hurt, my pelvis is heavy, I reach for the monkey pole and hoist myself up. On the other side of the shutters, it's a morning like any other. In the street, a car drives off, a mobile phone rings, children shout. Heels click on the pavement, a couple of women walk along quickly, chatting. Their steps recede.

So does Gabrielle.

Dancing queen.

67

The lovers of the périphérique

Léo was spending a fortune on taxis. He had a hard time getting the drivers to obey the law. No, the wheelchair wasn't luggage or a pushchair! He'd got the same driver, Césaire, a West Indian, three times in a month. On top of deafening him with the music of Compagnie Créole he charged ten francs extra for the wheelchair. One day, at a taxi rank, Léo spotted an old driver snoozing in his cab. He woke him up and made him act as referee. Césaire lost his case.

'It's in the regulations,' the old guy said. 'A wheelchair is inseparable from its owner; it's a personal item. Hey, Césaire, d'you charge your passengers for transporting their underpants? Well, it's the same for the gentleman's wheelchair. It's free.'

Césaire let him off the fare this time ('No problem!')

Léo was at home a lot. The nurse came in the morning while Camille was preparing breakfast. Darius had divided Léo's time into four parts: morning, afternoon, evening, weekend. He'd also assigned daily tasks: meals, shopping, cleaning, washing and dressing, physiotherapy, swimming and outings. He'd allocated a sum for travel expenses and placed ads for two live-in carers. He was offering accommodation, meals and laundry to a student, in return for them being there overnight.

Léo's girls came round every day to tidy up and prepare meals. The national employment agency, ANPE, sent Papou, a young guy originally from the Comoros Islands, to help Léo during the day. Within a month, everything was running smoothly, the kitchen was fully equipped, the pictures hung on the walls and the hi-fi set up. Léo felt at home at last.

In the bedroom above the desk, Darius pinned a notice board with the schedule for the week, from Monday to Friday. In the box marked 'Weekend' he'd written and underlined 'My goals': computer and Internet training, checking out welfare benefits, alternative therapies (acupuncture, nutrition, hydrotherapy, osteopathy, massage, transcendental meditation, hypnotherapy, yoga), holiday plans, driving lessons in specially adapted car.

Léo stared at the schedule covered in names, acronyms, addresses and telephone numbers: no time to get bored!

'By the way, you've forgotten something. When do I get to screw?'

Sylvia, who was tidying the video shelves, seized the opportunity to tell Léo, 'You'll get to screw when you're ready to make love. You'll make love when you decide to have a baby. You'll have a baby when you find the love of your life. You'll find the love of your life when you decide, at last, to get married. And you'll get married the day you've had enough of screwing around. It's time you grew up, don't you think?'

Léo agreed, but the sexual training techniques taught at Garches meant that his love life had to be tackled in two stages. First, he had to get his genital equipment going as often as possible. But who with? Secondly, it would be great if he fell in love. But he felt he was on the scrap heap. Alizée appeared every night in his dreams. He couldn't get rid of her. He'd found his photos of her, her letters and some ties she'd given him. His friend Frédéric had bumped into her at a party in Beaubourg. So she was back from the islands. Now that Léo was getting around town again, he looked out for her on every street corner.

Césaire, the West Indian taxi driver, dropped him and Papou in the Rue Vieille-du-Temple. There was a Mexican restaurant, El Taco, in the courtyard of the old Café de la Gare; the rest of the building was occupied by the Studio du Marais, a multi-ethnic dance school where Manon took salsa classes. She finished at nine so Léo suggested they meet for dinner at the Mexican place afterwards.

He chose a table in the window so he could watch the moving forms at the open windows. On both floors, he could see students repeating dance steps over and over, copying their teachers. The fashion for Latin dance was at its peak: samba, salsa, tango, flamenco. 'And one, two, three . . . one, two, three . . .' The dancing master clapped his hands in time to a piano, guitar or bandoneon. The Studio du Marais offered the first lesson free, so if you wanted to be clever, you could try out dance from the East, India, Spain, Brazil, Cuba; tap, or even acrobatic rock 'n' roll, without spending a centime.

Léo was green with envy as he admired the slender sweating dancers, full of energy and concentration. What wouldn't he give to be facing that Andalusian beauty striking the final pose of a *Sevillana*? Her proud, pained face looked up to heaven and her hands, in net gloves, were two black butterflies frozen in mid air.

A class had ended – a door on to the courtyard opened and a noisy group of young women spilled out, kissing one another goodbye before scattering. Léo knew which was Manon by her smile. He was seeing her for the first time, but they'd spoken on the phone so often that he'd have wagered 'his legs' it was her, the Brazilian girl. Her long ash-blonde hair was tied in a plait that swung down her back. Her olive skin was deeply tanned from her childhood in the sun, and she had the easy upright posture of someone who's lived by the sea and swum every day. She was just as Léo had imagined her: exotic, vivacious, with a hint of nonchalance.

She waved to a friend, then rushed over to the restaurant. Léo didn't take his eyes off her. By the bar a big smile lit up her face as she recognised him. She made her way through the tables like a cat slinking between puddles, deft, supple, agile. She seemed always to be in motion, impatient and captivating.

'I'm starving,' she said, kissing him on both cheeks. 'You know, this place is fantastic. My teacher's Peruvian. He can't speak a word of French, he just yells: *un, dos, tres*. It's brilliant, I love it.'

'Fantastic' and 'It's brilliant, I love it' were her favourite expressions. They attacked chips with guacamole. He ordered beer, chicken tacos and chilli con carne. Manon devoured her food. The appetite of a growing girl, thought Léo. But no. She talked quite openly about puberty, saying that by the age of twelve she was fully formed, had had her period, and had reached her present height of five foot nine. Nothing had grown since, apart from her mane of hair which she had trimmed every two months.

'For years, I was a beanpole, the tallest girl in the class!'

'I was always the shortest. I didn't stop growing until I was twenty-six and didn't really start shaving until I was twenty-eight . . . last year,' joked Léo.

Manon didn't react to this last bit. She admitted that

when her uncle François-Jean suggested she meet his friend she refused.

'I pictured some old muso with a beard, who looked like a teacher or something, you know, kind of an old hippie.'

'So what made you change your mind?'

'Your voice on the phone. And the things you said! You were nice and funny. That evening I mentioned it to Mum. She told me about your accident and that you'd only just got out of hospital. I couldn't believe it. We'd talked for over an hour and you hadn't said anything. I just went on about myself.'

'You were unhappy . . . far from the country of your birth, under a black cloud.'

'I feel better now. How about you?'

'You want to know if I'm under a black cloud too? Probably.'

'In that case, let's drink to the light. And if there's healing to be done, well, we can heal together!' She clinked her glass against his.

'Innkeeper!' yelled Léo holding up the empty bottle. 'Another one of these. We're thirsty!'

Papou arrived as they were finishing dessert. Manon didn't feel like going home. Léo suggested a game. Out in the street they hailed a taxi. 'I'm writing a song at the moment, but I've only got the first few lines. You can help me finish it.' He told the taxi driver to go to the Porte Maillot.

'What's the song called?' asked Manon.

'"The Lovers of the Périphérique". It's about a girl who meets a guy on the périphérique. She tells him her story.'

'Go on, sing it.'

Léo hummed: '*She met Eric on the périphérique / a golden boy, at the Porte Doré / who flirted with the chicks, at the Porte de la Muette / he said, "Where are you going?" At the Porte des Lilas / "Home to my parents, at the Porte d'Orleans" / Off with him she went, to the Porte de Bagnolet / He drove straight on, to the Porte de Vanves . . .'*

'Woww!' yelled Manon. 'Go on!'

'*He told her she was sexy, at the Porte de Bercy / then said, "What's your name?" at the Porte de la Chapelle / She answered, "Delphine" at the Porte Dauphine.* Your turn now!'

'Give me two seconds!' She got out her map of Paris. Léo went on, 'He found her a bit fussy, at the Porte de . . . Well?'

'Hang on, I'm looking. *Porte de Passy!*'

'Being a bit slow there. Come on, get with it! OK, let's carry on: *He got some action, at the Porte de Brancion* . . . And?'

'Excuse me,' said the taxi driver. 'We've reached the Porte Maillot. What do I do now?'

'Get on to the périphérique, and drive round.'

'Drive round?'

'Yes, drive round and don't stop until we finish the song! We can go past all the *portes*.'

'I've got one,' said Manon. 'Listen: *She sold maillots, at the Porte de Maillot!*'

'Didn't exactly strain yourself over that one, did you? Remember the guy got some action at the Porte de Brancion! So what does he do to poor little Delphine? Find something funny.'

'*He kisses her really well at the Porte de la Chapelle*?' suggested the driver.

'Hey, you keep out of it! You're not playing!' objected Manon.

'Yeah. Anyway, we've already used Porte de la Chapelle.'

'*He paid court* . . . No. *He declared his amour, at the Porte de Clignancourt.*' Manon was very pleased with this.

'You're going too fast! He has to kiss her first. *He kisses her on the lips, at the Porte de Sèvres?*'

'Not great. We need something a bit raunchier, like: *He tried to slide it in, at the Porte de Pantin!*'

'Well done, Manoushka! And how about: *He turned her on, at the Porte de Châtillon?*'

'*No, I don't know how you dare, even at the Porte d'Asnières!*'

'*Hey, don't try to be chichi, at the Porte de Clichy, or I'll be obscene at the Porte de Vincennes.*'

The taxi drove on into the night.

Manon and Léo were *as happy as you can get, at the Porte de la Villette / a veritable battle cry, at the Porte de Versailles / pure fantasy, at the Porte de Choisy / and rhyming hard, at the Porte Balard.*

They were happy, at the traffic lights . . . On the urban highway . . . And despite the traffic . . . Until daybreak . . . They were the only ones there . . .

The lovers of the périphérique.

68

Revelation

Evidence of the 'divine' caught Léo by surprise outside a porno-pharmacy, on the pavement at the Carrefour Réaumur-Sébastopol. Later, he remembered the story of Paul, struck down on the road to Damascus. Paul had fallen off his horse; Léo fell out of his wheelchair. The zealous Jew had his legs, so he could jump back on his steed; Léo remained on the pavement, long enough to realise that no one was paying him any attention. He had become invisible. He lay on his side, hoping to see Papou who was in the porno-pharmacy getting antibiotics.

Arses as round as apples, nice firm buttocks, shapely legs, full breasts, blonde hair gleaming in the sun and backs shiny with suntan lotion rising from gold G-strings – the full anatomical range of the beach babe was displayed in the pharmacy window. There was even a mirror in which Léo could see his reflection.

He was an advert for superfluous survival. His hair was dull, he had dark rings under his eyes, he was unshaven, his muscles were flaccid. He was lying in dog piss and looked like a tramp. In an office three floors up from the pharmacy, he'd just signed his first contract with the boss of Yes No FM, a rock station that was looking for journalists, in particular an expert on surf music, for the summer season. He'd signed up for fifteen sixty-minute programmes. Léo would be involved in music again. He couldn't play it, but he could talk about it – the Beach Boys, Jan & Dean, Dick Dale, a musical phenomenon that only lasted four years; the Beatles exploding on to the American scene in 1964, ending the fashion for beach boys, sending them back to their balsawood boards, flowery bermuda shorts, Thunderbird convertibles, choruses of *wap doo wap* and Fender Jaguars.

Léo was a huge fan of this happy tanned tribe. In the morning, they left a girl's body and flung themselves into the waves on a surfboard.

They worked in a surfboard shop in the afternoons, and at closing time rushed back into the Pacific rollers. Afterwards, they stopped off at home to pick up their guitar and then headed over to the club where they got up on stage and made the girls scream as they played 'Baja', 'Listen to the King of the Surf Guitar', 'Misirlou', 'K39' or 'Pipeline'.

This was the life Léo dreamt of. Not one of lying in shit, gaping at the behind of an Italian supermodel photographed in Miami. His wheelchair had rolled away and was stuck between two cars. It wasn't surprising that no one was coming to his aid – his collapsed form clashed with the summer atmosphere. Shop doors were open while tribes on wheels sped past: bicycles, rollerblades, scooters, skateboards – thousands of legs skating, pedalling, sliding along the asphalt. There was love everywhere: couples snogging, fondling, cuddling, all along the animated streets of the city. The June heat had uncovered shoulders, opened shirts, shortened skirts, shrunk t-shirts. The young looked carefree, radiant. As

Léo fell to the ground, a CD slid from his bag, a sixties compilation called *Summer of Love*.

He glanced again at his reflection in the mirror. Was that really him? That poor toppled thing? Hurry up, Papou! The coup de grâce came when he heard someone burst out laughing: he fell into a void, he became nothing, a mass of gaping wounds which would never heal. The guy was teasing the girl, his arm round her waist. They were walking fast, kissing, tongues entwined. She was stunning. She held her man by the bottom and nibbled at his neck. As they passed, Léo inhaled the vanilla scent of the long-haired Amazon. Her hair tumbled in thick black curls down to her waist, swinging like the mane of a wild pony. She radiated desire, the pleasure of the senses, the burning conquest of her orifices. Her man slipped his tongue into her ear, promising her a good time. The girl's clear, crystalline laughter shattered Léo's heart in successive waves. The couple ran across the road. A taxi hooted. His heavy head fell back and hit the tarmac.

He looked at the sky above the roofs. Pigeons fluttered outside the windows on the upper floors and squabbled on the sun-warmed gutters. An ambulance, siren blaring, went through the lights. Léo was shrinking inside. He was becoming dust. How long had he been lying there? Had he ever stood up? What he was going through was inhuman, unreal; he felt he was no longer alive, no longer among the living. He had nothing in common with his fellow man. It was as if he'd jumped off a train by mistake and left the walking world.

He felt blackness fill his heart and poison spread through his veins. The sticky tide rose to his throat, forcing him to close his eyes. The sky seemed to fragment. A dark stain in the shape of a cross danced before his eyes, then came to a standstill. He thought of Christ, of someone crucified. He felt his pain, the nails through his flesh. He saw his mother weeping at his feet, begging the executioners to spare her son. But he was smiling from the depths of his soul and had already forgiven: 'I will continue to the end, it is thus . . . It is written.' Léo caught his eye and tried to speak to him. A prayer he'd never learnt came to his lips, words that didn't belong to him – a plea, a cry for help: 'My God, this is too hard for me to bear. I've got no strength left, I've got nothing left. Tell me what to do, I'm listening, I've got no one but you. They tell me you're the Saviour, so save me.'

Léo was lifted off the ground. His body rose towards the light. Warmth spread through him, driving out the negative waves that had engulfed him. His heart started thumping again in his chest, as he felt himself enveloped, protected, comforted, lovingly carried. His grief receded. He was back in his wheelchair. Four people were standing around him: Papou, the girl from the pharmacy and the young couple from earlier on.

'You really gave us a fright there! Here, drink this.' The pharmacist gave him a glass of cold water.

'Are you alright? Me and my girlfriend saw you on the ground and we rushed over. Didn't we, Tatiana?' The girl was holding Léo's hand.

'You need a taxi. We'll come with you.'

Léo asked Papou how long he was in the chemist. 'Two minutes. I turned round and you'd disappeared. Did you hurt yourself?' He felt Léo's head, checking for bumps.

'The taxi rank's just here,' said Tatiana. 'Jerome, grab his bag.' They walked along the boulevard to the junction with Bonne-Nouvelle. Tatiana pushed the wheelchair, her man walked ahead. Léo felt lighter than a feather, as if he were flying along. At the corner, Tatiana skilfully tilted back the wheelchair to get it down off the pavement, holding it in that position until the lights turned red. Léo's head nestled against her breasts.

'You've handled a wheelchair before,' said Léo, making the most of the young woman's natural padding.

'My father had an accident when I was eight, so I'm used to it. What happened to you?'

'I was in a car crash, last year.'

'That's terrible. But don't worry, you'll get better – *inshallah*!'

A tourist with a big suitcase had got to the taxi rank just before them. He signalled to the driver of the G7 who was reading a paper.

'You should go first,' said Tatiana, speeding up.

'It doesn't matter, it's a lovely day, I'll take the next one.'

The tourist turned round and, seeing the little convoy, he put his suitcase down, indicating that he was letting them take the taxi. Césaire, the West Indian, got out of his cab. 'Ah, it's my mate on wheels. This way, I'll get you home. No problem!'

Jerome opened the back door and wheeled Léo into the taxi. 'Good luck, man! Take care!'

As she passed him his backpack, Tatiana perched for a moment on the back seat. She stroked his cheek, black eyes staring into his. The scent of patchouli filled the taxi. She kissed him on the corner of the mouth, long enough for him to run his fingers through one of her curls, then she hugged him. Léo felt the warmth of her skin under her t-shirt and the supple mass of her breasts. Like Alizée's breasts, in the old days.

'I know you've come back from very far away,' she whispered in his ear.

'If it was to find an angel like you, it was worth the journey.'

She closed the door. Her spicy scent lingered in the taxi for the whole journey, as if she were still thinking of him and he of her. Léo leant his head out of the open window. Today he had good reason to pray: 'Lord, send me an angel.'

He was no longer scared. He was no longer alone. When God saves someone, he always keeps his promises.

69

Teatime

It's teatime at Sylvia's and I'm expecting Manon. She's bought herself a bicycle. We talk on the phone every day. She makes me laugh. For her English oral exam, she lined up two outfits: jeans, which she wore, and a flimsy skirt, which she kept in her bag – just in case.

'If the examiner's a bloke, I'll run to the toilets and get changed!'

She only got a five. Perhaps he was gay? She was so furious that outside, as she passed a bus stop, she lifted up her skirt. An old woman called her a little tart.

'It did me good. I hate injustice! That teacher was an idiot!'

'Go on, Manon, speek me Ingleesh!' I didn't understand a word she said.

'OK,' I said, 'put your jeans back on.'

I explained that showing your arse might work at the lycée in Rio but not at the François-Villon.

'I don't understand how your country works at all,' Manon muttered, before hanging up. She was ringing from a call box at the Closerie des Lilas. She'd be here in half an hour.

Sylvia's sitting room opened on to a little garden,

surrounded by ivy-covered walls. Beyond it was the Russian ambassador's residence, where the shutters were always closed. Sylvia installed me under a sunshade with my legs propped up. From my chair I counted the floors of the building. It was July and all the windows were open. On the third floor a baby was crying (too hot, too heavy, too alone). A droplet of rain fell on the ground. The sky was turning black. A second droplet, then the whole family. In the distance, beyond Suresnes, a storm was rumbling.

'Sylvia? Sweetheart, it's raining, come and get me!' Where was she? In the kitchen, in her bedroom? I was an invalid, convalescing, pampered and cosseted, but they forgot me sometimes. I couldn't move, my wheels got stuck on the gravel.

I heard the front door slam. 'Darling, are you still alive? Quick!'

She'd just got back with pastries from the boulangerie. 'When is Manon arriving?'

'Soon . . . With the tide. Have you seen the rain?'

Sylvia burst out laughing when she saw me under the deluge. She placed my feet back on the footplates, then pushed me inside imitating an ambulance siren.

The storm was moving over Paris. There was a shout from the garden: it was my cousin, Gilles Brochard, delivering the tea. He'd been trying for years to convert me to the leaves of wisdom, to the evaporation of the spirit thanks to the miracle of boiling water. In his green mac, dripping from head to foot, he looked a bit like a decomposing plant, a living infusion. He'd brought his clay teapot from Yixing, and a box of oolong tea. 'Semi-fermented blue-green tea,' he specified, taking over the kitchen. He added, quoting Oscar Wilde: 'I have the simplest of tastes, I am always satisfied with the best!'

I liked the smell of rain, of wet earth, and the clouds coursing across the sky and this unexpected darkness that had surprised us in the middle of the afternoon, cutting us off from the rest of the world: a romantic curfew, devoid of danger – except, possibly, for Manon; I hoped she didn't get struck by lightning on her bike! I pictured her pedalling, blinded by the downpour, surrounded by cars slowing down at the lights by the Hôtel Lutétia, getting up on the pavement by Bon Marché, going down the Rue du Bac in the wrong direction before turning left into the Rue de l'Université.

Gilles and Sylvia carried me to the sofa. 'Let's have a cup of tea, that'll make her arrive.'

Before, I would have rushed out into the street to meet her. My little sparrow . . . She must be soaked to the skin! What would she be wearing today? She took such care with her appearance. She could only bear silk or cotton against her skin and would rather get cold than put on a jumper, jacket, coat, hat. Her latest problem was tights: 'I refuse to wear those horrible things on my legs!' She'd never known winter weather, never seen snow.

Sylvia raised a finger: the doorbell!

'It's your pupil,' she said, winking, and went to open the door.

'So you're giving lessons now, are you?' teased Gilles.

'Guitar lessons, music theory. I think I'll enjoy it.'

'I see,' he said, smiling conspiratorially.

He'd just caught sight of Manon, behind me.

'Léo, look at me! Have you seen the state of my clothes? I got soaked, it's a disaster!'

She made her way round the sofa to give me a kiss. She was barefoot. 'I got rid of my shoes at the door.'

Sylvia ran to get her a towel. Manon was wearing a white linen blouse and trousers. They'd become transparent.

'Lucky you're wearing underwear and this is a safe neighbourhood.'

She shrieked when she caught sight of herself in the mirror and covered her chest. 'You see, I'm naked even when I put clothes on,' she said. 'It's all Brazil's fault.'

'Didn't it rain in Brazil?'

'I was always in a swimsuit!'

'If you don't get changed, my cousin here is going to start walking,' joked Gilles.

Manon frowned as she peeled her soaked blouse away from her bra. 'Now I understand why this bloke was following me in his car.'

'He couldn't help it. You look like a fashion ad: Ralph Lauren, Hurricane and Shipwreck collection, 1997.'

'Or Zelda, without Fitzgerald, caught by a wave from the Pacific.'

Manon crossed her feet on the sitting room carpet while Sylvia dried her back.

'We look alike, don't we?' the Argentinian Sylvia asked the Brazilian Manon.

They both had olive skin, hazel eyes. Manon was as tall as Sylvia, and as blonde as she was dark, with a slender waist and long slim legs. Sylvia's large breasts were heavy and firm. Manon's were higher, rounder.

'Manoushka,' I said to her, 'you always do things the wrong way round! When you go out, you have to take a shower first, then get dressed, not vice versa.'

Sylvia took her hand. 'Come on, I'll find you something to change into.' The two women disappeared.

Gilles served me tea in a glass, Eastern-style. He thought I'd improved. 'You're moving your hands better, aren't you?'

I gave him a lesson on the tenodesis effect: when you bent back your wrist, the fingers curled inward, creating a grip between thumb and index. It meant you could hold a CD, piece of paper, pen, small spoon, champagne glass. With exercise, you could strengthen the wrist muscles and use them to hook things, pull down a zip and push on your wheels.

'Can you make a woman come?' asked Gilles. He was copying me, flexing and relaxing his wrist.

'Yes, thumb fucking.' I held out my hand, to'ing and fro'ing in an imaginary penetration.

'You'll develop a new sexuality. You'll really have to think about it. It'll be fascinating! Blokes are obsessed with their cock. As soon as they get a hard-on, they want to stick it in and spread their sperm! But you, you'll have to take your time . . . Time for love, time for women.'

'Seen from that angle, it's quite appealing.'

'Yes, so where's the problem? You can love, give pleasure without necessarily using your prick, can't you?'

'Great, I'm going to become a lesbian.' There were so many new paths to explore.

'Talking of girls, where've they got to?' Gilles headed to the bathroom. I heard him yell and stifle hysterical laughter. I was stranded on the sofa; I tried to grab my wheelchair but it was too far away. Lesson number one, Léo: never part with your wheelchair! Don't forget, your wheelchair's your legs! My gaze panned round the sitting room and entrance hall like a camera fixed on a tripod.

'Hello, anybody there?'

Gilles came back, looking mischievous, and put on a CD. A Japanese gong sounded. My cousin bowed. 'Merry Christmas, Mr Lawrence!'

Against the background of Ryuichi Sakamoto's chords, Manon and Sylvia entered on either side of the sitting room, dressed as geishas. They'd put their hair up in buns, stuck through with thick needles. Under kimonos cinched at the waist they were wearing sandals with wooden soles that clacked on the parquet. They looked delightful! Radiant, Manon put her hands together and bowed, then did a little Sino-Japo-Indo-Arabo-techno dance, moving her hips and bending her body, supple as a reed. I realised how essential dancing was to her. She floated, her movements were natural, expressive, instinctive, in both time and space. Her hands fluttered like a pair of capricious, inquisitive butterflies. Her kimono tensed, parted, pulled tight over her curves, particularly her buttocks, which were as round as apples.

That evening, we ate supper by candlelight. Manon left her bicycle behind and Gilles drove her home. Sylvia let me use her room and she slept in the sitting room. Papou came over to wash, undress and put me to bed. It took us ages. The most tedious part was having a shower. We used a plastic garden chair placed under the stream of water, and an ergonomic ring to protect my bottom. Sylvia helped transfer me from one chair to the other. Manon's things were hanging up to dry in the bathroom (her trouser label said 'size 36'). She was there, invisible, in her crumpled white outfit. I pictured her asleep on her front, sucking her thumb, her hair all tousled, her nightdress hitched up to her waist.

My body relaxed under the boiling hot water. It was the only way to ease the increasingly severe muscle and nerve pain. I was sleeping for longer. I always prayed before going to sleep and asked my dead loved ones to help heal me. Manon said I should seek St Anthony's protection and made me repeat after her: 'O glorious St Anthony, light of the scriptures, faithful servant of Mary and all-powerful friend of Jesus, hear my fervent prayer. Grant me clarity of spirit and help me regain' – we drew up the list together – 'my legs, my hands, my back, my stomach, my breath and my voice. Help me to avoid Satan's tricks and the traps that he sets me to afflict me and make me lose my way. Let your noble light guide me for the greater glory of God, for all eternity, Amen.'

It was good to have a direct line to heaven.

70

Manon

Sylvia woke me up early the next day. While Papou was dressing me, she made coffee and toast. Gilles and Manon arrived at around 10 a.m. to take us to the church of Saint-Pierre-du-Gros-Caillou. The service was at 11. The sky was a beautiful, immaculate blue above slate roofs warmed by the sun. Manon was wearing a short white lace dress with a silk slip underneath. She had matching ribbons tied in her long gold hair, which hung in two plaits down her back. Gilles wheeled me to the front row. Manon winked at me. To the left of the altar a statue stood staring at us; it was St Anthony. Manon went to light a candle, before kneeling on the prayer stool. I admired the nape of her neck, her back, the hollow between her shoulder blades, her slender wrists as she raised her hands in prayer. A ray of sunlight pierced the stained glass window, covering her dress with patches of different colours. A halo of light seemed to make her stand out from the rest of the faithful thronging the central nave. She returned to her seat beside me and the organ announced the start of the service.

Before Communion, during the sacrament of reconciliation, she took my hand. As I felt her warm fingers intertwine with mine, I was filled with gratitude towards whoever was up there lavishing so much attention on my soul. I felt as if I had woken up after a night of terror. I knew that Manon hadn't come into my life by chance; nor was she forbidden fruit, although at that crucial moment I wouldn't allow myself to look ahead. Why not? I had no idea. I just had to look at her to see how happy and loving she was. We were so alike. We both loved the sun, the sea, the heat, music and dance. We were both exiled, we had both lost what was most dear to us. Deprived of the beauty and vitality of the land where she grew up, she'd found someone to make her laugh and sing. I, who had thought I was nothing but an old, out-of-tune mandolin. Our unhappiness disappeared as soon as we looked at each other.

I caught my breath: my imagination was running wild – since losing the power of sensation, it was all I had. And I hadn't dreamt this. 'She was holding my hand, she was holding my hand.' I repeated these words to myself as if they were the lyrics to a song I was afraid of forgetting.

After lunch in Sylvia's garden, Gilles took her and Manon for a walk in the Jardin du Luxembourg. It was too hot, so I opted for a nap. Sylvia drew the curtains in her bedroom. I didn't hear them get back. The sound of music made me prick up my ears. '*Agua de Beber*': guitar, percussion and the warm voice of Astrud Gilberto, the diva of bossa nova. I could hear Manon singing as she moved around the sitting room; a wild child with bare feet. I pictured her dancing on the parquet floor, leaping on to the sofa, balancing on the little oak bench. The kitten purred in Brazilian, but got carried away with her acrobatics and fell over.

'Shit!' exclaimed the young lady. 'I've buggered my knee. Ow, ow, ow! Léo, I've hurt myself!'

She jumped on to my bed and burst out laughing. 'Did the big baby have a good sleep?'

'Carry on singing, Manoushka, I love to hear you. But if you smash your face, do it in time to the music . . . and quietly, please.'

'Hang on, I'll be right back. I'm going to put on another song.'

From the sitting room, she made me play a guessing game: who? What? When?

'It's someone who talks too much. Come here, Manon, and shut up.'

She sat cross-legged on the bed. Music started up again in the sitting room.

'Well?' she said, and her eyes shone.

'It's old, sweetie, but it's beautiful. "*Manha de Carnaval*", by Luiz Bonfa, from the film *Orfeu negro*.'

'Well done, my little ang . . .' Her voice trailed off. Manon held her hand to her throat, lay down and nestled against me. I stroked her hair, her forehead, her cheek. She kissed my hand then pressed it against her chest.

'I'm so comfortable with you, so happy.'

We looked at each other in the dim bedroom. Our faces moved closer. Something burned in my belly. After brushing her lips against mine she gave me her tongue in an intense, passionate kiss. A little pink serpent, devouring me and taking my breath away. One of her dress straps slipped down; I started to put it up again but she pushed my hand away.

Manon lay down on top of me, as light as a feather, and wrapped her legs around mine. I felt her mouth on my neck, then her tongue licking the edge of my ear. I put my arms round her waist, and stroked her from her hips to her sun-burnished shoulders. Manon removed the other strap and her dress slid down to her waist. What exhilaration on discovering her breasts! I'd expected them to be smaller than two wild pears, in keeping with her slim figure. Ah, Léo had lost his connoisseur's eye! Manon unclipped her bra, liberating full, heavy breasts, whose whiteness accentuated their voluptuous mass. Her skin smelled of sweet almonds.

She placed one breast on my mouth. I sucked her nipple, then moved over to the other one. They were hard, and unusually large. Two erect little appendages that swelled as I sucked, nuzzled and nibbled them, setting off spasms that shook her torso and made her moan. A mass of blonde hair cascaded over my face and shoulders. I put my hand on her forehead; I didn't want to make her stop, just to show her that I was in control of the situation.

Manon arched her back and moved so that I could kiss her stomach, which was flat and tight as a drum. Crouching over my shoulders, she gripped me between her thighs. She started rocking her hips and I understood where she was taking me. I put my hands on her buttocks, following their curves beneath her panties: a triangle of white cotton that she pulled aside, placing her sex against my mouth. When she felt my tongue, she bucked and moved away but she came back immediately, pressing down this time. A strange, wild rodeo. My head trapped between her thighs, I thought of my battered cervical vertebrae.

She was rocking harder now and her pleasure was wetting the lower half of my face. The shadows of the room played on her face and upper body, revealing a teenager who was no longer that: she was tigress Manon, shameless Manon, lover Manon, woman Manon. Without realising, she said things between moans: 'Ye-es,' 'Nooo,' 'Ahh,' and a surprising, 'That's good, my love, that's so good. Take my pussy, take it.' Her cries changed whenever her body experienced a new sensation.

She was also fighting herself, shaking her head as if she were ashamed of what she was doing. I thought she must be embarrassed at being on top of me, straddling my face in order to reach her climax. And I thought this must be a new, intense experience for her, because she'd gone off like a rocket, with all the vigour of youth. She must have been planning this for some time. She had nothing to fear from me.

What if I was her first? Or perhaps I wasn't. Wouldn't that be simpler? Come on, Léo, stop talking rubbish. Maybe it was only me who was worrying and asking myself pointless questions? Was I afraid that she'd take off her knickers and decide to make love to me? What if she was a virgin? And what if she wasn't? Everything was moving so fast. I wanted her but I was scared. She was half naked, I was still in trousers and a t-shirt. Things were hotting up under there but she'd have to get my damn jeans off for me!

The music had stopped. Manon was dripping with sweat, her hair was a mess. Sitting on my stomach, her crumpled dress round her waist, her face expressed both ecstasy and suffering, like a child emerging after a week in bed with a fever. She got up, rubbed her eyes and stretched her back.

'Ooh, baby,' she sighed, 'this is going too fast . . . too strong.'

Yeah, I was with her on that one. I held out my hand towards her mouth; she swallowed my thumb and played with it, pushing it back and forth between her lips.

'Look at the state of my dress!' she sighed. 'I think I'll have to take it off. Oh, what happened to the music? Back in a second . . .'

She stood up on the bed and her dress fell off. She picked it up with her toe and sent it flying across the room.

She took two bounds on the bed, three across the floor and her little arse disappeared into the sitting room.

Where had Sylvia got to? She must be with Gilles.

Manon reappeared in the doorway against the light, just as *Corcovado* started up on the CD player. She paused dramatically, standing there in her little white panties.

'Hey, sweetie, why don't we go away together, somewhere far away?'

'Far away – where?'

'Wherever you like, Manoushka. You choose.'

'In August?'

'Er, no, I know a really great girl who's taking me to Brazil then.'

Manon grabbed a bolster and started to stifle me with it.

'Bastard, you can't go there without me! It's my country.'

She was a fury, pulling my nose, ears, hair. 'Repeat after me, or you'll regret it! "No-Brazil-without-Manon-No-Brazil-without-Manon." Understood? OK, now you!'

The little demon kept the pillow over my face. '"Nobazilwivoutmano!" I promise, my love, I promise!'

Reassured, Manon lay on her side, her back pressing against me. I wrapped her in my arms and blew warm air on to the back of her neck. She shivered. 'Another cuddle and then I have to get home. But I don't want to go . . .'

The doorbell rang; Sylvia letting us know that she was back. Damn, she was early!

71

Deo gratias

Manon has an answer to everything. Last time, she stayed the night. We had dinner and then she got into my bed. She played for about half an hour with the TV remote, then I heard music. 'A mix of jungle and drum 'n' bass,' she yelled. It was time for her exercises and singing practice. I was finishing the text for my radio programme which was being recorded the following day. I typed on my computer keyboard with one finger (before, I used two), then printed it up: seven pages for a one-hour programme. Papou ran me a bath. As I passed the bedroom, now turned into a disco, I saw Manon on the bed, doing her exercises in time to the music: headstand, handstand, abs, stretches, splits. She was in a world of her own, with her music, her dreams.

I was splashing around in a hot bath when Manon looked round the door. 'Can I get in the bath with you? Wait, I'll get candles and music.'

When she came back, she closed the door, turned off the light, took off her pants and t-shirt, and then sat facing me, crossing our legs. The steam, the glow from the candles on the tiled walls, Youssou N'Dour on the stereo, Manon shampooing her hair . . . I was dreaming. The accident had never happened.

'We're like an old married couple, aren't we?' she said, rinsing her hair.

'You're the old one. Me, I'm just starting out: I've got to learn to walk, eat on my own, dress myself, work.'

'A big sixty-kilo baby, that's what you are! D'you want me to wash you?'

Manon got behind me, slid her legs round my waist and massaged my neck and shoulders. She spent a long time on the twelve-centimetre scar that ran down my neck: a fine line dividing my cervical vertebrae in two, through which my former life had escaped. If science ever found a way to repair the spinal cord, a surgeon would have to reopen the wound: cut along the dotted line. Parting the flesh, he'd inject a miracle chemical into the spinal canal, awakening a new man.

The first time we made love, I told Manon I was sorry I couldn't offer her my 'former' body. She yelled at me, 'I couldn't give a shit about your "former" body, Léo! I love you as you are. If you'd met me before, you'd have fucked me and dumped me like all the others. I know you by heart!'

Now that I spent time with priests and was trying to return to the Christian faith, my old demons were pestering me. My relationship with Manon troubled me, though never for very long. And she couldn't have cared less about my Judeo-Christian hang-ups. Her parents gave her total freedom. One day her father cycled over with her and we all had tea together. Manon called him by his first name. When it was time to leave she said to him, 'I'm staying the night, there's a sofa bed in the sitting room. Give Mummy a kiss from me, I'll be home tomorrow.' He smiled and asked me if I minded. I told him frankly: 'Your daughter's my sunshine, my lucky charm . . . And she makes wonderful pasta!'

'You see,' added the young lady in question, 'no man can do without me, so you'll have to get used to sharing!'

He called her a 'demonia' and, before leaving, told me to shut her in the freezer if she became unbearable.

In the evening, after her shower, she joined me under the duvet, whispering: 'What a day, I'm exhausted.' She stroked and kissed me and made sure I was hard, before easing herself very gently on to my penis. I enjoyed her pleasure; my own felt too distant, even if the mental excitement made up for that. And there was always her tenderness, and the vertigo induced by her breasts that she gave me to suck as consolation. So I could spend all my time on her and, despite my countless amorous experiences, I realised that on the subject of female orgasms there was a lot I didn't know. In the old days I was a selfish male, a poor little prick puffed up with pride and pretentiousness.

With Manon, I rediscovered love, women, kissing, patience, language ('Come on,' she'd say, 'tell me a story'). I learnt to read on her skin the countless erogenous zones concealed behind an ear, elbow, toe, finger, hair, tooth. Manoushka's pussy was the eighth wonder of the world, and as capricious and demanding as an English lawn. Maintaining it was a huge undertaking; I spent whole nights at it. We'd start lovemaking late, and what with sliding and kissing, sucking and biting, penetrating strategic hollows, spanking and stroking, modest silences and crude words, anodyne chat and erotic tales, we'd glance at the alarm clock and it would be 5 a.m.

I slept badly and restlessly so sometimes I sent my little blondie packing to the sofa bed in the sitting room. She stood, grumbling, at the foot of the bed, rubbing her eyes

('See, Léo, you take me and then throw me out!'). As she was putting on her nightie, her buttocks within reach, I caught her between the thighs and, moving up to her stomach, pulled her towards my mouth, hungry for her skin, gold triangle and warm bitter folds. She let me enter her with my tongue, my fingers, and had another orgasm before crossing the room, staggering, with her bum showing because her nightie ('Petit Bateau – age 14') only came to her waist. She'd grown too fast. Me, I'd shrunk too soon.

Still . . . back to the subject of religion: I was asking myself questions. I went to confession. Was the sin of the flesh really a sin? Should I give it up? Surely this was too heavy a price to pay when you'd ended up a tetraplegic? The good Lord understood, the good Lord forgave . . .

Brother Samuel, the prior at Sainte-Cécile, had become a friend. One day I invited him out to lunch and he suggested holding mass. In my sitting room. Amongst the nudes, pin-ups, electric guitars, limited edition photos by Jean-Loup Sieff, pictures of Laetitia Casta wearing Victoria's Secret and photos of my exes in swimsuits. On my bedside table in the next room, only five feet from the altar which Brother Samuel had set up on a bridge table, there were two polaroids: Manon naked on the sofa reading *Bibi Fricotin*, and Manon facing the wardrobe mirror, in micro-shorts and bustier, in a very upright dancer's pose, on tiptoe, a curved arm raised.

After communion, Brother Samuel sat next to me, his head resting on my shoulder. I opened my heart to him.

'The thing is, Sam, I moved in here three months ago. It was pretty hard starting a new life that seemed empty, except for small stolen moments of pleasure. It all seemed derisory compared to the spectacular collapse of all my plans. Our religion tells us there's life after death. Well, I discovered that there can be death in life. But then, at the beginning of the summer, a friend introduced me to his niece so that I'd give her music lessons. This girl, Manon, turned up, I saw her smile, her beauty . . . she's been an incredible source of love . . . and . . .'

'You realised you were no longer alone, that someone was watching over you.'

Sam held my hand between his; he smiled at me with brotherly affection. I wanted to go on, say more, confess, but he shut me up. 'It's God's grace, my friend, it's God's grace! Let's pray together and then go to lunch, I'm famished!'

72

Alive

After the holidays, Manon drifted away. She had a new lover. She told me as she slipped under the covers, one night in September when I was no longer expecting her. She'd tapped our secret signal on the window: a Samba 2/4 time. When I felt a warm damp patch on my shoulder (she was crying and asking me to forgive her – but for what?), her body trembling against mine, I realised how much I'd miss her and how hard, if not impossible, it would be to fall in love with someone else because I'd be afraid of being left and hurt again.

In the morning, she stuffed into her bag all the treasures she'd left in my drawers, in the bathroom cabinet, on my desk, in the kitchen – her photos, books, CDs, wash things, the underwear drying on the radiator which reminded me of her when she wasn't there. I felt that without her my life would consist only of departures, sudden abandonment, managed loneliness.

This was so like Manon: she cried as she told me she was leaving and begged me never to abandon her and always to leave my door open to her. What about my heart? And my body? But I was already on the other side of the mountain; the slope of break-ups doesn't necessarily end in a ravine. Her love had been like a diamond: pure, luminous, uncompromising, limpid, precious.

What was the searing pain of parting compared to the glorious weeks we had spent together? Shouldn't I be happy that she had enriched my life for a time, rather than bemoaning my loss? I loved Manon, and her desertion, cruel as it was, wouldn't change my feelings. On the contrary, she could count on my love forever. Her future would probably be more eventful, more dangerous than mine. She could do with a loving older brother and lover, a caring ally, to fill her sails and watch her put out to sea, waiting for her to return, whether she was brave or bewildered, confident or troubled. This was the promise I made her as I cradled her in my arms and dried her tears.

She clung to me more tightly and slipped her leg between mine. Her blonde curls covered my smooth chest. As a teenager, I dreamt of having a mat of chest-hair to impress girls; I even bought creams to encourage its growth, for all the good it did – I remained as hairless as an egg. But now, this crown of golden hair, this wheat field spread over me, represented – thanks to Manon – my regained manhood. I might not have a single hair on my chest, but I had the prettiest girl in France, in Europe, on the planet, in the universe, on my heart.

'Hey, the music's stopped,' she said, surprised.

It was true. For three months we'd lived on bossa nova and not much else. Today, the crotchets, minims and quavers had deserted us. Silence. The best thing for saying goodbye. No raised voices, or false notes, or histrionics, just the sound of the shutters in the wind. A natural ending, no pretence. I love you.

Even as you close the door gently behind you, clasping

in the bottom of your pocket my spare key which you'll never return.

Didn't I give you my heart? So keep it warm, Manon. And come back when you like . . . Even without warning me. Even without loving me.

Only death arrives unexpectedly. And today, I'm alive.